An Island
Lost

Y0-AGR-396

C.A. LARMER

Published by Larmer Media
Goonengerry,
NSW 2482, Australia
www.calarmer.com

ISBN: 978-0-9871872-4-6

ABOUT THE AUTHOR

Christina Larmer was born and bred in Port Moresby, Papua New Guinea, educated in Sydney, Australia, and went on to work in London, Los Angeles and New York. A journalist, blogger, editor, teacher and author, she now lives with her musician husband and two sons in the Byron hinterland of Northern NSW, Australia.

www.calarmerspits.blogspot.com/
christina.larmer@gmail.com

Also by C.A. Larmer

The Agatha Christie Book Club Series
The Agatha Christie Book Club
Murder on the Orient (SS)

The Ghostwriter Mystery Series
Killer Twist
A Plot to Die For
Last Writes
Dying Words
Words Can Kill
A Note Before Dying

The Posthumous Mystery Series
Do Not Go Gentle
Do Not Go Alone

Non-fiction
A Measure of Papua New Guinea:
The Arman Larmer Surveys Story

Available at Amazon, Apple, Smashwords, B&N…
www.calarmer.com

For Dianne and Michael

I'm enormously indebted to my parents for the magic and
wonder of childhood holidays on remote Doini Island in
Papua New Guinea's Milne Bay.
I'd also like to thank the Neville family for their help and
hospitality while researching the book, and the people of
Doini who opened their hearts and my imagination.

Without Doini, there is no Island Lost.

PREFACE

Once, long ago, the people of Asaro in the highlands of Papua New Guinea lost many good men in a bloody tribal war with a vicious neighboring clan. They were so devastated by their loss that they could not let the matter rest. One moonlit night they immersed themselves in the nearby river, cloaking their bodies in the thick gray mud. They fashioned grotesque masks of oversized ears and giant, protruding nostrils from the wet clay and then crept back to the village of their conquerors.

Surprised by these ghostly visitors, appearing like phantoms from the surrounding bush, the conquering villagers fled, screaming, into the hills beyond.

And so the Asaro people were victorious in their defeat.

PART 1

NEW YORK CITY—TREADING WATER

October 21: There are nights when I look down at myself from above and burst into tears at my sorry sight, hunched over and scribbling frantically in my journal, my dinner for one half-eaten beside me, my true love elsewhere trying to build a new life...

The rain was pelting down when Vilia got the call. She had just ordered a skinny latté in her usual haunt on the corner of Twenty-first and Ninth and was enjoying watching her fellow New Yorkers bolt for cover, scurrying in every direction as though a few drops might dissolve them on the spot. *Really, they could have just listened to the weather report.* The weatherman had said 4:35 p.m., and that's exactly when it hit, give or take a minute. She hadn't really intended to head out but his certitude had her intrigued; even after all this time, and she liked to put it to the test, to face nature head on and see. And so she had idled along Twentieth, one eye on the brewing clouds, the other on her watch, and only when it struck 4:30 p.m. did she enter the café. And again, she had been rewarded. Down came the rain. Mankind 1. Mother Nature nil.

"It's Jane, Vil," came a thick Australian accent down the mobile phone. "Jane Logan, from Cairns."

"Jane?" Vilia sat back, stunned. "Oh, hello. How are you? Is everything okay? How's Bob?"

"No, no, we're fine, love. It's about ya mum."

Vilia shifted in her seat.

"Where are ya, love? You sitting down?"

"Yes I am. What is it, Jane, what about her?"

There was a pause, a clearing of the throat, then: "She's gone, Vil. The cops just let us know." Another pause. "I'm so sorry."

Vilia frowned, feeling suddenly irritable. She could see her day crumpling around her.

"I'm sorry? What do you mean, she's gone? Where's she gone? Exactly."

She took a quick sip of her latté.

"Oh dear, I'm not making myself very clear. Um, ya mum passed away, love. She's, er, dead."

Vilia dropped the cup down with a clunk. "I see." She paused, shook herself a little. "Right. Okay then." Took a deep breath. "So what happens now?"

There was also an intake of breath at the other end. Whatever Jane was expecting it was not this. "Oh, er … well that's what we want to know. You want us to organize the funeral? Look, it's no trouble—"

"Um, I need to think. Can … can I call you back? Can we talk later?"

"Of course, love, of course. You alright?"

"I'm fine, Jane. Fine."

"You can stay with us, when you get here. If you like."

"No. Thanks. I'll probably just stay in town, at a hotel. But I really do have to go. Um, I'm right in the middle of something … but thank you. Thank you for letting me know."

There was another inhalation at the other end, a strengthening of nerves. "Look, Vilia, I know that you and your mum weren't—"

"I am fine, Jane. Really. Give my love to Bob, yeah?"

"Oh, okay then, love. We'll talk later?"

"Absolutely."

Vilia sounded almost chipper as she hung up the phone and returned to staring at the view. She hadn't asked her old neighbor how her mother had died but she already knew; had been expecting it for decades, if truth be told. Yet now that it had finally happened, she was just slightly surprised. Her mother had come this far, why top herself now?

Vilia's mother, Genevive Lea, had lived and, it turns out, died in the far north of Australia in a town called Cairns. Tourists flocked to Cairns from the far reaches of the earth to snorkel its magnificent Great Barrier Reef—350,000 square kilometers of what is considered one of the great natural wonders of the world. In her thirty years in Cairns, however, Gena had never bothered to witness the wonder, preferring instead the solitude of an ordinary little beach several miles north of town and one street down from her house. She would wander down there daily, ritually resting her skinny limbs on the warm, white sand and stare out to sea.

As a child, Vilia would sit beside her, singing quietly to herself and watching her mother watch the ocean for what seemed like an eternity. She contemplated the older woman's gaze, so expressionless at times it sent an icy chill down her little spine and made her aware, even at a tender age, that her mother was not the full quid. Genevive was not insane, she knew that, she was simply blue. Whatever the hell that meant. It's the word Gena used on those bad days, trying to make light of her depression and explain it somehow to a daughter who sat furrow-browed beside her, wondering what on earth she'd done wrong. Again.

"I'm just a little blue today, darling. I'll be right tomorrow." As though she just had a headache.

Yet the blue would often drag on for days and Vilia would eventually lose her patience, willing her mother to snap out of it or, at the very least, assure her that it wasn't her fault, that it wasn't Vilia who was making her so damn sad. But Gena never said that and Vilia was too scared to ask. On particularly bad days, she would take measures into her own hands, flinging her little body down the beach and into the ocean's depths. And there she would remain, fighting the boredom and waiting for her mother to shake herself out of it and call her back in. Sometimes it took an hour, sometimes two, but at least she was out of the blue and focusing on her daughter again, towel in hand, the whisper of a smile upon her lips.

Once, of course, it backfired. Vilia was just seven years of age and had been swimming for what seemed like forever. She splashed about in the shallows, floated on her back as best she could, her skinny limbs unable to buoy her up for long; and on Gena sat, staring blindly out to sea. Time ticked by, Vilia grew restless, then weary, then red hot with anger and was ready to give up, to drag her wrinkled body back in when she noticed Gena stand and simply walk away. Not so much as a second glance. Vilia dropped her legs to the sand and stood up, gobsmacked. Fortunately, kindly Mrs. Logan from next door was watching from the esplanade and enticed the young girl out.

"She's not well today, love. Come stay with me for a few days until she gets back on track." (It was Mrs. Logan who would eventually explain Gena's depression to Vilia, but not before she was twelve and the damage had already been done.)

When it was box jellyfish season, during the wet season (between November and March), and only dogs were allowed to swim, Vilia would sulk angrily on shore slapping sandcastles together or scrounging for shells, as angry at her mother's silence as she was at the jellyfish. She hated her more in those months than in any other.

She remembered a beach from days gone by where the shells were large and plentiful. There were oval white ones and triangular, brown, speckled ones and, from time to time, enormous pink and white ones shaped like miniature gramophones which promised the sounds of the ocean if you put them to your ear, although if truth be told she never heard more than an eerie whistle.

One summer Vilia made herself some jewelry from the tiny, hollow shells deposited along the sand, and wore the clinking necklace with such enormous pride, every day for one full week until its scratching and tinkling wore thin. Then she tossed it aside, never to be worn again. The next week, straw hats made from dried palm fronds became her obsession, and soon after, oversized board shorts created from yards of luridly colored material purchased at the Cairns market on steamy Sunday mornings. Mrs. Logan had lent Vilia her old Singer sewing machine, and she improvised the rest, thrilled with the results until a new hobby came along.

The summer she turned fourteen, Vilia discovered the joys of sailboarding, and everything else faded into oblivion. It was the Christmas holidays and she was fretting for a new activity when the first brightly decorated sails started bobbing into view. The twin boys two houses down got their own sailboard first and, after much persuasion, let Vilia try her hand. Her first few goes were disastrous; she could not grasp the concept of harnessing the wind and was too puny to pull up the waterlogged sail. She spent most of those early hours toppling into the ocean and frantically scratching her way back on, as fearful of the venomous jellyfish as she was of being thought a failure.

But on the fifth go everything changed. After much time coaxing the boys to give her another go, and only after their own fatigue had forced them to relent, Vilia slipped a floppy T-shirt over her swimmers, and old sandshoes over her feet, stepped onto the board and began sailing out from the shore. She sailed through the rippling waves that collected close to the shallows and past the old rock that jutted out from one side of the bay, on into the setting sun. She sailed for what seemed like forever, then, knowing the boys would be cursing her back on land, she pulled one end of the boom in close to her chest and released the other end so that it lost its grip of the wind and began fluttering madly. She grasped the sail rope, dropped the sail down a little, and, clinging to the rope for support, stepped carefully around the board so that she was facing back towards shore. Then she pulled the rope towards her chest, grabbed the boom again, first with one hand, then the next, waited for the right gust of wind and harnessed it once more. Within moments she was sailing back home, smoothly, swiftly, without a single falter. When she returned to the shore, she brought the board in close and stepped off onto the sand, discarding the boom as she did so. The boys stared, open-mouthed, dumbfounded.

Vilia was bone dry.

From then on she was smitten. She had harnessed nature at last, and it exhilarated her. Finally the young girl was in control.

That night she asked her mother for her own Mistral sailboard and Gena, glad of the distraction, had readily agreed. By her fifteenth birthday, Vilia was the strongest junior sailboarder on the bay, leaving the twin boys for dead as she ploughed through wind and wave. But even as she skimmed across the water's surface, land fading behind her, she knew it was only a temporary reprieve, that to really be in command, she had to stop turning back for shore.

And so, the day after her school graduation, Vilia piled a suitcase of clothes and the old Mistral into her car and bid Cairns and her mother good-bye.

She made the occasional, guilt-riddled phone call home and received the odd letter in reply, but Vilia had not seen Cairns or her mother since.

Soon Vilia would have to return, to the house of her youth and the memories of a mother who had been dead as long as she could recall. The funeral would be superfluous. Eventually, when the rain cleared and the streets filled to bursting again, she paid her bill and departed. Any smugness she felt had now dissipated. There was another storm brewing and this one, she knew, was beyond anyone's control.

The floorboards protested below Vilia's feet as she entered her apartment and flicked on the light. The room sprang to life and she glanced about at something that may or may not have moved in the corner. She deadbolted the door and applied the chain, debating as she always did whether this was such a good idea, especially if someone was already inside. She slipped off her shoes wearily. It was just loneliness playing with her nerves. She glanced at the clock above the fireplace she never used, and noted that three hours had passed since she first stepped out. But what had she done? What had she achieved? She had spent most of that time skulking through the streets, furious at her mum and New York and the clouds that still sat like a dark scowl across the skyline.

A small red light flickered furiously from the answering machine in the living room but she headed straight for the kitchen, opened the freezer door and pulled out a microwave meal. Honey Baked Chicken. She scratched about for another. Only Veggie Lasagne and something that resembled roast pork. She stuck with the chicken, shoved the door shut and cracked open the box to reveal a small plate covered in sheer wrapping of plastic and frost with a shriveled piece of white meat in one pocket, baby carrots and stunted green beans in another and a yellow iceblock of sauce in the last. She plucked a fork from a drawer and pricked absently at the cover several times, then placed the lot inside the microwave, pushing 'Instant cook,' 'Rotate' and 'Start.'

As the meal circumnavigated the microwave, she returned to the living room, flicked on the TV, pressed 'play' on the answering machine and then swept past it into the bedroom to tug off her jeans. She found her tracksuit neatly folded and placed on the edge of her bed, and put it on while the machine chatted away to her from beyond.

There was a message from Jane Logan, sounding anxious, telling her of important news. "I'll try and find you on your mobile," she had concluded, clicking off suddenly.

You found me alright, Vilia thought, now scrounging through her draw for socks. She located two woolly ones, noticed they were odd colors and poked about again.

Another voice was speaking to her now, this one was less anxious, more commanding, more assured.

"Vilia, it's Alex. Call me." A pause, a lightening of the tone. "I heard about your mum. You need to call me, sweetie. We can talk." Then he, too, was gone.

With her feet now warm, Vilia padded into the tiny bathroom to remove her make-up.

"Ohhhhh," she groaned, scowling at her tired reflection, and tried not to meet her eyes again as she scrubbed and rinsed and removed the day's grime.

It would be a long night, she knew that, but she would get through it, because that's what she was good at. And so she set a place at the table, retrieved her meal, poured a glass of wine and sat down to eat. When she finished, she washed her plate, glass and cutlery and put them away, then she returned to the bedroom to grab a small leather-bound journal that was resting beside her bed. Back in the lounge room she switched off the TV and began to write.

And write.

And write.

And as the words poured out, her breathing began to shorten and her chest began to heave and soon she was dropping giant, wet tears upon the page, and she was brushing them away furiously as her pen continued to skid and slide and try to make sense of her mother and her life. She had spent most of hers despising Genevive and then herself for not understanding the depression. *But I was a child*, she wrote. *A child!* She should have opened up to me. She could have at least been honest.

And then, *Forget her, forget her, forget her! She doesn't deserve all this.* And it helped dam the flow. Many pages later, she put the journal aside.

"You'll be fine, Vil," she told herself. "You'll fly home for the funeral, you'll pack up her stuff and you'll come back again. But no more tears, now. Not for her."

That night she dreamt of a tiny child, swimming alone in a stormy sea, one hand waving frantically to a woman who would not see. She awoke with a start, drenched in sweat, and reached across the bed. But he wasn't there, of course he wasn't there, Liam hadn't been there for months. But this one was all her fault. And so she turned back, tucked her legs underneath her, and cried herself back to sleep...

PART 2

CAIRNS—SEARCHING FOR LAND

August 7: I'm home at last and I know I should be happy, overjoyed.
It's what I want, what I've been asking for. But there's no joy. Just a
kind of emptiness because he isn't with me.
I'm giving birth to a new era and his heart is elsewhere.

We often underestimate the power of our senses but you
need only return to a place of past significance to be
reminded how potent they are. We may think we have
cleansed ourselves of that past, disposed of it like two-
dimensional snap shots into the album of life, confined now
into neat little rectangles of fading color, void of texture,
taste, sound and smell. But step back into the past proper
and we see how a certain thickness of air, humming of
silence or the taste of salt in the sea breeze will send us
racing through corridors of familiarity so shocking, we
realize that the past never really went anywhere.

It had been fifteen years since Vilia had stepped inside
her mother's house, but one whiff brought that past flooding
back with an intensity she wasn't prepared for. There was the
lush aroma of well-watered plants and the thick, moldiness
of her mother's many books weaving their way in disorderly
queues along every wall and available surface, and in stacks
up to the ceiling, like a stairway to the sky. There was the
dung-like smell of old mosquito coils and, most surprisingly,
the smell of Genevive Lea herself. It was a scent indefinable

but undeniably hers, lingering at every turn, as though she were still there.

"Hanging around to haunt me," Vilia hissed into the darkness.

Her mother had always been like a ghostly presence, lingering in the corners of her life but never quite coming into focus. She dashed from room to room, pushing up the window blinds and thrusting open the glass louvers not so much to let the air stream through as to release the ghost of Gena.

Genevive had lived in a creaky old beach house in the coastal suburb of Sunside Bay. She had lived alone, as far as Vilia knew, but then what did she know? They hadn't spoken in so long.

"I'm so sorry, love," Jane Logan had said when they finally met up outside her mother's house.

"It was suicide, wasn't it?"

Her neighbor looked shocked. "Well, we don't really know that for sure, love. I mean—"

"How did they find her?"

"Her body washed up to shore."

Vilia caught her breath.

"Scared the bejesus out of a morning jogger," the older woman was saying. "Coroner reckons she'd drowned sometime overnight. I've got his details inside somewhere."

But Vilia was no longer listening. She had sat down on the pavement with a thud.

After a few minutes, the elderly woman softly added, "They say she was stung."

"Oh, God."

Vilia dropped her head into her hands.

"Bloody crazy of ya mum, love," Jane's anger was edging out her empathy. "Everyone knows you don't go swimmin' this time of year."

Yes, Vilia thought, everyone including Gena.

Vilia forced herself to swing open the door to her mother's bedroom. The bed had been stripped, the side table cleared of the usual clutter of pill bottles and prescriptions, and this room, only this room, smelt of strong disinfectant, a kind of fake lemony scent. Someone had obviously cleaned it. Probably Jane, she thought, and ventured no further than the door, which she quickly pulled to. She would find the strength to return later.

The house was a large one for a single woman, with three bedrooms, a large living area that opened out on to a flyscreened veranda, and a decent sized kitchen complete with its original cooker, the type highly sought after by Yuppies back in Sydney. Vilia had always opted for gleaming new appliances—fresh, clean, devoid of past. She noticed, too, that the living room had barely changed since last she was there, and the observation choked her. The furniture, mostly beige and '70s in style, was all still in place and nearly worn through, a testament to Gena's self-imposed exile. And then, of course, there were the books.

Gena loved to read. It was her enduring passion, second only to the beach and, for reasons Vilia didn't understand, never mutually inclusive. Gena only read at home and always something long and thick and difficult to grasp. Vilia used to linger over the bookshelves of her friends' parents, admiring the soft, gold-embossed covers that creased at the corners and featured women with heaving bosoms, or men in trench coats under a foggy, moonlit sky. These stories were enticing. These stories she could follow. Gena's were always beyond her reach.

But that was nothing new. Hadn't Vilia, in effect, grown up on a different shelf than her mother? Hadn't she watched (silently at first) while her mother wandered by, like a servant, quietly serving meals, keeping house, getting her off to school, with very little in between except the occasional unexpected morsel—a quick smile, a slight tap on the top of her head. But none of the real parenting she had witnessed elsewhere:

"So tell me about your day, dear."

"Don't speak with your mouth full, please."

"There'll be no TV for you, young lady, not until you clean your room!"

She was the envy of her friends, of course; they longed to be left alone. It was company Vilia wanted, and conversation and discipline and order. And when she failed to find all that, she settled for the sea.

Vilia's eyes wandered to an old painting on the wall. It was of small wooden huts clustered along a bleached white shoreline.

"Where are the huts, Mummy?"

"Somewhere far, far away."

Like a fairytale, she thought now, but probably Fiji, and then, hearing a car pull up outside, she turned away.

"How are you, Vili?" Alex Fielding called out as he closed the door of his Saab behind him and, checking it was locked, made his way up the rickety stairs to where Vilia now stood.

"No one will pinch it here," she told him as they kissed each other hello.

She led the way inside and, finding some instant coffee and sugar in the cupboard, prepared him a cup. He liked a little milk with his coffee, she remembered that, but today he would have to make do.

"No milk?" he asked, as she expected he would and she shook her head.

"No bickies either, sorry. The pantry's virtually empty."

"Surprise, surprise," he replied and she avoided his eyes.

Alex had never met Gena but he knew the story.

"Lots of dying plants, too, I see."

He brushed his black fringe behind his ears and Vilia shrugged her shoulders. Bitching about her mother had proven a therapeutic pastime while the woman was alive, but now she wasn't up to it. Not in this house. Not now. It just wasn't right. Alex had no such reservations.

"I suppose she's left you a billion debts to clear, and God knows how you'll ever sell this old dump."

"It's not a dump," she shot back, and then: "I'm leaving that to the agents. I called them yesterday."

"You don't muck around. I forgot that about you."

"We haven't seen each other in a while, have we?" Softer, trying.

"Over a year, sweetie. At least now you can come home, hey?"

"What do you mean?"

"Well, I don't mean here, obviously," he said, glancing around the kitchen with his nose crinkled. "I mean now you can move back to Sydney, where you belong."

Vilia blinked several times. "You think that's why I'm in New York? Because of Mum?"

"Oh Vili, I *know* that's why you're over there."

Vilia slammed her cup down on the kitchen bench, sending coffee flying. She scowled, then reached for a dried up sponge from the sink and swiped at the mess.

"Jesus, Alex. I've got a bloody good job there, you know. I wouldn't have anything remotely as good if I lived in Sydney."

It was true, she did have a good job, one she knew her friends coveted. Vilia was the personal assistant to the Australian Consul General in Manhattan and while it was only a clerical role, it brought with it a small sense of power and prestige. She felt safe there, cosseted somehow in a city most people found threatening. In return, she kept everything running smoothly for her boss, an elderly gentleman with a severe lack of patience. He had been through quite a few PAs before he met Vilia, but they clicked instantly. He demanded perfection and, for the most part, she provided it. On those odd occasions when she failed to, her own mortification was worse than even his bite.

A very small part of Vilia's job was to run the Down Under Club, a social organization designed to help antipodeans meet up for work and play. It organized social events, assisted with housing and provided networking opportunities almost impossible in the closed Manhattan business scene. And she loved it, not because she was social, quite the opposite in fact—Vilia's good friends could be counted on one hand—but because she got to help other lost souls find some familiarity and direction in a crazy new world.

Of course her boss hadn't flinched when she'd asked for time off. Why would he? She hadn't had a day off in two years.

"Not everything in my life is about her," Vilia spat.

"Whatever you say, hon." Alex buried his face in his cup.

He'd forgotten her temper, too, her impatience with the truth. But he remembered enough about her to know when to shut up, and so he did.

They both sipped their coffees, avoiding the other's eyes and through the silence she heard the sounds of her childhood start up like a symphony from the past. The cicadas buzzed shrilly, their mating call climbing high above the fig trees and then ceasing with such precision that all that was left was the echo of their song bouncing from branch to branch, before, on some silent directive, they resumed their piercing cry. A kookaburra camouflaged within the trees laughed aloud from time to time as though mocking their call, or, Vilia thought sullenly, perhaps it's me she's mocking. The dull roar of the ocean, just meters away, set the backdrop for this tropical tune and, yearning for a sail, or even a swim, she settled on a beach walk and returned inside to change into sneakers.

"Walk?" Alex said, startled. "The funeral's in less than an hour; you'll be late!"

"Well they're hardly going to start without me, are they?"

"Look, Vilia." Alex grabbed her hand, held it tightly within his. "Do you want to talk about it? You know?"

"I'm not going to fall apart, Alex, I'm okay."

"I wasn't talking about your mother."

"Neither was I," she replied and then offered him a small smile. "I gotta have a walk; it's been ages. I won't be long. You wanna come?"

"God no! Walking is for dogs!"

She laughed at this, felt good to be laughing, and then disappeared outside, leaving him to fidget uneasily in the dead woman's house.

Sorting through Gena's things was not as traumatic as Vilia had expected. There were no more tears—she had shed enough, she told herself, more than she deserves—and she would not be keeping mementoes of a woman she'd rather forget. So she simply piled everything from the living room and kitchen into a dozen boxes for giving to the Salvos or dumping at the tip. The decent furniture would be left in place until she sold the house, although she balked a little at the thought of selling it. This surprised Vilia. Why wouldn't she sell it? It had never really felt like her home.

Alex had ghosts of his own to appease. His parents lived just north of Gena and were 'beside themselves with excitement' that the prodigal son was in town.

"Better do the right thing," he told her, rolling his eyes, feigning disinterest.

Yet she knew, deep down, he looked forward to seeing them. His parents were elderly, adoring. They would throw open the netted door and welcome him with open arms and a cup of their finest green tea.

"Not an espresso in sight!" he sniffed, and she'd laughed and waved him off.

"I'll be all right," she told him, but she secretly relieved.

This was something she needed to do alone, without his running commentary. And she made good time of it, clearing out every room but one by late afternoon. With a strong cup of coffee in hand and her stomach in her shoes, she plodded towards her mother's bedroom and stared at the shut door meekly. For a brief moment she considered knocking before shaking herself out of it and pushing the door wide open. She turned on the light.

The room was bathed in a soft amber glow and dust glistened like tiny snowflakes where strips of sunlight snuck in through the curtains. Placing her coffee down, she flung the heavy drapes aside and threw open the windows, wondering as she did so whether this was the first time in years that the room had seen real light. It was certainly the first time Vilia had seen it without the added filter of a guilty conscience.

As a child she would often sneak in while Gena was out, peering around anxiously, desperately, believing that the answers to all her questions would be lurking somewhere in this yellow interior. Today, as she chewed absently on the edge of her cup and allowed her eyes to wander lazily about the room, it did not dawn on her that, in fact, they were.

Gena's old double bed was wedged against one wall, a small closet disappeared into the shadows of another wall, and the bedside table sat incongruously sparse considering the mess in the room. Most of it, like elsewhere in the house, was made up of books stacked haphazardly against the walls and underneath the furniture. There were shabby piles of newspapers and magazines, too, and Vilia wondered why her mother had bothered with the sea. A simple flick of a match would have done it.

But it was the old dressing table that caught her attention. As it always had. It was Gena's ode to the past and the only surface of the room that wasn't jammed with books. The table was also surprisingly sparse with little more than an old hairbrush, some antique jewelry and a nameless World War II medal. The dresser was antique, the dark wooden style of the early '20s, with two small drawers and a large oval mirror cluttered with fading black and white photos. Vilia's own dressing table, a sleek blonde-wood piece she had purchased at an upmarket New York design store, was crowded with perfumes and eye creams, moisturizers and make-up, a cornucopia of cosmetics to beat back time. Gena's dressing table was not a workbench for life, it was the altar of her mausoleum, a place to sit and stare death in the eye.

Slowly, Vilia stepped towards the table and surveyed its dusty exterior. Photos had been stuffed ad hoc around the mirror and sticky-taped in almost every space so that, peering into it now, she was allowed only the smallest glimpse of her own face between the faces of the forgotten. And she recoiled at her image, sickly yellow in this light, her green eyes wide with awe and uncertainty, her thick auburn hair dancing all about. She felt like she had stepped back in time. She looked fourteen again; uncertain and unkempt. And she flung one hand up to pull her frizzing locks back behind her ears, angry now that a morning spent straightening the hair, lacquering the ends, applying make-up, had come unstuck so quickly.

She looked away, furious, and back at the faces more vibrant on paper than she felt in the flesh. There were images of several young men amongst them and she once dreamed that one of these, the most dashing perhaps, was her dad. She had asked about him more times than she cared to admit, and Gena had always been evasive. Unapologetically so: *"He left before you were born." "Forget him, he's gone."*

"But I need to know, Mum," she would implore. "I have a right to know."

And, still, the silence, a deafening, unforgiveable silence that would eventually turn her daughter away.

The neighbors, however, were a little more articulate.

"Your dad ran off with another woman," one of the Parlour twins once said as though remarking on the weather and she recalled his words like a slap across her freckled face that stung for days afterwards, that still stings today.

"Tell me something I don't know," she had said, sighing so nonchalantly he was caught by surprise and looked away, red with the blush intended for her.

And then he had wandered off, bored with this game. But she was the loser, she knew that even then as she watched him leave, the answers to all her questions left suspended on his lips, stopped forever by a lie. She had chosen dignity over denunciation and sacrificed truth in the process. And so she would sneak in and stare at those photos gloomily, wondering which was him and wishing he were there.

Because she knew everything would be okay, if only he were there.

As the years passed by, the young woman let the faces dissolve from her memory, pretending eventually that she didn't care. But looking at them now, she knew that wasn't true either and her heart caught in her throat. One of these men could be her father, she thought, and yet now she would never know. She would never have the chance to track him down, to find her other half, however much a cad. How dare she not tell me, she thought.

How dare she keep him from me.

Vilia plucked the pictures carefully from their perch and placed them on the bed to keep. There were old postcards, too, with barely legible scrawl and these were added to the pile along with the medal and several of her mother's scarves which were dangling down the side. So much for no mementoes.

Vilia was about to turn away when she remembered the cabinet drawers. She placed the keepsakes aside and tugged at the handles. They appeared to be locked in place. She glanced around the cabinet top again for the key, but only dust remained. She checked below the drawers and rubbed her fingers up along the sides, around the legs and behind the mirror. Nothing. Her curiosity was turning to impatience and she considered forcing the drawers free. Then it occurred to her. She dashed back out into the kitchen where, earlier, she had flung down her mother's house keys, and studied them more closely. There were six keys in all, two belonging to the front and back doors and a third to her mum's old Torana. The other three were unknowns and one of them was antiquated and rusting around the edges. She returned to the bedroom and applied it to the lock. At first it would not budge and her irritability returned. She tried again, applying some extra pressure, and, after several seconds, freed the drawer from its hold. It flew open and out, flinging an old brown envelope across the room, several papers dislodging and fluttering about before resting on the floor.

Vilia sprang upon them guiltily and stuffed them back inside the envelope that she then placed carefully upon the bed. She didn't know what it was, she didn't even try to look, there was time for that later. More cautiously this time, she unlocked the second drawer and, finding it empty, locked both drawers up again. Then, with the sun fading fast, she placed everything in a box by the door, changed into some swimmers and headed for the beach towards the sailboard hire shop she'd spotted the day before.

"Thirty-five bucks an hour," the young man in charge announced, "but we close up in 'alf an hour, so that's as much as I can give ya."

"That'll do it," she replied, handing him the cash.

"You know jellyfish season has just started? Not many about yet but ya wanna be bloody careful. We hire wetsuits, might help."

She smiled. "Don't worry. I won't be falling in."

He considered this and smiled back as he selected a wide board with a medium-sized sail that was resting on the sand, just out of reach of the rippling water.

"You new 'round here?"

"Just visiting. Do you think I could take the racing board?"

His eyebrows lifted a little but he returned the junior-level board to its place and handed her the shorter board without saying another word.

Placing her gear aside, she set off for one final sail down memory lane. The sudden, erratic gusts of wind that once taunted her childhood strength, now failed to send her flying off and she sneered at them, teasing them to try. She calculated their strength and maneuvered her sail accordingly, preparing for the extra gale that heralded the open sea, steadying her feet and hugging the sail to her chest. No sooner had she cleared the bay, she turned about and tacked back in, never losing sight of the shoreline just as she had made herself do all those years ago.

Forty minutes later, revived but unspent, she returned to the house to find Alex waiting, one foot tapping quickly on the post against which he leant.

"Jesus, you didn't go swimming did you?"

He could not understand her fascination for the sea. He was the chlorine pool and banana chair type.

"Got a death wish like your mother?"

He snapped his lips shut, hadn't meant to say that, then added, "Hurry up, sweetie, and wash that gorgeous body of yours. We've really got to go. You've got that appointment with your mum's lawyer, remember?"

Vilia hadn't forgotten. His name was William Hanes and he had called her at Gena's house not long after the funeral, insisting she stop in to see him before she departed and, reluctantly, she had agreed.

"Don't look so glum," said Alex. "She could have left you a million dollars, you never know."

"Yeah and she might rise from the dead and give me a cuddle, too. Let's just keep some perspective shall we?"

Soon after, she was buckled into Alex's Saab as he drove her back into the heart of Cairns.

Bill Hanes's office was small and cramped, and shared premises with a printing company and a Thai takeaway underneath. Hanes had told Vilia he needed her to come in and tie up her mother's loose ends and so she had appeared as promised, her clothes neatly ironed, her hair secured tightly behind her. She wanted to look orderly, look like she was in control, even if she didn't feel it.

"I'll need to see two forms of ID," Hanes said as soon as they'd shaken hands, and she fished through her handbag for her passport and driver's license. It was Australian, but she had a New York one, too. It was one of the first things she had done when she arrived in the Big Apple, sitting for her local licence, not because she had a car or even anticipated needing to drive, but because it enabled her to—and that was all that mattered.

Hanes motioned her towards a chair. He was a small, tubby man, in his early sixties with a deep, confident voice that belied his scruffy exterior. His shirt looked a little old, fraying slightly around the collar and his bright red tie was loosely slung around his neck in a vain attempt at formality. His spectacles were steel gray and forced his thick white hair into tufts where the metal met his ears.

He looks like a clown, she thought absently and sat down in the chair opposite him. Hanes took his own seat and then studied her identification, glancing up at the woman before him and then back down again.

"You look just like her," he said, and Vilia frowned.

"Gena and I were nothing alike."

It sounded bitter; she hadn't meant it to come out so fiercely.

"Not your mother, your grandmother, Miriam."

Vilia's throat drained dry. "Sorry?"

"Oh it's quite haunting!"

He was delighted by the discovery and sifted through the file in front of him to produce a tatty old copy of a black and white photo. She took it from him and came face to face with herself.

"That's ...?"

"Miriam. See the resemblance? It could almost be you."

The photo showed a woman with thick hair swirling about her face, dark from some angles, light from others, a mass of contradictions just like her own. Also like Vilia's, this woman's features were undefined and covered in big, dark freckles, like white china splattered in mud. Vilia used to fantasize about wiping her face clean but this woman suited her splotches somehow, and her cocked eyebrows dared you to suggest otherwise. She looked like she could handle anything, she looked the antithesis of Genevive. *And me for that matter,* Vilia thought, handing the picture back with a shrug. She had never been told about her grandparents, had certainly never met them, and this late in the game she decided she didn't want to know.

"So, what is it you wanted to speak to me about?" And then: "Do you think I could have a cup of coffee?"

He returned the picture to its place and made her a cup, spooning fine brown powder from a can that he located atop the photocopy machine. He filled up the kettle from the sink in the toilet and then waited for it to boil, placing the cup in front of her, before saying another word. It was bitter and tasted like day-old dregs, but she drank it regardless.

"As you obviously didn't know," he said, returning to his seat, "I was your mother's solicitor and executor of her last will and testament. Just as I was for the rest of the family, at least for a while."

She glanced up at that word and then back at her drink, blowing on the murky brew and waiting for him to continue. Family. What a foreign concept.

"As you can see from these papers," he said, producing sheets and sheets of old legal documents, "your mother has left you everything."

Hurrah, she thought, and smiled weakly at the lawyer.

"So there's the house in Cairns, the car—an old one I believe, you probably won't get much for that; the government bonds; a few bits of jewelry; Tubu, of course; and some shares, although they don't add up to much I'm afrai—"

"Too-boo?"

"Yes, Tubu. You still have quite a few years left on the lease but it is costing you each month so you'll have to decide what you want to do with it. I know a good property lawyer here in Cairns but of course you might want to see one up in Moresby. They'll understand the local law better, obviously."

Vilia shifted in her seat. "Excuse my ignorance," she began, "but what is Tubu?"

Hanes dropped the paper he was reading and stared directly at her, his bushy white eyebrows raised like snowcaps above earth-brown eyes.

"What do you mean?" she repeated, her own eyebrows now raised.

"The island," he said.

"What island?"

"Tubu Island."

He grabbed the will back up and began reading through it again. "Yes, yes, it's all here. It's yours, I'm sure of it ... yes, yes."

"I don't know about any island."

The lawyer frowned again and then continued burrowing through the file.

"Really? Seriously?"

"Seriously."

Her brain was starting to feel a little cloudy. She didn't like that cloudy feeling. She shook it a bit and put her coffee cup down. Hanes looked mystified.

"You've never been up there, then?"

"Up where?" Now she was losing her patience.

"Papua New Guinea. Just directly above Australia, the other half of Irian Jaya? Your island, er, Tubu Island is just near the Eastern tip, I believe, in the Milne Bay."

"New Guinea?" Images of her mother's old oil canvas— the wooden huts, the bleached white sand—flashed before her eyes.

Hanes took a deep breath.

"My apologies, Miss Lea. Your parents ... and then, of course, just your mum, has held the lease on a small island up north for, ummm ..." He scanned his papers again. "Let's see, April 21, 1970 ... yes, just on thirty-six years. It's a fifty-year lease all up. A wonderful little spot I believe. Your mother spoke of it often."

"Not to me she didn't."

Vilia's face was burning hot with embarrassment. *How could you not tell me this, Mum, this?!*

"I assumed you knew, that you both visited from time to—"

"No."

"You weren't born up there?"

Vilia shook her head emphatically. "No, I was not. I was born here, June 7, 1973. Check my birth certificate if you like."

He thought about this. "Yes, yes, that would be right. Many of the expats gave birth down south. But I'm sure you lived there as a baby."

He began to do some sums in his head, nodding as he went. "Yes, your mother must have taken you straight up after you were born, and then of course you both returned here after ... well, after your father ..."

His voice trailed off, he tried for a smile. "Oh, well, in any case, the island's yours. I guess that's good news then, eh?"

Vilia just stared at him, looking ready to explode and he turned away quickly, immersing himself in his papers again. Now he was the one blushing. He felt mortified for her. How could Gena not mention Tubu?

"I'm just sorry I don't have more information for you. I have this copy of the lease."

Hanes handed her a fresh photocopy of an old land title deed dated 1970 and stamped with the Australian administrator's seal. Below it was her mother's floral signature, faded almost into obscurity, beside what she soon realized was the signature of her father, Jamison Lachlan Lea. She stared at his steady, strong strokes unblinking for several seconds. Something thick had caught in her throat. She could barely breathe.

Hanes continued, "Australian guy called Jonah Johnson runs the place now, has done for many years. Not that he gets much compensation from your mum as far as I can tell.

Just a small retainer each month, which your mum's allowed for in her will."

Vilia didn't appear to be listening.

"I ... I can give you his details ... let me just write them down."

He scrounged around his desk for a scrap of blank paper and, not finding one, tore the bottom half off a used piece. He jotted down some numbers and placed it before Vilia, her eyes now glazed, her lips pursed shut. What else could he say? This woman made him nervous, and he was used to the mother.

"I'm afraid that's all there is in this file about it and there's not much more I can tell you. I just thought ..."

"Never mind." She had found her tongue and was breathing heavily in short, hungry bursts. "It's not much use ... to me ... anyway. If you could contact ... um ... that lawyer you mentioned. That would be good."

"You thinking of selling?"

"I ... I don't ..."

She broke off then, shaking her head violently from side to side. After several seconds she looked up at him with a start and tried for a smile.

Hanes smiled back, equally as confused. "I just need you to sign a few things, but we can do that another time. How long you around for?"

"Hm? Oh, not long."

"Look, there's no hurry. I can post you in New York. Probate won't take too long."

She stood up and nodded blankly.

"You can have this copy, if you like."

He held out the deed she had left on the desk and she hesitated briefly before plucking it from his hand. Then she turned slowly and departed while the wooden huts whirled like a cyclone through her brain.

"You've got what?!"

Alex was excited by the news, his voice bubbling over with unabashed glee.

"An island, Alex. Up in Papua New Guinea."

"New Guinea! What the hell was your mother doing with an island up there? Wow! A whole island! She was a bloody millionaire."

He laughed heartily at this but Vilia couldn't even muster a smile. He sobered up quickly, his eyes darting about in his head.

"How on earth could your mum afford a bloody island? And why on earth would she have one? How absolutely marvelously eccentric of her!"

These were questions Vilia had not yet answered for herself and she let out a long, deep sigh.

"I don't know any more than that, Al. I need to have a good look through her things. Maybe she won it in some freak raffle or the lawyer's got it all wrong. I just don't know."

"But why wouldn't she have told you about it? Why all the secrecy?"

"Alex, I don't know."

Vilia's voice had turned high pitched and he glanced across at her. He placed a hand over hers.

"It'll all make sense. Eventually. Go through her things, find some answers. Do you want me to help you?"

"No, no thanks. Let's just get back to the hotel. I need to get my head around all this."

Alex started up the engine. "You're due to leave tomorrow, aren't you?"

"Yes."

"You'll have to change your flight, sweetie."

"Maybe …"

"Well you can't go back to New York now!"

Vilia swung her head towards him. "Alex, just get me back to my room, please. We'll talk later tonight. Okay?"

He shook his head at her and pulled away from the curb.

That evening, after Vilia waved the anxious Alex away, she ordered room service, took a quick, cool shower and then pulled out all the papers she'd retrieved from her mother's house.

Perhaps the answers are all here, she thought as she dusted them off. It'll all make sense in a minute, you'll see.

But it didn't. Instead, Vilia was left with an aching headache and even more questions than she knew how to answer. There were really just three pieces of correspondence that were of interest and it seemed to Vilia that they had been left like tantalizing clues to some mystery her mother would not share with her—one last story beyond Vilia's reach.

The first was a telegram dated June 16, 1976, and commissioned by the PNG Police Department from a place called Samarai.

"DEAR MRS LEE (sic)—STOP—WE REGRET TO INFORM YOU THAT WE HAVE NOT BEEN SUCESFUL (sic) IN OUR SEARCH—STOP—WILL TELEGRAM WITH MORE INFO AS WE FIND IT—STOP—PROVINCIAL POLICE COMMANDER RILEY—END"

The next letter, dated several months later, had been hurriedly handwritten.

"My dear Gene,

Just jotting a quick note while Gary gets some goods. We're in Samarai and the talk here is tremendous. Oh how you must be hurting, you poor dear. Our prayers have been with you ever since you fled so quickly, so rightly some weeks ago—although none of us much feel like going to the church these days for your incident, and the other. Poor Betty has been a trembling mess and looks in on her kids—and husband—every second she can, fretful that they too will be taken from us in such a horrible way. None of us trust our help anymore and even the Whilhelms are packing up to take leave.

My prayers are with you,
Pam Beazley"

It had been addressed to Vilia's mother, care of Miriam Miller at an address she had never heard of in Cairns. She wondered, briefly, whether her grandmother had lived there. Still lived there. But it was all too much to comprehend just now. A grandmother still alive? Yet one more person who had failed in their duty to her?

She couldn't let her thoughts go there, not now. She had business to attend to, and so she turned her attention to the third letter. It was just a scrap of paper, fondled almost beyond legibility, but it was that letter that grabbed her heart in a headlock. It was dated earlier than the others, 1973, the same month of Vilia's birth, and addressed to the women's wing of the local Cairns Hospital.

"My darling Genevive,

The coconuts are coming along nicely and Toia tells me we should be harvesting soon. Old Hettie has blessed the crop would you believe! So we should be in for a winner (or so the workers think). How are you and the baby holding up? Miriam tells me all is well, that you are well, that the pregnancy is going as planned. Oh I hope so! I miss you so. The plantation is nothing without your cheerful face. And now baby will make three! Mary is plumping the pig for your return. And please do not fret, the baby will fare well here, we have everything you need. And Samarai is close by. I am more excited than even you would believe.

All my love and Godspeed,

Jamie"

That night, fueled with raw emotion and a kind of raging despair, Vilia had decided enough was enough. *To hell with it all,* she had written in her journal. *I'll put the cursed place on the market and get on with my life. MY LIFE!*

By morning Vilia knew that was impossible. Ignorance might have worked beautifully over the past decade but she always knew, deep down in the patched up place she called her heart, she would have to face reality one day. She would have to seek out some answers, to stop pretending none of it really mattered. And it seemed now, as she reread the pages left behind, that that day had finally come.

Vilia delayed her return flight home, dressed quickly and then pulled a business card out of her bag. She dialed the mobile number at the bottom.

"Bill Hanes speaking."

"Bill, it's Vilia Lea. From yesterday?"

He caught his breath. "Yes, Vilia? How can I help?"

"You mentioned about my dad?"

"Yes?"

"I'm just wondering, well, I need to know."

There was another pause, this time longer. "How do you mean?"

"I mean, do you know what happened to him? Why my parents split? Why my mother was here in Cairns?"

"Look, do you want to come back in? I can meet you at the office in, say, half an hour?"

"No." She shook her head. Swallowed. "Can we just get this out, please?"

"Vilia, all I knew—all your mother and your grandmother told me—was that he went missing. I don't know exactly what happened, the whys or hows, but I believe it was devastating for your mum and it brought her back here to Cairns. She ... and you of course, stayed with Miriam for a short while, somewhere in town as far as I recall, and then you moved to the beach address."

"And Miriam?"

Again he paused. "Look, I'm not too sure what's happened to your grandmother. Not long after your mum moved back, Miriam got her own lawyer, broke off contact with me."

"Why would she do that?"

"No idea, that's something you'll have to take up with her. Provided she's still alive of course."

"And her lawyer?"

"I've probably got his address here somewhere. She must have given it to me to forward anything on. I'll hunt it down for you. Look, Vilia, you should know your mum cut Miriam out of her will, left everything to you and that was that. I never asked why, not really my business to, you understand? But, I guess I could do some scrounging around for you. If you like."

"No," she said hurriedly. "It'll be fine. Thanks."

"Look, I've been thinking. It needs to be said: your mother was wrong not to let you know about the island, about your grandma, your history. She should have clued you in, that would have been the right thing to do."

"Well, we weren't exactly on talking terms," Vilia offered.

"No." He did not sound surprised. "And, well, there's something else." He hesitated. "After your dad disappeared, well, your mum … um, she wasn't well after that."

"No, she was clinically depressed. I eventually worked it out."

He sounded relieved. "That's right. She had a problem, Vilia, but she wouldn't seek any help, no matter what Miriam said. And I do know Miriam tried, I do know that."

"Well she didn't try hard enough," said Vilia flatly.

"Yeah, fair enough, fair enough. Look, if there's anything else I can do for you, you just give me a bell, okay?"

"I will, thanks, Bill, I appreciate it."

She hung up, her head still cloudy, and stared outside. Rain pelted down like glass bullets from the sky and it was an unwelcome annoyance. She would not be able to turn to the sea, to grasp it by the tail and give it a good shake while her troubles stayed firmly back on land.

Instead, she made her way down to the hotel café, hoping a change of scenery would help things clear. But of course it didn't and she tried to quash the questions that kept racing through her brain, making things worse:

What happened? Where did my father go? How could he possibly be missing?!

She sighed and looked around, brushed one hand through her hair and tried to calm down. There was an answer to it all, there had to be. A man doesn't just go missing. A woman doesn't suddenly return home with only a baby and a bunch of question marks. She doesn't slip into a lifetime of depression for nothing.

Vilia took a long gulp of her coffee and ordered some breakfast. She had made a decision and it heartened her. It helped, momentarily, to clear the fog.

No more hiding in New York. No more staring out to sea. It was time to take a trip far, far away.

It was time to visit Tubu Island. The place where it all began, and the place where it fell apart.

PART 3

PORT MORESBY—DIVING IN

January 18: Why am I back here at this place, so hot and crass and crammed with such ugliness, such reckless despair? I long for the order of home with its freshly mowed lawns and neatly paved roads, and faces that don't stare at you like the alien that you are.

There was turbulence at thirty-thousand feet and Vilia could feel her stomach tighten. Liam's prying hands should be somewhere between her thighs now, she thought, not thousands of miles away in New York strumming his Les Paul instead. His hands were not unlike hers—long, skinny fingers, fair, Irish skin—stronger, though, and calloused from hard work. His hair was soggy brown and overgrown, unwashed and unkempt. His lean body was splattered with freckles and, if he was at home, he was no doubt naked, his disdain for clothes still fascinating her even after all this time. The image sent a small smile to her lips and was quickly replaced by a heavy sigh.

She should not be thinking these thoughts. She was not worthy of them.

She turned her attention, instead, to the flight attendants who were keeping busy up the front. She had chosen to fly Air Niugini and realized these were the first Papuan locals she had ever met. Or, at least, they were the first she remembered. Yet she felt instantly comfortable with them, admiring their quiet, softly spoken grace, the way they went about their work seriously, almost too seriously, as though they were playing a part, the role of an efficient hostess. They seemed awkward in their starched uniforms and overly made-up faces, and she wondered what they were really like when the engines had stopped and the passengers had departed. *I know all about role-playing*, she thought as she watched them, *it's been my life's work*.

The plane, a large airbus, had flown out of Cairns, over the Great Barrier Reef, and she spotted vivid blues and greens and the white frothiness of clouds as they went. But, after an hour and a half, as they began their descent towards Papua New Guinea's capital, Port Moresby, the brightness was soon replaced by a drab brown.

So much brown, she thought, her eyes glued to the small window at her side.

The earth below was sun-scorched and thirsty, uninviting. She spotted a small shanty town beside what appeared to be a dump, and several other clumps of fibro houses wedged into the dusty, treeless folds of the surrounding hills. They circled over the main harbor and she was momentarily mesmerized by a smattering of wooden huts standing awkwardly on stilts in the sparkling sea. Beyond them was the township, a cluster of tall buildings beside a harbor crammed with container ships. Then it was back across the parched land, above smoky fires dotting the hillside and past a hunchback-shaped hill with gleaming white townhouses.

Those must be for the expatriates, she thought.

Then down, down to that ugly brown land. She closed her eyes as the tires made contact and cursed herself silently.

Chasing ghosts again.

Within seconds of stopping, passengers were leaping up and reaching for overhead luggage, offering polite good-byes as they vied for the best aisle position to beat the rush to customs. The man beside Vilia wrestled for his spot in the aisle and tried not to meet her eyes. He was a consulting engineer and had seen all sorts on his twenty-year commute to Moresby: young blokes with dollar signs blinding their good sense and reluctant wives joining them for as short a trip as possible before fleeing down south to fresh groceries and department stores and white people in control. But this woman seemed different, more displaced than any of them.

She's an odd one, he thought. *Polite enough, sure, but there's something about her. She doesn't belong.*

Vilia hadn't explained exactly why she was flying up, had said something about checking on a few things, but the engineer had his suspicions.

Maybe she's a journalist, investigating the latest government (corrupt bastards). Or maybe she's one of those bored city types, looking for adventure. Crikey, she'll find it up here, that's for sure.

He spent a few minutes warning her of the dangers of the capital, of the criminals who rampaged through the suburbs carjacking and killing for the sake of it, axes in hand, woolly beanies atop their heads; and of the daily pack rapes and the way the local police turned a blind eye to it all, but she didn't appear to care and so he gave up and dug his nose in his finance magazine.

"Good luck with your trip," he leaned down and whispered eventually when her inaction sparked some sympathy. "Hope you don't get TANGFU'ed."

Before she had a chance to reply, he was off down the aisle and out into the blinding light of the exit door. When the plane had almost emptied, Vilia grabbed her handbag and followed, allowing herself to be politely ushered across the tarmac and towards the arrivals hall.

The heat in that brief walk was like nothing she had ever felt before. It was staggering. Furnace-like. Unexpected. So when the doors swept open and she passed into the air-conditioned interior she felt an overwhelming sense of relief. As though she had escaped something. For now.

The arrivals terminal was almost empty and surprisingly modern, washed in white with enormous, brightly painted faces of ceremonially dressed villagers adorning the walls. She joined a small queue for the swift shuffle to the customs desk. There a young black man proceeded to scrutinize her passport photo intently while Vilia glanced around at the few other white faces in the throng. They smiled encouragingly at each other with that 'we're all in this together' air, and she felt more like an outsider than she cared to admit. *I lived here once,* she kept reminding herself. *I have a right to be here.*

"You from Cairns, eh?" the customs officer asked, a scarlet smile encircling an enormous, flat-topped nose. His eyes were so black she could not tell where the pupil stopped and the iris began. They were stunning eyes, laced with the thickest set of eyelashes she had ever seen. And above them were a motley collection of small, tattooed stripes, blue in color and almost like idle pen marks. It was as though someone had wandered up and scribbled away on his forehead. His nails were chewed raw and his uniform faded blue, and she noticed his teeth perfectly matched his ruby-red lips. She was later to learn this was from the effects of a small green nut they chewed called *buai* or betelnut. When mixed with lime (made from crushed burned sea shells) and *daka* (the fruit of the pepper vine), it resulted in a sticky red substance which not only provided a sedative effect, but needed to be spat out and was usually done so at will, leaving bloody streaks across footpaths, buildings and cars.

But this guy seemed lively enough and she nodded that, yes, in theory at least, she was from Cairns. He seemed happy to hear this, stamped her passport with gusto and ushered her past him in the direction of the luggage carousel.

The bags had not yet arrived and no one seemed too surprised by this, fanning themselves with their passports or leaning against the walls. Vilia made a beeline for the toilets and tried vainly to repair some of the damage that the brief walk through the furnace had caused. Her hair, previously straightened to salon perfection, had turned into a thick bowl of frizz, and several drops of sweat trickled slowly down her face. She dabbed a tissue at them and reapplied some lipstick, then scowled at her reflection and returned outside.

The baggage carousel had cranked into motion and a few bags were finally dropping down towards the impatient travelers. Eventually, Vilia spotted her own and, pulling it onto a stray trolley, carefully made her way through the quarantine section. It was a breeze. It seemed nobody was too interested in checking anyone's luggage and they simply shrugged her on, to the exit and out to the waiting crowd.

By now she had steeled herself for the stifling heat but she was not prepared for the sea of faces that stared openly at her as she slowly wheeled her trolley outside. There were hundreds of people hanging around, some sitting on mats as if they had all day, and they all kept their eyes firmly upon her, as though they had never seen such a spectacle. Some even looked delighted. She shook her head angrily, hating the attention. She spotted several white men standing guardedly to one side, but there was no question she was an oddity and it sent wary shivers down her spine. Clutching her bags closer, she weaved her way towards a sign that said 'Transfer' and what she hoped was her escape.

Yet she hadn't counted on her airplane dropping from the sky.

"It's missing?" Vilia repeated to the woman at the transfer desk who was busily picking away at some lurid red nail polish that was holding fast to her short, gnarled nails.

"What do you mean it's missing? Exactly."

The officer stopped picking, looked up and glanced around, then waved lazily at a passerby before turning back to Vilia with obvious indifference.

"She no stap at Alotau, now," she remarked in Pidgin English. "You go speak to Kenny."

Kenny was more cheerful and appeared to speak good English, so she lightened up a little and managed a smile.

"The woman over there," she said slowly, pointing behind her in no set direction, "happened to mention to me that my 4:25 p.m. connecting flight, PX154, to Al—al—ahh—teeow—"

"Alotau," he corrected.

"Yes, Alotau, is, well, missing."

And she laughed then because it sounded so absurd.

"What does she mean and is there another flight?"

He glanced at some forms in front of him and then back at the bedraggled woman. "What is your name?"

"Huh? Oh, Vilia Lea, L-E-A."

He perused the forms deliberately and then shrugged his shoulders at her. "It's either still in Alotau or it's crashed. Who knows."

"Crashed?"

"Yes, why not?"

Well, you couldn't argue with that. "So what do I do now?"

"Ahh, you come back tomorrow."

"Tomorrow?"

"Yes, Misis, 12:15 tomorrow. We have another flight to Alotau."

The wonders of modern scheduling she thought, and asked, "But what do I do now?"

"You go to the hotel, Travelodge in town. This is the best hotel for you. Then you come back tomorrow. Yes?"

Vilia scowled. No, this was not what she had planned. She didn't want to spend any time in the capital. She had heard what a dirty, dangerous place it was; she didn't need this added distraction.

"Thanks, Mum," she hissed under her breath as she turned towards the road.

Within seconds a crowd of men, hands waving frantically, began tugging at her luggage. Before she had a chance to react, the keenest of the lot was already pulling her away from the terminal, towards his battered taxi. At first she tried resisting, she should really check the prices, ask around, but the overwhelming heat and the man's insistence wore her down and she let him push her into his cab's smelly confines.

"Travelodge!" he stated, as if there could be no other destination and then added, "15 kina!"

She nodded blankly and slithered back into the seat, feeling a sense of dread in the pit of her stomach. This was not part of her plan.

The drive took less than half an hour along winding hills and over pothole-plagued streets. There were several shanty-style suburbs along the way with rundown stores and blinking neon signs suggesting a bygone wealth that the loitering masses no longer enjoyed and she wondered how depressing this must be for wide-eyed tourists who had imagined paradise. Eventually they detoured onto a brand-new freeway that seemed almost incongruous amidst all this poverty, like a slice of LA had been dumped in the middle of a ghetto. She held tightly to the car door as they weaved in and out of traffic, missing other vehicles by inches, horns honking, passengers hanging on to the backs of pickup trucks for dear life. By the time they reached the coastline, her knuckles were white and her eyes firmly shut. Better not to watch.

"You don't enjoy the journey," Liam once told her. "You just want to get there."

"That's rubbish," she'd replied, but she knew he was right.

Vilia was an impatient person at the best of times, never stopping to look out the window, head always down, wanting to be there *pronto*. It occurred to her then how well he knew her in such a short time, how she had opened up to him so blindly. She thought she wanted him to know her, to truly understand her and yet the truth was, the thought terrified her. She wasn't worth knowing. Eventually he'd find that out. Perhaps that was why she left him. She was just saving time.

Liam's favorite part was the journey. Getting there was the anticlimax, the whimper after the bang. They hired a car once and drove north, through Connecticut to the small seaport of Mystic. A journey of just 134 miles and Vilia wanted it over and done with, as soon as the speed limit would allow. She longed to be there, to be checked into their cozy B&B, to be wandering the streets, searching for a restaurant, to fall wearily into each other's arms in a bed made of fresh white sheets that someone else would clean. But the towns and roads in between were just window dressing.

Liam, on the other hand, wanted to enjoy the entire journey, including every inch along the way, stopping to smell and taste and prod it a little before moving on again. And he had had his way. The trip took them two days. They detoured inland, down unmarked roads and through uninteresting villages, stopping at every opportunity shop and rickety old bridge along the way. They even stopped overnight at a dingy roadside motel because no one else would ever choose to stop there, not if they had an alternative. And they did have an alternative, she tried to tell him as she frowned at the flimsy lock and the sticky carpet and the pickup full of rednecks that was pulling up next door.

"I've already booked us a place in Mystic, they'll be expecting us!"

"It'll be an experience," was all he replied, because that was the kind of person Liam was, and the kind of person she wished she could be.

But as she sat wedged deep into her taxi seat now, appalled by the brown poverty and the heat, her eyes firmly shut, she doubted she would ever get there, and wondered why she cared.

A gust of cool, salty air caught her by surprise and Vilia opened her eyes to find they had exited the freeway and were now rattling along the coastline, past a yacht club housed within a gated compound and beyond it, a mass of bobbing, gleaming yachts. It heartened her somewhat and she sat up and released her grip. They passed a bustling harbor and then detoured up through the main town, past shop fronts and high-security blocks of units with bored looking security guards at each gate. At the top of the hill she looked out to a spectacular view: a coconut tree-lined beach, a flat blue ocean beyond it and what appeared to be several sailboards whizzing along the shoreline. She watched them, surprised, before her driver did a sharp right-hand turn pulling into the gusty driveway of the Travelodge Hotel.

Horseshoe shaped and a little shabby, it was sanctuary nonetheless and she fumbled with the currency, paying her driver carefully and shaking her head at his beaming face as she clambered out. The hotel bellboys had already claimed her luggage and she followed them into the air-conditioned lobby, a wave of relief suddenly washing over her.

This is a bit more civilized, she thought, looking around her at the plush lounges and the massive artifacts. She presented herself at the reception desk, secured a room and locked herself away in it for the night, never noticing the startling sunset that bid her first day in the tropics good night.

People watched her, the stranger in their midst. And she wondered if they wondered who she was. What could possibly have brought her here? She clearly didn't belong. Her new flight to Alotau did not leave for almost an hour and she was waiting in the domestic departure lounge with a shifting crowd of travelers. When one ogling group gathered their bags and disappeared out the departure gate, another group was quick to take their place, glancing around the room inquisitively before settling their dark eyes on the nervous looking white woman again. There was the faintest hint of air-conditioning but it could not appease the heat that curled around her as she sat, rendering her lethargic, numbing her brain, luring her to slumber. But she must not sleep. She shook her head a little, jiggling it awake, and tried not to meet their eyes. Wishing they'd look away.

PX154 was now scheduled for 1:25 p.m. It had already changed twice since she arrived and she wondered if it would change again before departure time.

As in the international terminal, these walls were also decorated with cartoon-like characters, dancing, beating drums, carrying produce in string bags, but they weren't as large or as bright, and at intervals there were signs prohibiting smoking and the chewing of betelnut: *No ken kaikai buai hia.*

But it was the smell that overwhelmed her, a kind of mold-meets-cheap-soap-meets-rampant-body-odor stench that was growing increasingly worse as time dragged on.

"How's your Auntie Tilda?" she heard someone say.

A group of Australian missionary-lookalikes had nestled in nearby as though designating this the White Zone and she watched as a young local woman, who had been breastfeeding beside her, quietly hoisted the child up, lips still sucking away, and swaggered across the aisle to take her place beside her own. Vilia was appalled by this voluntary apartheid but loath to move away. It was too dramatic a gesture and, besides, her legs were not up to it. The tallest of the whities, a man with an unruly beard and crisp white socks pulled up over skinny calves, was talking in a subdued tone about his Aunt Mathilda in Maroochydor.

"She died," he said solemnly. "Very suddenly I'm afraid. She went to mass one morning. Then straight to the hairdressers—who, would you believe, are called 'Curl Up And Dye'?"

"No!" someone gushed beside him, clearly delighted.

"Oh yes, my man. And that's exactly what she did. She got home, didn't even bother to put her groceries away. Just curled up in bed. And died. Heart failure. She was seventy-one."

Vilia sighed. She was weary, hot and sweating from the armpits. Half an hour to go.

She remembered her first flight. Two weeks after her sixth birthday, beside herself with joy. It was a Boeing 707. Cairns to Sydney. She recalled the thrill of departure, the delight at dangling so high up, clouds like cotton wool peeling before her eyes. And small joys, too: the large plastic plate with pockets of treats. Squishy plastic earplugs too large for her ears. Waxy paper bags inviting you to vomit.

And then a slow dive as they returned to earth again. They stayed in a small motel where Vilia sat staring at the television more enthralling here than it had ever been at home. And her mother had come and gone, sometimes smiling, sometimes not. A quick trip to a pizza place and then back in the air and home again. She once cherished this as her first trip. Now she knew that was a lie.

Everything was now a lie.

Small black children staggered about like drunkards, their bellies protruding, their mouths drooling, their bright clothes mismatched and oversized. Eventually a white girl dressed up like a dolly joined them in play and to Vilia it was a lovely sight.

"Are you a missionary?" came an American accent and she looked up to see a young man in desert print uniform, taking the seat beside her.

She shook her head no.

"I was here three years ago, as a missionary," he told her. "I'm a US Marine now, from Ventura County, California, originally. Near Santa Barbara?"

She nodded, yes.

"Now I'm on a peacekeeping mission on Bougainville. I haven't seen any action, though." He sounded disappointed. "I'll probably go to Iraq next."

"Well I guess you'll see it there," she said finally, fidgeting in her seat, wishing the time away.

The plane that eventually whisked Vilia from the heat of Moresby into the cloudy sky was more like a rattling tin can than a jumbo jet. In fact, it was an Air Niugini Dash 8. Thirty or so seats and a cup of cold tea and bickies to keep you entertained. She nibbled her Scotch Fingers and stared glumly out the window. She smelled disgusting, had already changed her socks and was now wishing she'd thought to include a change of shirt and underwear, some antiperspirant, perhaps.

But then, who was there to impress?

The plane was almost full, half local, half expat, and there was a young white man just in front, still wearing dark sunglasses, too cool to lock eyes or smile. Others offered tired glances, encouraging smiles. The man beside her, a Papuan from Mt. Hagan, told her his flight had been canceled twice.

"I got TANGFU'ed," he said, and in response to her raised eyebrows added, "Typical Air Niugini Fuck Up."

"Ah, that's what it means."

They both laughed.

"Government regulations prohibit smoking," came a booming voice over the intercom, "and the chewing of betelnut."

And the man let out another red-toothed laugh.

They were gliding well above a thick rug of clouds and she had lost sight of the splattered reef beds below. She longed for a view, something to distract her from the questions that kept popping up, niggling at her nerves: *Why had she come? What was she hoping to find?*

She pushed them back down again, unable to answer, and thought about Tubu instead. Vilia had learned a little since her initial conversation with the lawyer, Hanes. But not enough. The island had been privately leased by a succession of expatriates since the early 1900s, her father the last in a long line of starry-eyed copra producers who poured their heart and savings into what was largely an unprofitable plant. His disappearance (abandonment? death?) had screeched it to a halt until the current caretaker, Jonah Johnson, had come in and cranked it up again. As far as she could tell, Jonah had never known her father and she wondered now what he could possibly tell her, how much use he could be. But Jonah seemed pleased enough to hear from her and, over a crackling phone from the island, had issued her with instructions and advice.

"Bring plenty of canned goods," he'd said, "and matches and mozzie coils and the biggest bloody bottle of RID—

tropical strength insect repellent—you can find. Oh and don't forget ya cossie!"

That comment made him chortle and he signed off while she sat simmering by the phone. She wasn't coming for a holiday and she didn't intend to stay.

The plane's engine suddenly sounded like it was about to conk out and Vilia glanced outside, relieved to see the cloud thinning out and then slipping away to reveal the lush green carpet of Gurney just below. Rows and rows of bushy oil palms covered the entire area, with rivers of dirt roads running through and the occasional coconut tree and white tinned roof. She spotted the airport, another glistening tin roof, and the long, wet gray airstrip just ahead and was glad when they finally landed, shuddering to a halt beside a sign welcoming them to Gurney Airport, "Outlet to the Milne Bay."

Only then did she release her shoulders from the fortress they had formed around her neck and, as she was prone to do, let out an enormous sigh.

Gurney is fifteen kilometers from the bay and its small capital Alotau, and Vilia was eyeing the empty bus stop with skepticism when a rusty Toyota four-wheel drive creaked to a halt beside her.

"Need a lift into town?"

The driver was a mixed-race man in his late twenties. His black hair was tinged almost blond around the front and its fuzzy ringlets had been secured in a ponytail down his back.

"No, no, I'll manage, thanks."

He hesitated a second, then shrugged and continued driving down to the small terminal where he parked and disappeared inside. Vilia gathered her bags closer and leaned out along the road, looking for signs of a bus. None were forthcoming and she noticed that the locals were starting to dissipate, leaping onto passing trucks or weaving their way on foot along the dirt highway. Sweat slowly trickled down her spine. She waved off the mosquitoes that were buzzing about her face and began chewing on her lower lip, wondering what to do.

"Sure you don't want that lift?"

It was the young caramel-colored man again, leaning out of the window of his 4WD. "Looks like the bus has come and gone and you're probably in for a long wait." And still she hesitated. "Look, I don't bite, eh?"

Vilia smudged her lips into a smile. "Of course not. Thanks, that'd be good."

His name was Roger Talis and he was full of the kind of youthful exuberance she couldn't even recall ever having.

"What brings you to these parts, then?"

"Oh, just traveling through," she said.

"Well, it's a top spot. I help my dad at the liquor store in town. Big business there, no doubt about that."

"You like it here?" She tried to conceal her doubt.

"Aw, it's alright. 'Course, I ran off down south a few years back before I realized that serving up burgers at Mackers wasn't quite my life calling. So I came home."

To serve up beers, instead, she thought.

"I make this trip every week," he explained, guiding the vehicle carefully along the wide, muddy road that weaved from the airstrip and towards the sea.

It had potholes the size of small craters and he maneuvered each one like a pro, swerving the vehicle from one side of the road to the next. Luckily, there was little passing traffic although they did overtake a red PMV, full to overflowing, its passengers gawking out at her, a variety of names scribbled in the dusty sides.

"It's not often I get company. It's … it's nice to have company," he was saying, and she smiled, then looked away.

They drove quietly for some time and she surveyed the long grass that lined the highway and the scattered coconut trees, some with their heads chopped off. The palm plantations had given way to a lush forest and there was an occasional rusty shed that seemed so at odds on its own in the wild. There wasn't much to admire and Vilia felt a million miles from Manhattan and her other life.

Roger glanced at the young woman and then quickly away. He opened his mouth to speak but something stopped him and he concentrated on the road ahead, embarrassed by the silence. She didn't look like a backpacker, he thought, had no spark in her eyes.

"It's certainly green here," she offered and he glanced across, surprised.

"Yeah, had a bit of rain. Not like that hole Moresby. Spend any time there?"

She nodded.

"Bet it was a dust bowl. Hate the place. They call it the New York of the South Pacific, y'know? Lots of rascal gangs. You meet with any trouble there?"

"No, I wasn't really there long enough. Just overnight."

"Travelodge?"

"Yep."

"Yeah, well, pretty safe there, I guess. Safer here, though. We're lucky, kinda hemmed in by a giant mountain range. Keeps the riffraff out."

He was referring to the rugged Owen Stanley Ranges to the west of Alotau which, with no roads cutting through, served as a natural Great Wall and kept the crime levels in this eastern region relatively low.

"So how long you stayin' in Alotau?"

"Hopefully I'm not."

"No?"

"I just need to get to the ..." She consulted a scrap of paper clenched in one fist. "The Masurina Trading Wharf. Apparently there's a mail boat leaving later this afternoon. I'm heading to one of the islands."

"Great! Which one?"

Vilia tugged at some curls that were cutting into her neck. She wished he would turn on the air-conditioning.

"It's called Tubu—"

"Jonah Johnson's place?"

My place, she wanted to correct him. "You know Jonah?"

"Aww, seen him around the traps a bit, you know? Good bloke."

"That's a relief."

"You don't know him then?"

Too many questions, she wanted to tell him. "Actually my parents used to own it and, well, my mum passed away recently and left it to me. So I'm going to check it out."

"Really?"

He turned his whole body to stare at her then, his eyes wide.

"Wow, lucky you, eh? You never been there before, then?"

"No." She felt foolish. "Well, not since I was a young child."

He went silent for several minutes, as though satisfied, but the truth was he was digesting the information, sorting old memories out in the recesses of his brain.

"Your parents," he said eventually and she turned back to him, eyebrows raised. "They weren't the Leas, were they? You're name's not Lea, is it?"

She hesitated. "Yes ..."

Something hot hit her stomach. It contorted defensively.

"You knew them?"

"Well, not me." His tone was suddenly wary, he was no longer meeting her eyes. "Heard about you guys, that's all."

"Yeah, well, I'm just back to check the place out." She wanted to slip underneath the seat. "Just for a week or two. I've gotta get back to the States. Got so much work on at the mo—"

"The States, eh? Whereabouts?"

"New York.'

'New York?!"

This also had him stunned and he turned right around in the cab again to stare at her.

"Gee, I haven't met anyone from New York before."

"Well I'm not from there, just working there."

"Same difference. What you do there?"

She hesitated. She was happy they'd got off the subject of her parents but these questions were all too much.

"Bit of this and that. How long until we get into town?"

"'Nother ten minutes or so," he said and, sensing her discomfort, returned to silence.

But everything was different now, she could feel it, and she knew she should ask Roger what he knew about her parents but she couldn't bring herself to, couldn't get the words out. All of a sudden, Vilia was back in Cairns, sitting next to a taunting twin boy, pretending not to care.

But that's why you're here, she told herself. *Just ask him!*

Yet still she remained mute.

Eventually they rolled into a small, shabby town with dusty roads that barely scratched a path around one block. Basic fibro stores lined the road and boasted western wares: *Pepsi, Winfield Cigarettes, Fanta Is Best!* Men and women, children, dogs and chickens loitered everywhere, others sat on mats selling dirty brown and green fruit and veg, and buai, daka and plastic bags of lime. The road continued around the coast and towards a busy harbor. Roger maneuvered his vehicle past some workmen towards a small shed sign posted 'Masurina.' He parked under the shade of a mango tree.

"Run in there and see if someone knows when the next boat's running. I'll wait here. Just in case."

Vilia did as instructed, returning a few minutes later her face forlorn. "I missed it," she managed to say.

"Damn!" He jumped out beside her. "Had you booked? Did they know you were on your way?"

"Well, no. It was yesterday. My flight from Moresby got changed to today and I figured there'd be another boat today."

Roger looked incredulous for a minute and shook his head. "Not likely. They wouldn't go daily—that'd be far too good service for this place."

"Oh," she said. *How stupid of me not to check.*

Roger scratched his hair vigorously, releasing several ringlets from their hold.

"Wait here," he said. "I'll see what I can do."

But there was nothing to do. The mail boat was not due back for days.

"I've got another idea," he announced, waving her back into his truck. Then they sped back along the coastline into town again.

"What have you got in mind?" Vilia asked, feeling helpless and hating it.

"It's a long shot but I saw Kyle O'Brien 'round town yesterday. If we're lucky, he'll still be here and you can get a lift with him."

"He owns a boat?"

"Light aircraft."

Her heart plummeted. Not another tin can.

"His island neighbors yours and he could easily drop you off if you chip in a bit for fuel."

"Fine, no problem, and you don't think he'll mind?"

"Well, that's the thing," he shot her a quick glance. "The guy's a bit odd. Bit of a loner, more than anything."

"Fabulous."

"Look, it's your only way. Try and sweet talk him." He smiled then, a radiant white smile, full of mischief. "Anyway, I reckon I know where we'll find him and that's a start."

The eminently named Royal Alotau Yacht Club was really just a weather-beaten fibro shack with a scruffy old beer garden out the back. It was the antithesis of the grand structure she'd spotted in Port Moresby the day before and her heart sank as she followed Roger inside. Small, smoky and reeking of stale beer, the club was scattered with an assortment of mostly white men, many of them bearded and sweaty looking with beer bellies protruding below raggedy T-shirts and over faded board shorts. Flip-flops were the standard footwear, and most had caps on their heads. There was clearly no dress code here. Several guys waved at Roger but they all kept their eyes firmly fixed on the woman by his side, their mouths pursed shut, their eyebrows raised in that lopsided, territorial way.

Vilia maneuvered her own mouth into a smile and followed Roger out into the beer garden, grateful to get away. He had chosen well, deliberately no doubt; there wasn't a soul in sight.

"You're in luck. I spotted Kyle on the way in."

Vilia glanced around.

"He's inside. I'll get us a beer. You might need it."

He winked cheekily and disappeared back inside while Vilia dropped her head into her hands and muffled an internal cry.

I don't belong here, what am I doing here? Oh God, what have I done?

This place was too strange and unpredictable for Vilia Lea. She had grown up with strange and unpredictable; she did not need it now. And she didn't need to rely on perfect strangers to survive her day. Or at least she wished she didn't.

"Here you go," Roger said as he placed the beers down. "South Pacific lager, it's a top drop."

"Thanks. What do I owe you?"

"Oh bugger that. My shout."

"Look, I hope I'm not keeping you from something?"

"Yeah, a boring afternoon in the shop! Dad'll be pissed off but that's nothing new. Nah, don't worry about it. This is the most fun I've had all month!"

"Glad to see I'm so entertaining," she said, smiling weakly and clicked his glass.

As they drank, Roger pointed out Kyle O'Brien who was sitting by himself at the bar, reading a newspaper. Vilia was expecting someone shorter, gruffer, with a giant chip on one shoulder, so his clean-cut, boy-next-door looks caught her by surprise. He was clearly just a few years older than her, in his early forties perhaps, with thick, brown hair that was cropped short and just starting to gray, but his body looked in good shape and he had taken some care with his clothes so that it wasn't just the distance of his stool that set him apart from the other men. He had a crisp, blue and white collared shirt on, long brown shorts and chunky work boots. Like Vilia, he looked transplanted from elsewhere.

"No point putting this off," she told Roger, taking another swig of her beer as she stood up. "Wish me luck."

"Good luck, hey. You'll need it!" He chuckled into his beer again.

Kyle didn't look up from his newspaper when Vilia took the bar stool beside him and she thought it odd, considering every other eye in the house was back upon her. She cleared her throat.

"Kyle O'Brien?"

"Yep," he said, still immersed in his paper.

"I was wondering if you could help me." He continued reading. "My name's Vilia Lea."

For a moment nothing happened, then it must have registered. His head snapped up, his eyes whipped across to hers.

"Lea?" he said, his sun-chapped lips stretched across his face as though he couldn't quite believe it.

"Yep, Vilia Lea."

It was amazing, she thought, the reaction this name was getting. His eyes were the palest of blues and they were staring at her expectantly, almost as if he was waiting for the punch line. She stammered on.

"I hear, um, that you have your own plane ... and, er, might be flying out soon." She swallowed hard. "I really need a lift, I missed the mail boat and it won't be back until—"

"You want to get to Tubu."

It wasn't a question but she nodded her head anyway. He didn't hesitate.

"I leave at four. Get yourself to the strip by quarter-to, and you've got yourself a ride."

"You mean Gurney?"

"No other strip I know of."

Then he put his beer to his lips and, once again, looked away.

PART 4

TUBU ISLAND—SWIMMING ABOUT

January 21: His eyes lit up as the island came into view and I can still recall his body, twitching with anticipation, sweat dripping unimpeded down his face. I am simply flat. And furious for being here.

Coconut trees stood to attention as the four-seater Cessna teetered towards earth, only their fronds swaying in the wind, like an audience clapping at the rattling bird and its pale entrails. Within seconds the tires touched down and Vilia's groan, long and low, was lost in the engine's drone. They rattled to a stop beside a small wooden shed with 'Tubu' chiseled into one side, in case you'd lost your way. From the far end of the airstrip, an old rusty yellow tractor materialized and a man began waving furiously as he ploughed it towards them.

Vilia felt a wave of nausea come over her and she wished they could just swing the plane around and fly off again. Up until this point, the whole experience—her mother's death, the lawyer's revelations, the mechanics of getting here—had been almost surreal, something from which she could be detached. But now, standing on terra firma, the past roaring towards her with a giant smile, was like standing in the middle of a storm. And she hated it.

The trip across had been like the calm before the storm, surprisingly serene and enjoyable. Part of her wished it could go on forever. It was as though she were sheltered in a cocoon, suspended in time and space. Despite what Roger said, Kyle had been polite enough but then there hadn't been time for very much more. He was initially preoccupied with the take-off and, once they were in the air, the roar of the engines had made conversation almost impossible. She guessed, though, that he was the quiet type anyway, quieter even than her, and she admired that in him, despite Roger's comments.

Kyle clearly recognized the Lea name and knew all about Tubu, but he didn't have that hungry look in his eyes. He didn't need to know everything, to prod her for gossip.

She thought then of Alex, of his almost insatiable appetite for her life. He had tried to talk her out of the trip, of course. Told her it was no island paradise she was going to.

"The crime rate there is appalling," he had said, and she had shrugged him off. But it didn't stop him from texting her just minutes before her departure from Cairns: "Call me. 1st thng. B safe! XO"

No, Alex, she thought, *not now. I have other things on my mind.*

This flight was different from the last two. It was her first light aircraft and she had expected to feel fear or trepidation. Instead, there was a kind of exhilaration. She watched, enthralled, as they left the muddy inlets and wind-battered waters of Alotau behind and began flying directly east, along the velvety green hills that were fast being frosted by the mist and, in some places, coated whole.

The Cessna was loud, but not disconcertingly so, and she enjoyed the slight breeze that filtered through as she sat strapped in behind Kyle, her groceries stuffed in beside her. Roger had kindly helped her navigate the trading store (for tea, biscuits, bread, cordial, matches and the like) and then the market place for what little fresh food they could find. She settled on sweet potatoes, bananas, lemons and pumpkin. Behind her was her luggage and, below, a breathtaking view. They had been following the line of the mountains around the mainland and were now leaving it for the open ocean which, to Vilia, resembled a satellite map—a mess of black, blue, purple and white where clouds and waves and reef and islands clashed to form ever-changing patterns.

Clouds lolled past her like lazy passersby, some in more hurry than others, and Vilia understood for the first time how a person could want to learn to fly. There was a sense of freedom in this kind of flying, a certain detachment from the land. She felt a little like a conqueror, too, as they ploughed noisily through the sky from which they should be falling. Once again she was beating Mother Nature at her best.

"That's Samarai!" Kyle called back to her against the engine's drone and she followed the line of his finger to a tiny, circular island below. She'd heard the name before, recalled it from her mother's letters.

We're in Samarai and the talk here is tremendous.
Oh how you must be hurting, you poor dear.

Vilia scrutinized the island more closely. She had read a little about it on her flight to Moresby, courtesy of Air Niugini's glossy in-flight magazine *Paradise*. It informed her that Samarai was once the thriving colonial capital of the region, mostly because of its deep-water port, but, looking down at it now she found that hard to believe. It was tiny, just twenty-four hectares in area and completely covered in neat rows of houses with thin roads and a perfect little oval in the middle. There were old wooden houses on stilts and a lush cliff on one side, and on the other the all-important port, cluttered with boats. It had been destroyed during World War II when the Japanese came close to invading Australia, but was still a commercial port and also served as the main supply town for the islands around it. She wondered if her father had moored there once, too, to stock up on supplies.

"Tubu!" Kyle yelled again and this time she saw a larger island wing into view.

This one was the antithesis of Samarai, a kind of sprawling mass of coconuts and rainforest, of a searing mountain and a ragged shoreline that resembled opals where the reef and sand merged. And there didn't appear to be a sign of life on it, not a neat little road nor a house to be seen. That is, until they circled a little closer and she spotted a tiny settlement facing northwest and almost overshadowed by the lush mountain behind it. Kyle kept flying, though, above that mountain and back around to the other side of the island, to a cleared grass airstrip about ten hectares long and one hundred meters wide. It was just meters from the beach and facing slightly south. He took the plane down smoothly and landed, taxiing the final leg to the shed.

Vilia wondered if Kyle would stay, what the protocol for island drop-ins was, but he seemed in a hurry to get going. He helped her alight then hauled her things out, dumping them in the shed, before returning to the aircraft and giving it a quick once-over.

As soon as Jonah was in ear shot, he yelled out a quick, "G'day, Jonah, you 'right?"

Then he jumped back into his aircraft, called out, "Clear prop!" as he revved up the engine, his door still open, then took it down a few revs, pumped a few pedals, shut his door and taxied off again, down the grass strip.

Within seconds he had escaped back into the sky.

"Good to finally meet ya," Jonah announced when the roar of the engine had subsided.

He produced a grubby hand to shake and seemed unaffected by Kyle's obvious snub.

"Welcome to Tubu. I was expectin' ya yesterday. Get TANGFU'ed, did ya?"

Vilia nodded and the old man burst into laughter. She could feel her temper rise.

"Yes, well, it would have been nice to know the mail boat doesn't go daily."

"God no, not around here!"

He raised a hand to wave at the departing plane.

"So grumble bum came to your rescue then? That was bloody lucky."

"Yes, it was lucky," she replied.

He glanced upwards again. "We better get a move on. The light's fadin' fast."

He piled Vilia's things onto the trailer with the deftness of a man half his age, then motioned for her to jump aboard.

"There's no pillow, love, but it's better than walkin'." He chuckled at this.

They chuckle a lot here, she thought, still smarting from his casual attitude.

Jonah was a skinny man, in his late sixties, made up entirely of muscle and bone with short, shaggy gray hair, just starting to recede. His stubbled face seemed kindly and his body was splattered in enough grease and dirt to know this guy wasn't afraid of hard work. In fact, he had been clearing away some bush at the far end of the strip when he heard the plane circle overhead.

"Which is lucky again," he cried out as he cranked the tractor up. "If I was back at the house you'd have been in for a long, dark wait."

He wasn't exaggerating. The journey between the strip and the main house took over an hour, although the distance on a gravel road would easily have halved that. The grass track had been cleared up to the width of the tractor, so the flatbed trailer, which was wider, protruded into the long grass that fringed the road and cut at Vilia's skin as they swished past. Things dropped on her, too, and she swiped frantically at them with one hand as the other tried desperately to cling on.

They drove along the coastline for several kilometers, weaving beside thick mangrove and coconut trees which leaned out across the beach as though on the look-out for something. And on the other side: their cousins stood impossibly tall and erect, their wares hanging like bulging breasts, threatening to drop. Beyond them was a mountain carpeted in lush rainforest and it was up into the hills they rattled and roared, scattering birds and insects as they went.

As the coconuts gave way to palms, the dirt turned to mud, a clay-like sludge that turned the tires into skates, slipping and sliding on the road while Vilia held her breath. Above them the fading sun was slowly being eclipsed by the canopy, and vines hung down, tugging at the intruders as they passed. The air here was thick and moist and for the next ten minutes they drove along at a slow pace as Jonah tried to keep the vehicle on track. He glanced back, smiling, from time to time and Vilia waved assuredly in return, pretending she was fine, but seething inside.

I suppose you could call this an adventure, she thought, *but it's not one I asked for.* This one had been foisted upon her.

Soon they were rolling back down the mountain and the coconut trees returned. So, too, did the coastline, and through thick mangrove Vilia could see the ocean roaring dark waves towards the shore. The sun was fast setting and the sky had turned an eerie orange hue. Vilia yearned to get there, wherever 'there' was. She didn't want to be caught out here when darkness dropped.

"Nearly home!" Jonah called back to her, and then swung around to negotiate what turned out to be the trickiest part of the journey, a rocky coral ledge that was masquerading as a road.

The mountain's jagged torso climbed up on one side and waves crashed erratically against the coastline on the other. The width looked barely able to take the tractor, let alone the wider trailer, and the dirt ground had given way to jagged rocks and coral. Vilia felt a chill run through her.

This wasn't an adventure, it was dangerous and stupid.

She wanted to jump off but her cries to Jonah went unheeded. He clearly couldn't hear her above the noise of the engine and waves. Clinging on to the side, her knuckles draining white, Vilia wondered how they could possibly make it, but Jonah didn't hesitate, simply changed gears and roared on.

At one point they leant so far to the right, she expected them to topple onto the rocks and down into the sea below, but within moments they were upright again. Then, a sudden lurch to the left sent her gear flying across the trailer and she reached out for it, unwilling to relinquish her own grasp, before a bump to the right nudged it all back into place.

Vilia closed her eyes and screamed silently inside. This was her worst nightmare, of course, and she couldn't believe her life—her beautifully organized life—had come to this. But then, miraculously, around the bend, a thick, grassy road appeared and they chugged off the coral and onto the earth.

She felt her entire body release and relax. She was almost euphoric. It was the feeling you must get, she thought, when you stepped off a rollercoaster ride.

Jonah slipped down a gear and turned back to her with a wink and the broadest of smiles that showed he thought the whole thing was a hoot. *He must love putting the tourists through that,* she thought. But she wasn't angry, now, just wildly relieved.

And something else, too, something she couldn't quite place.

They were now heading back inland on the final leg to the main house, and it proved to be a cinch by comparison, so she sat back more easily and breathed normally again, taking in her surroundings. She could still hear the ocean, just, through the thick trees to her right, and on the other side she spotted a clearing fenced by hibiscus trees. Within, a small thatched hut sat on stilts, barely visible in the encroaching dark.

"That's the guest house!" Jonah called back to her, but didn't stop, kept chugging along towards a distant light, and the soft roar of another engine.

Within minutes they were passing through a mesh fence, past what looked like chicken pens, veggie gardens and a few old sheds, and beyond all of that, an old wooden house, also on stilts. Jonah spluttered the tractor to a stop beneath the sprawling fig tree out front, and leapt down from his seat. Vilia simply sat and stared up at the building before her.

Her heart sank. The main house was a shambles. Painted in a myriad of shades, most of them now peeling or faded, with random bits of wall missing and rusty gutters hanging loose in spots, it looked ready to topple over. It was teetering on its stilts like an aged invalid, barely able to hold itself straight, and had clearly been badly battered by winds and rain. There was a work area underneath and a rickety staircase leading up to it at one end, and at the other, a giant cement tank upon which a rooster crowed, evidently unaware of the time.

"Yeah, she's old," Jonah said, referring to the house, "and even a little ugly, but she's home."

He grabbed one of her bags from the trailer where she still sat, clutching on to the sides.

"Come on, I'll show you 'round."

The house rattled beneath their feet. The floorboards were faded white and the paper-thin walls were littered with holes, the windows barely covered by dilapidated fly screens that she just knew would offer no resistance to the mosquitoes that buzzed outside. It was mostly open-plan, with a long, wide hallway that led between the kitchen on the east side and the living area on the west. In between, several doors led off to guest bedrooms. Jonah's room, the main bedroom, was beside the bathroom at the back. He had made some attempt to pretty the place up with giant, white clam shells full of fresh pink frangipani, but it did little to make the place seem any less shabby. It was old and in serious disrepair.

Why doesn't he renovate? she wondered, trying to keep the disgust from her face.

In the living area, there were several mismatched sofas, all faded and fraying, and against one wall a tall bookcase was jammed with books, most of them, she was delighted to see, falling into the category of pulp fiction or penny dreadfuls. She smiled despite her disappointment. Gena would not be impressed. But then, for the most part, Vilia wasn't too impressed either. Had she really been expecting a whitewashed villa with sweeping verandas that lead down to the sea? She had a sudden urge to bring out the Ajax and drape everything in crisp white cotton sheets.

"Got the generator runnin' now," he said, helping to explain the dull roar she could just hear off to one side. "But we don't usually run it at nights. We're spoilin' ya."

He pointed to kerosene lamps scattered about the place, hanging down from the ceiling and up against the walls.

"These usually do the job. 'Course I'm always in bed by sunset. Oh, come and meet Mary."

He marched back down the house, shaking the foundations as he went, and into the kitchen where a woman with black and gray-speckled hair was washing dishes. Two large gasoline freezers were rusting away against one wall and everywhere ants were busying themselves, on benches, in the pantry, all over a bunch of rotting bananas.

"Meet Mary," Jonah repeated as the native woman stopped her work and smiled bashfully, her hands still plunged in the soapy water.

He said something to her in a language Vilia did not recognize and the older woman clasped her soapy hands together with apparent delight and nodded her head towards Vilia.

"Mary's been here as long as I can remember," Jonah said. "'Course she was a young woman when I first landed here, but then, none of us are getting any younger!"

He laughed at this and led her back out to the hallway and into one of the guest rooms.

"So she knew my parents?" Vilia asked.

"Oh yeah she did, love, but you won't get much out of her. Doesn't speak a word of English. Not even good at Pidgin. Now, here we are, this is one of the guest rooms."

It was basic but clean, a single wooden bed placed strategically under the window.

"This is my room?"

"Yeah, I reckon. Of course there's also the old guest house ..."

"Oh?"

"Yeah, but you'll be all alone up there, so ... well, we'll see."

She didn't mind alone. She was used to that.

"I'd prefer the guest house."

"Well, it hasn't been cleaned up. It'd be a lot more comfy here. Still, we'll take a look at it later. First, though, my favorite spot!"

He led the way out a screen door to a wide veranda that lined the front of the house and looked out on the sea beyond. It was newer than the interior and recently painted, with a rope hammock covered in cushions hanging to one side and a staircase reaching down to a trimmed lawn below. Potted ferns flowed down from both ends and a small table laden with old magazines, a kerosene lamp and mosquito coils sat in the center between two enormous, faded arm chairs. Below her the lawn paved a path towards the beach, a rich magenta wall of bougainvillea separating grass from sand, and beyond that, the sea, a thick mass of surging darkness. There was just a sliver of moon tonight and it lent a kind of spookiness to the place.

Vilia wondered about her parents then and tried to see them here, sitting quietly hand in hand, looking out to sea. But all she conjured up was Gena's skinny white frame, watching, wondering, alone.

Always completely alone.

There had been touching, once, when she was a small child. But even now Vilia wondered if she had made that up. Hadn't there been an occasional hug from her mother? A gentle stroke? A loving kiss? It was all so long ago, how could she be sure memories had not merged finally with dreams? Or with childish longing? What she did remember clearly was her mother's placid features, so calm at times it brought her daughter to tears. If only Gena could unsettle her docile smile and cry along with her, or laugh or scream. An ugly, agonizing scream would have been preferable to her amiable nods, her predictable glances away.

Always away.

Outsiders called Gena 'introspective,' a 'dreamer.' Vilia saw it as indifference and disregard. In any case, it enabled her mother to be left alone to read her books or stare out to sea, as time marched wearily on, and her daughter sat brooding in the background.

Jonah reappeared carrying two cold drinks and, wiping several of the magazines off the table, sat one down in front of her.

"I always forget how mesmerizing this view is," he remarked.

But it wasn't the view she was looking at, she wanted to tell him, it was the ghost of parents passed.

"I won't be staying long," she declared after some time and he looked up from his glass surprised. "I'll probably catch the next mail boat back. Just so you know."

He went to say something, then stopped, shrugged and eventually muttered, "Rightio then." He got to his feet. "Now let's see about this guest house."

The guesthouse was a ten-minute walk back from the main house, through tall grass and a forest of coconut trees that separated the two houses like a platoon of soldiers, at ease in the breeze. They took kero' lamps with them, to light the way, and Jonah was laden with sheets, towels and a mosquito net. This house was in better shape than the main one and its walls and roof were covered in dried banana fronds in a traditional grass hut style. A seashell pathway led up to it and Vilia stared at the shells absently. *They must be painful under bare feet*, she thought. Enormous spider webs greeted them at the front door and it was clear it had seen many guests lately, but not of the *Homo sapiens* kind.

"We do get the odd backpacker passing by," Jonah explained, clearing the webs with a single swipe of one hand. "Your mum hasn't been here for a long time as you know, although Miriam did spend several months here a few years back."

There was that name again. The grandmother she never knew.

"Sad to hear she passed away, though," he continued and Vilia realized now that she never would.

He flicked a light on—"Connected to the generator," he said with a wink—and led the way inside. The place was dark and hot and creeping with insects. It featured one room broken into two smaller cubicles for bedrooms, a kitchenette on one side and, beside it, a tiny bathroom. A set of steps led down from the bathroom to a back garden, neatly mowed and edged on three sides by hibiscus plants that were not yet flowering. It was solitary and quiet. She decided to move in immediately.

"Okay then," he said, surprised. "I wasn't sure you'd fancy it but, yep, no probs. I'll get one of the guys to bring your gear up soon as poss. Let's get back to the main house for some *kaikai*."

On the way out, he turned back to her and said, "Your dad built this place himself you know?"

"No," she replied, bristling a little. *Of course I didn't know.*

She slammed the screen door behind them.

February 3: This place is so wild and alive. There are sounds I have never heard and smells and sights! I want to close my eyes and then open them, to my other life.

That first evening Vilia felt cravings for a panang curry brought in a little plastic bucket to her door by a polite Thai guy with a meek smile, but she shrugged off the image and went around to the front of the house where Jonah was piling bits of dry wood into an old brick barbecue. He threw coconut husks in too, and then a splash of kerosene which ignited the lot with thunderous delight. Later, when it had settled down, she watched him pile sweet potato and pumpkin onto the hot plate and then a large fish speckled red and white. He called it a Red Emperor.

When they returned upstairs with the food, Vilia noticed Mary had set up a table on the veranda with a candle to eat by. It was certainly warm enough to eat outside but it was so dark she wondered why they bothered. Various noises prickled her attention, creatures lurking frighteningly close by, and beyond that the roaring of the black sea. Mary had also placed large glasses of gin and tonic beside each plate. Vilia didn't drink much normally, she preferred her senses straight up, but that night the gin comforted her and she let it lead her to that place where nothing really mattered. She didn't want to think too much and, worse still, to feel. When she got there, she sat in a dazed kind of stupor staring into the darkness. It didn't seem so spooky now, more soothing, like a blanket.

Or, perhaps, she thought morosely, *a blindfold*.

Vilia recalled her first night alone at the age of eighteen in the 'Big Smoke,' Sydney. She had driven out of Cairns and away from her mother like a prison escapee, one foot firmly on the pedal, her eyes darting every now and then at the rear vision mirror, desperate to flee but racked with guilt and dread nonetheless. She was making sure that where she had come from was still firmly planted in her mirror, fast disappearing from sight. It took thirty-six hours on the freeway and another sixteen stopping off in crummy roadside motels she could barely remember now, as though she had wiped them from her past. But she did remember the relief she felt when she got to Sydney. She knew she should have been scared, but she was thrilled and relieved and ready for a new life.

That's when she met Alex.

She'd been in Sydney a week, had already rented a small art deco studio apartment in an inner-city part of town called

Potts Point. She wasn't sure how she'd pay the rent, was using her meager savings for now, and on the lookout for work—perhaps she could pull off waitressing, she told herself—when she began wandering the streets. She had meant to stop at the edge of her suburb, to turn around and head home, like the good girl that she was, but her feet would not hear of it, as though the very act of stopping and turning was too defeatist. Not today, they told her. Today you'll do as you please.

And so she walked on, through unfamiliar streets, past foreign stores and alien faces. A Greek Orthodox church here, an old pub there, a cluster of young guys ogling her from one corner, a bustling cafe spilling patrons into her path on another.

Then she saw the bookshop. And stopped. It looked misplaced in this grungy street of beer-swilling blokes and greasy food bars and perhaps that's why she sought refuge there, flinging the door open and stepping inside. Or perhaps it was because of her mother, a momentary reminder, a subconscious reconciliation attempt.

Alex was behind the counter but didn't bother to say hello, so she wandered from stand to stand, half looking at the books, half wishing herself home. She quickly settled on a novella and placed it on the counter, fidgeting for her purse.

"Complete crap," he said and she looked up surprised.

He was leaning his long thin torso across the counter, his thick black hair sheared into a military style, short back and sides, with one white streak above his left ear. She later learned it was his pride and joy, that streak, his one attempt at anarchy. In later years he would replace it with a rat's tail and then a bobbled plait down one side.

"I'm telling you, sweedie," he had chirped, "don't waste your dosh."

"Well it looks fine to me." She handed him some notes.

"This book is for pretentious prats who spend more time scanning the *Herald*'s bestseller list than reading real literature, and by the look of you ..." He paused then and eyed her from head to toe. "You are as far from pretentious as I am from a Catholic priest."

Vilia wasn't sure how to take this and he flashed her a smile.

"It's a compliment, sweedie. So, where you from?"

"I live in Potts Point," she replied.

He turned his head to one side as if to say, *Yeah and I'm King Kong*, and she quickly added, "Cairns, originally."

His eyebrows shot skywards.

"FNQ ... really? I should've picked it."

Now she knew he was making fun of her and Vilia slammed the book back down on the counter.

"Can I have the book, please?"

"Oooh, a touchy one." He smiled. "I'm also from Far North Queensland, doll, from Mossman, heard of it?"

"Of course." She was surprised.

Mossman was a small country town on the fringes of the Daintree National Park rainforest, just north of where she grew up. Full of rednecks and hippies and very few people resembling this guy.

"How long have you been here?" she asked.

"Long enough to know I won't be going back. How about you, sweets? Looks like you're just off the bus to me."

She laughed then. "Pretty much. A week."

"My, that is virginal. Welcome. How do you like it so far?"

"It's okay."

"You run away?"

Vilia considered this for a moment. "That would suggest I had something or someone worth leaving," she said at last. "And I don't reckon I did."

Alex was delighted by this answer and laughed heartily. It was the beginning of many hilarious moments the two ex-Queenslanders shared together over the next few years. As it turned out they were both running away, she from neglect, he from the complete opposite. Alex's parents were old-style cane farmers, as ocker as the earth they toiled and as adoring as any parents can be. In fact, he found them overly adoring, fussy, desperate for him to take over the farm, and completely incapable of accepting that their son was gay. And so, feeling suffocated, he, too, had escaped to the big smoke.

Despite a five-year age gap, the pair soon became best of friends, eventually moving in together. Yet while Alex made the occasional trip home, Vilia could never be convinced to join him. Not, that is, until her mother's funeral, when they flew up together. Her first trip home since she'd left.

"I need to call Alex!" Vilia declared, startling Jonah who had also slipped away somewhere, gin slithering through his veins.

He shrugged towards the house. "You'll notice your mobile don't work here, no range at all, but we've got an old phone in the lounge room, there's dialing instructions beside it. Costs a packet though, watch the clock."

It took some time before Vilia managed to get through and when she did her good mate seemed further away than he ever had when she lived in the States.

"Alex? Alex, it's Vilia, can you hear me?"

"Vili, sweedie! How are you?"

"Missing the real world," she replied and then proceeded to give him the dramatically abridged version of the past two days.

"I knew you shouldn't have gone," he said, sounding worried. "What's the island like? Tiny?"

"Huge actually."

"What's the caretaker like? An old loony? How are you supposed to spend your time?"

"I am here for a reason, Alex, don't forget." The G&T was quickly wearing off. "Look, I can't talk for long, this is gonna cost a fortune—"

"Well when do you think you'll be back? There's a Sydney Dance Company show starting up next week that I really think you'll enjoy."

"Oh, I'm not sure."

"See all the things you're missing running off to the bloody tropics?"

"I know, I know. Alex, I really have to go, but I'll be in touch."

"Tomorrow night, call me tomorrow."

"It's expensive from here, Al."

"Yeah but I'm going for that advertising job and you'll want to know how it went."

She frowned at herself. "Oh, I forgot about that. Good luck with it, I know you'll do fine."

"Oh we hope so! I can't even think what to wear, what do you think I should wear?"

"The pinstripe, of course."

It's what he always wore to the impressive job interviews he never seemed to get. Over the fifteen years she'd known him, Alex must have gone for more than thirty interviews for everything from journalist to personnel officer to publicity coordinator for a leading retail chain. Yet somehow he was still selling books in dusty old shops where the clientele was thinning and large book chains were casting ominous shadows from every side. She admired his persistence, though, and his unwavering confidence in himself.

"I have to go, Al," she told him. "Take care and good luck tomorrow."

As the phone cluttered onto its stand, she felt a wave of melancholy wash over her. Her watch said 8:00 p.m. It was too early for bed and yet every cell cried out for sleep. She made herself a cup of strong tea and returned outside.

"So what usually happens now?" she asked Jonah who was still nestled in his seat.

"It's called sleep," he replied softly. "But I know what you Big Smokers are like—can't even look at a bed until both hands are pointin' north."

"Yeah, well it is kind of early."

"Which is why we have a fine selection of books ... although if you ask me, you look buggered. It won't hurt to get an early one in."

"But eight o'clock!?"

"It's just a number, love. I hit the sack when the sun does and am back up to greet her in the mornin'. It's worked for me for thirty years. Besides, that way I don't flog the generator so much."

"Speaking of which, what on earth brought you out here in the first place?"

"Ohh, that's a bloody long story, love. You really want me to go into it?"

She indicated her watch. "Hey, I've got till midnight, remember?"

He chortled and then settled back into his chair and told her his tale.

Born on the outskirts of Darwin to a couple with too many kids and too little cash, Jonah Johnson idled from one odd job to the next as a young man, restless and unsure of himself. One year he labored on the steamy construction sites that later became the bane of the Gold Coast skyline, the next he headed south to pluck oranges or west to drive cattle. Yet nothing really stuck.

"I considered joining the Navy," he said, "anythin' to keep me occupied. And then I saw the ad."

In the mid 1970s, the *Brisbane Courier Mail* ran a small advertisement for a cattle business in Papua New Guinea.

"They wanted someone with a bit of experience and, well, I'd done a bit of farm work so I applied. Barely knew where PNG was let alone what the job involved, but I applied for it anyway. And I got it."

"Oh, so Tubu?"

"Patience," he said. "Told you it was long 'un. So, I headed up to Lae, where the job was and, well, I guess you could say the business was a dismal failure."

He laughed at this. "I kinda took to the place, though. Besides, I was pushin' forty and couldn't keep runnin' forever. And I'd paid good money for the blasted plane ticket—which the buggers never reimbursed I might add— so I figured I might as well stay and make a go of it. That's when I met ya mum.'

Vilia's heart skipped a beat.

"I found work and board at a small tea plantation in the highlands. Been workin' there about a year when I heard that a white woman was lookin' for a caretaker for some island in the Milne Bay. I liked the idea of movin' to the coast— highlands can get bloody cold, y'know? And they're a tough bunch out there. But I wasn't real sure I wanted the job, tell ya the truth." He paused then, not meeting Vilia's eyes. "Anyway I met your mum and saw how eager she was to get someone on it, so I agreed. My plan was a month, max. And now look at me, thirty years later!"

He chuckled a little and then settled back into his seat. But Vilia's curiosity was now piqued, she needed to know more.

"What did she say to you? Why did she have to leave? Was she living here at Tubu then?"

"Had been. Wanted to move down south."

His tone had lost its ease and he blinked slowly as though clearing away the cobwebs of a story long forgotten.

"Let's see," he said, finally, shifting in his seat. "What did she tell me ..."

Genevive Lea was a wisp of a woman, even back then, he recalled, with stringy limbs and long, ashen blond hair. Her freckled skin looked as though it had seen a lot of sun lately and he remembered cold sores bubbling up on her chapped lips. She had put on a little lipstick but that, and the crisp cotton dress she was wearing like a coat hanger dangling from her bones, did little to detract from the frail appearance she presented when he first saw her in the lawyer's office in Alotau. He remembered being startled by the woman and began to wonder whether he'd made a terrible mistake in coming.

The idea of hiding away on an island had seemed tempting at the time, even at the age of forty, and it wasn't just about the weather. As one of a brood of kids he longed to have his own space. Hell, his own bedroom would do the job. *But an island? All to himself?* It seemed too good an opportunity to pass up. Then there was the added bonus of being his own boss or at least not having the real boss there, breathing down his neck, pointing out all the things he was getting wrong, again.

But the truth was, he was happy enough, too, on the tea plantation, and much of that centered around the childish crush he had developed on the plantation owner's daughter, Nicola. The problem was, at forty, he was far from a child and while she, at seventeen, still was one, she had her sights set further afield even than him, something Jonah failed to realize until a sudden tropical downpour opened his eyes.

Nicola was quite a beauty. Of German descent, she had her father's chiseled features and her mother's long, olive limbs. Her hair was snow white and always worn long and down, despite the heat. It was clearly her crowning glory and she often brushed it forward, across one shoulder where she would stroke it softly, her hazel eyes staring out across the tea fields seeing not the plants nor the men who labored away, but another world, one far away.

"I'm going back to Germany," she told Jonah that afternoon when the storm had halted work and they'd both sought refuge in a storage shed nearby. Nicola occasionally helped out on the plantation, although she did so reluctantly, and today she welcomed the storm, grabbing Jonah's arm and dragging him away from the fleeing workers who were headed for the main work station, to the shelter of this solitary shed. His pulse had accelerated at her touch and his mind raced with possibilities as they ran. By the time they got inside, he was dizzy with anticipation and looked around frantically for a dry spot to lie, but she stopped at the doorway and turned back to stare at the storm.

"I hate this place," she spat, glaring out at the haze. "What is there here for me?"

Jonah caught his breath. "Me!" he wanted to yell and if she had turned she would have seen. But she offered him not a glance, just stared out and sighed.

"What am I supposed to do? How will I ever meet the man of my dreams?" And then, "Oh, everything's so *provincial*!"

Gutted but pretending not to be, Jonah joined her by the door. He did not know what to tell her. His experience with women was limited to idle conversation, perhaps a little small talk after sex and God knows there hadn't been a lot of that. He didn't attempt to answer, simply followed her gaze outside. And that's when the cloud lifted. They were standing in the same spot, staring at the same view, but he saw only beauty, nature at its most magnificent, and wondered then if beautiful people had trouble seeing beauty elsewhere. Even when it slapped them in the face.

"I'm leaving, you know," she continued, her tone defiant. "I'm going back home to Munich."

He wanted to laugh then. She had been born in this land, had probably trod on German soil twice in her life, and yet it would always be her home. Papua New Guinea was not good enough for her. He'd never been to Munich but he'd seen pictures and thought it an ugly place, with too many old buildings below a dirty gray sky. When it rained there, it rained soot.

"You'll get there, then," he told her.

"Of course I will," she spat, swinging around finally to meet his eyes, hers now fiery with what he thought was determination. Later he realized it was uncertainty and fear. It was the same look that Vilia tried to conceal now as she sat across from him, desperate for the details that would only serve to slice her heart to shreds. And so, determined not to keep punishing his own, he hitchhiked his way to the coast and organized a meeting with the lawyer.

As he shook the lawyer's hand firmly, Genevive had emerged from the shadows and extended one skinny arm towards him. She seemed almost ghostly, despite the sunburn, and he felt instantly ill at ease. Her eyes looked at him but they did not appear to see and her grasp was so slight he thought her fingers would fall to bits in his craggy hand.

"Thank you for coming, Jonah," the lawyer, an Englishman by the name of Sebastian Cone, had said and, directing them both to seats, got straight to the business at hand.

"Mrs. Lea, here, has an island directly south of Alotau. Not sure if you know the area? It's not far from Samarai. She needs a good caretaker—just a temporary position for the moment. It's operating as a copra plantation, which I see you've had a bit of experience with—"

"I work on a tea plantation, mate, not copra you understand?"

"Yes, but you help manage the place, is that correct?"

"Yeah, that's right, but ..."

"You manage a team, you oversee the work, you do the books?"

"Yes, well, no. Not the books. Don't do that side of things."

The lawyer waved one hand in the air. "Simple mathematics." He paused. "You seem like an intelligent man. We simply need someone to keep the place going for a while until we, er, until Mrs. Lea here decides what to do with it. There are six workers and their families currently living on the island so there's plenty of help there if you need it."

"And if it was to shut down?"

"Then we would pay you duly for your work and you'd have copra plantation experience up your sleeve."

"And the staff?"

"They would remain." It was Genevive's voice, barely audible from the chair beside him, but firm nonetheless.

"Yes, well ..." Cone said, a little hesitantly and it was clear to Jonah that this had been a point of contention. He coughed.

"In any case," he continued, "the main focus for now would be keeping the grounds in shape and the bush from taking over the main house and gardens until we decide what to do with it."

He looked back at Gena then, his eyes widening a little as though making a point, but she stayed silent, staring straight ahead.

"So you're thinkin' of sellin'?" Jonah asked.

"Well, that's not really your concern. We would still ensure a six- to twelve-month contact depending on what you think you could handle."

"If anything, six," he said dubiously.

"Jolly good, six to start with. Do you think you're up to it?"

"Well, as I said, Mr. Cone, I've never done copra before—"

"Ahhh, easy as pie," he scoffed, uninterested in Jonah's objections. "Tea, coffee, copra, whatever. All it needs is a bit of common sense and a lot of elbow grease. You'll be fine."

"Well, I'd have to think about it," Jonah continued, determined to turn the job down.

It was more responsibility than he cared to take on, and it all seemed a little odd to him, this ghostly woman and the bossy lawyer. What was she doing with an island she didn't want, anyway, he wondered? And where was her husband?

"Well, then, Mr. Johnson, you go away and give it some thought. We'd appreciate an answer as soon as possible. I want to get Gena and her girl out ... They need to leave by the end of the week so we are looking at a replacement as soon as possible, you understand. We'd be most appreciative.'

"Jesus, that soon."

Jonah was shocked. This was all happening too fast to make any kind of sense. He'd get the hell out of there and call the toffee-nosed lawyer from the tea plantation to tell him thanks but no thanks. He didn't need this kind of headache in his life. He wasn't sure what trouble this scrawny lady had got herself into but it wasn't his job to rescue her.

"Yeah, well, I'll be in touch," he said quickly and, nodding uncertainly at them both, fled outside.

The sun was beating down hard that day and he made his way to a local bar to get a beer and commend himself on a narrow escape. He was just sinking his lips into the fluffy white head when he noticed the woman had followed him in. She seemed uncomfortable here, her eyes darting around the room warily and then resting on Jonah by the bar. She glided over, her hands clutching a small bead bag in front of her, and climbed onto the stool beside him.

"I need your help, Mr. Johnson," she said, staring down at her lap.

She was so frail, Jonah wondered if she would slip right off the stool.

"Look, ma'am," he began, trying to sound sensitive, not sure exactly how. "I'm not the bloke you're lookin' for, that's all. I'm not equipped for this sort of thing, wouldn't know where to start. I'm just a drifter, see, a bit of a bum by my dad's account. You need someone reliable, someone who'll stick around if that's what you want."

"There's never any assurance of that."

She said it so quietly he wasn't sure he'd heard right.

"Look, you wanna a drink?"

"No."

She shook her head emphatically and then turned her whole body around so that she was facing him, her eyes now zeroing in on his.

"You seem like a good man," she said. "I'm not asking for a commitment. Just stay a month, see how you like it."

"Why don't you just sell the place? Sounds like you're headin' back home anyway, what do you need a place like that hangin' over your head for?"

And where's your bloody husband? He kept that thought to himself.

"I can't sell it," she replied, her voice lifting a little. "That's not an option. Not yet. Please, give it a month. Just one month is all I ask. I know you'll love it, I just know you'll want to stay."

You don't know me at all, lady, he wanted to bark back but her eyes were so insistent, her whole body twitching with nervous anticipation, that he could not find the courage to disappoint her. He was terrified she would shatter into a million miserable pieces right in front of him. She was clearly close to tears. He did not want a scene. And so he agreed. One month. And that was all.

"Oh thank you, thank you, Mr. Johnson," she sobbed, her shoulders throbbing, and he thought she would break down anyway, crying like a baby in a shanty bar full of expatriate men and mangy dogs.

But she pulled herself together suddenly and the tears that had threatened to spill dropped back into her eyes. Only her trembling voice gave her away.

"My lawyer will see to the details. You will not regret this."

And then she was gone, slipping out into the sunlight. He didn't know what her story was but he knew it was a sad one and he guessed it involved a man.

You're a bloody pushover, he scolded himself and angrily ordered another beer. One month, he'd give her, that was it. Then he'd tell them both where they could shove their bloody island.

Tubu turned out to be more work than he expected and he spent the first week cursing himself incessantly and rehearsing his resignation speech over and over again. But before he knew it the month was up and the copra plantation, which had been at a virtual standstill when he arrived, was starting to show a little promise. His vegetable garden, too, was starting to come good and he was buggered if he was going to hand it over to someone else to enjoy. Perhaps he'd stay another month or so, see if he couldn't knock the main house into a bit of shape.

It was old and beaten up, even back then, and why it hadn't been properly painted and decked out with flyscreens was beyond him. The veranda out the front could do with a little extending too, he thought, and made a note to call old lawyer Cone at the end of the week for some more funds to help him out.

Sebastian Cone had been more than generous and while the caretaker's wage was not great, Jonah had been assured all the financial help he needed to clean the place up. It wasn't until a prospective buyer dropped by one day on his gleaming white yacht that Jonah understood why. Cone was clearly hoping to sell the place off, and fast, and Jonah's job was to knock it into shape for a profitable sale. He wondered what Gena's views on the matter were, and did not think she would approve.

The buyer was a large Dutch man with a bald head and enormous eyes that shot about the place furiously. He told Jonah he owned a string of islands to the east but was looking for something closer to Samarai, the main port island in the region. The Dutch man's priority, it soon became clear, was money and he was disappointed to hear that the plantation did not run at a profit.

"More a hobby farm than anythin' else," Jonah explained.

"What the hell for, hobby farm?!" the man boomed and then his eyes had stopped long enough to flicker with understanding. "Oh, that is right. This was young Lea's place, yes? Now I see."

He left soon after and never returned.

Another potential buyer sailed over within the month, this one from New Zealand, with his wife and son in tow.

"Were those sandflies that attacked me as we came up the beach?" the woman, a short fat thing with a bouffant hairstyle that would have been hell in this heat, snorted.

"'Fraid so,' Jonah replied gladly. These people didn't deserve Tubu. "All the beaches are plagued with them but it's nothing a little RID won't fix."

"RID?"

He couldn't believe she didn't know what RID was. It had become his best buddy in these parts, a strong-smelling white liquid that gave the mosquitoes their walking papers. Dab a bit of that stuff on and it's so long stings.

"Mind if we look around?" the husband interjected and Jonah just shrugged. Wasn't his concern.

They started with the main house, peering into the rooms and scrutinizing the woodwork, whispering to each other conspiratorially. Jonah wanted them to understand he couldn't care less one way or the other what they thought of the place. It wasn't his, see, he was just the caretaker. But still, after they had sailed off in a blaze of complaints, he had to admit relief. Genevive wouldn't have liked them. They didn't belong here.

And so that first month turned to two, and then, before he knew it the year had flown by. There was the occasional visit from unimpressed investors and long, quiet spans which he grew to relish more and more. Gena seemed happy enough for him to stay on and showed no desire to sell the place, despite Cone's best efforts. Jonah was happy, too. He always found one project or another to keep himself occupied, and the copra plantation was coming along nicely. Despite being promised six strong men, only three had remained on the island when Jonah got there, but between the four of them, they had the place sewn up. Besides, two of the men's young boys showed promise and would be helping out in the next year or so.

And that's how he began to think. Not in terms of weeks or months, but long-term. As Gena had predicted, he had soon fallen in love with the place, despite its stinging sand and crashing coconuts.

"And you're still here," Vilia said quietly when his voice had trailed off.

"Be hard to leave now," he replied, and she wondered at this.

Didn't he get lonely? Didn't he crave a lover's touch? Didn't he long for civilization, for some kind of comfort in his old age? She couldn't imagine living here for thirty years. She wouldn't have lasted that first month.

He stood up, stretched his lean limbs and emitted an enormous yawn.

"It really is past me bedtime. The sun'll be wonderin' where I've been. Want me to walk you back to the guest house?"

She shook her head no. But her stomach was in knots. There was so much she wanted to ask him, so many questions about the past. But she was tired, too, weary from the long journey and the bombshells of the past week. Another day of ignorance wouldn't hurt.

Jonah prepared Vilia a kerosene lamp and placed it down beside her.

"I need to turn the generator off now, love. This'll light your way to the hut. I've already had Mary clean it up a bit for you. Personally, I reckon you'd be more comfortable bedding down here, but, well that's up to you. G'night."

Yet Vilia was determined to stay in the guest hut. She still needed her space, even on this expansive, almost uninhabited island, and so she took the lamp and made her way there, tripping about in the long grass as she swerved from the pathway and back on again. Weariness had already taken hold by the time she flung the front door open, so she did not notice whatever might have been lurking in the shadows. She undressed somehow and fell into bed, enveloping herself with the old gauze mosquito net. Within minutes she was asleep dreaming of her mother sipping beers with a fat German woman in a dingy, dog-riddled pub.

February 21: I don't care for the island. This is someone else's dream, not mine.

A strange call woke Vilia from her sleep.

Kwa! Kwa! Kwee! Kwee!

She peeled open her eyes to discover her body cocooned like a butterfly in her net and thrashed about frantically, searching for an escape. Eventually she found the opening and wriggled out, noting as she did so that the hook that held the net had broken overnight. Her restless dreams had done the rest. Below the window the crowing continued. Whatever it was, she wanted it dead. Beyond that, she could hear the erratic crashing of water against land.

Her things had been brought up the night before so she rifled through her bag for a swimsuit and sarong. She wished she had brought a sailboard.

"What? And get your toes nibbled off by sharks? Those waters are plagued with them," Alex had warned her. "Don't even think about it."

"But I'll go insane. You know how much I love sailing."

"Besides," he continued, "how will you ever transport the thing? I can't imagine what hell it'll be. Just take the basics, sweedie, you can windsurf when you get back."

He was right, she knew that. But it didn't curb her regret. If ever she needed to disappear into the wind, it was now. Vilia pulled on a white, wide-brimmed hat and oversized sunglasses and made her way carefully along the track towards the sound of the ocean and what she assumed was the beach. Sprawling mangrove formed a barrier between land and sea and this path met up with the main road that had brought her from the airstrip along the rocky cliff face. She followed the road around and came across a slim pathway down into a small bay just around the bend from the main beach. This was where Jonah's yacht was anchored, bobbing about in the bay's calm sanctuary. It was low tide she guessed by the water marks, and there was barely a ripple in the ocean suggesting strong coral reefs beyond. And reef sharks, too, no doubt.

Questions began forming in her mind, but she tried to push them back. She didn't want to think about anything now, she just wanted to be calm.

Vilia strolled along the sand for a while and noticed hundreds and hundreds of sea shells, dumped like unwanted litter along the beach, fading and forgotten. Most of them had been starched white, their once vibrant hues long forgotten on their journey to these shores. Most were broken and felt like jagged glass under her soft feet. She winced a little as she stepped over them and tried to find clear sandy patches as she made her way down to the water's edge. A large circular object caught her eye and she bent down for a closer look. It was a Nautilus shell, complete, black at the tip and spreading out into a miniature gramophone, painted red like zebra stripes and then the brightest white. She picked it up and placed it to her ear.

It didn't sound like the ocean to her. Just a deep breathing, like that crank call she got last March, just before she met Liam.

"Huuuuhhhhhhhhh ..."

Heavy, soulless. She tossed it back down and turned her attention to the sea. The ocean, as crystal clear as any travel brochure cliché, was like some sort of odious drug that lulled her into its depths and assured her for several sweet minutes that nothing else really mattered. She did not think of her father or her mother, or the way Jonah had described her, nor did she notice the sandflies that first morning as they hovered around her like unsettled dust, tiny particles clinging to her skin as she carried them like an ocean liner out to sea. She didn't notice the rip, either, as it directed her away from shore and towards the sandy bay that heralded one edge of main beach. She just bobbed about, clearing her mind. Forgetting.

Suddenly there was a whoosh.

She dropped her legs to the sand but there was nothing there. She looked about frantically, she had floated out too far, she needed to get back in. Suddenly black shadows lingered everywhere she looked. She imagined hungry jaws snapping at her, tearing into her, pulling her down. She began swimming frantically towards shore, her legs flailing about in all directions, her hands wading, grabbing, grasping at nothing, splashing water up into her eyes, stinging them. Then, like a life raft from the ocean floor, she felt the sand beneath her and clawed her toes in, pulling herself upright with her hands, thrusting her thighs harder through the rip of the morning tide, harder, faster.

And finally she was out, dripping and heaving and panting uncontrollably. She flung herself on the sand and only when her toes were free of the frothing liquid did she dare to look back. There was nothing there. Not so much as a splash.

"Ouch!"

She felt her first sting, like an injection straight into her arm. And another, and then another. She looked down and spotted them at last, the little midges, feasting merrily on her virgin skin, and she swiped them away frantically. She grabbed for her towel and dashed up the beach and back on to the road where the insects were loath to follow. Itchy red splotches were already starting to form all over her body and she cursed and scratched and swiped the empty air.

"No wonder nobody wanted to buy the bloody place," she snapped beneath her breath, wiping away sudden tears.

Before Vilia made her way to the main house for breakfast, she clenched her teeth through an icy shower, washing away the tears and scrubbing the salt from her skin and hair. She tried to ignore the wasps that buzzed around her, seemingly peeved at having their peace interrupted, and concentrated instead on cleaning and scrubbing and getting the job done. Afterwards, she donned something cotton and flowing, and pulled her unruly locks back into a tight, dripping ponytail, but she couldn't settle her nerves, and she wondered at this as she climbed up the steps of the veranda.

Jonah was nowhere to be found so she grabbed some bananas and pawpaw from the kitchen and made herself a strong cup of cheap, instant coffee. She missed her espresso machine. The sooner she was back in Manhattan the better, she thought, returning to the veranda.

"She rises!" came Jonah's voice behind her and Vilia managed a smile as he climbed the stairs to join her.

"I see the net needs fixing," he added, taking a seat. "Stopped by the hut to bring you this."

In his hand he produced a coconut, freshly dehusked, with a small hole at the top. "Take a sip."

Vilia stared at it.

"Coconut milk's a good elixir for the morning," Jonah said.

It was more watery than milky, and almost bitter in taste but she drained the nut dry. He took it from her and, with a sharp piece of wood, cracked it into half a dozen chewable pieces. He handed her half.

"I'll have to teach you how to open one up yourself."

Vilia dug her lower jaw into the hard meat and wondered if he'd been listening when she said she'd soon be gone. Cracking open coconuts was not high on her agenda.

"You don't have an antidote to blasted sandfly bites, do you?" she asked.

"Nope. They'll take a few days to settle down, just don't scratch."

He tossed her an old bottle of RID. "And next time you take a dip—douse yourself first."

His lack of sympathy irked her. And it reminded her of Liam.

"So you ready to look over the place?"

"Um, before we do, I need to ask you a few questions about my parents," she said and it caught him off guard.

"Oh plenty of time for that later, love, let's go meet the staff."

"Jonah, I came here for answers, not to ingratiate myself with the locals. I need to know what happened, I need to know about Dad. That's my priority, okay?"

Jonah sat back down and cleared his throat.

He considered this a moment and then said, "You sure you really want to know, Vilia? Have you really thought about it?"

"Only for three decades, Jonah. It's time."

"Okay then. But first let me tell you about these people, yeah?"

Vilia sighed, irritated.

"The first thing I noticed about them when I got here was that none of them spoke the local language, and they barely spoke English. Mostly Pidgin English or Motu."

"So? What's that got to do with anything?"

"Patience, Vilia, this is important," he said. "There was such a strong Missionary presence here, most of the locals speak pretty good English in this province, and they certainly speak one of the dozen or so local languages. That's the whole point. The original staff had all been brought in from somewhere else. They're not locals, not by a long shot."

She didn't see what this had to do with her father but she let him continue.

"They became my mates pretty fast after I got here. I helped them with their English, they helped me with my Pidgin and Motu. They'd been shipped in especially from other territories, some came from the Solomons, some from as far away as the Highlands if I recall, and it took me a few weeks to uncover why."

He took a deep breath. "It seems the island's inhabited by evil spirits."

Vilia stared at him. "I'm sorry?"

"The locals believe the place is evil, and they want nothing to do with it."

She was trying to grasp what he was getting at. "So that's how my parents got it so cheaply?"

Jonah shrugged. He'd never taken the superstitions seriously, he told her, but enjoyed teasing tourists and scaring off buyers with tales of its eerie past. But it was the locals who told it best, their tones hushed, their eyes wide with reverence and fear. These were superstitious people who lived by such tales and, they insisted, died by them, too.

"*Masalai stap long ailan, tru!*" one of the workers, Toia, had gushed of the evil spirits that lived on the island.

Weary from a long day's work, and still trying to get to know the workers, Jonah had invited them back to the main house for a beer, an offer they considered with great trepidation. Only Toia had come, the others too humbled to accept the white man's invitation. Toia had no such qualms and proved as good a drinker as he was a talker.

"Longpela taim, cannibals stap long Tubu," he began in Pidgin English, telling the tale of the headhunting inhabitants who lured friendly villagers and passing missionaries to the island and then ate them for dinner, keeping their heads as trophies to ward off aggressive neighbors and turn evil spirits away.

And then one year the cannibals began dying off, one by one, with a mysterious illness that their resident witch doctor diagnosed as the wrath of the Gods before he, too, was consumed by the curse. Neighboring villagers rejoiced in their deaths but dared not step foot on Tubu lest the evil spirits ran rampant with no new skulls to keep them away.

And so the island had remained uninhabited until 1921 when the resident magistrate at Samarai had acquired it on behalf of the government of the day and requisitioned it for lease to industrious expatriates. And there had been a steady stream of them. First it was semi-cleared for a cattle project with staff quarters built near a flash manager's residence. When that faltered, it was turned into a piggery and sausage-making factory, followed by extensive market gardens and then the copra plantation. But none of them flourished and the locals knew why. The island was cursed. It was inevitable. Lea was just one in a long line of cursed lease holders. So when he fronted, thirty-six years ago with stars in his eyes and a virginal bride by his side, no one expected him to last. And when he disappeared, no one was very surprised.

No one, that is, except his young bride.

"So what happened to them?" Vilia asked anxiously, slamming Jonah back to reality and the matter at hand.

She was not particularly interested in the island's history or its ridiculous superstitions.

"What do you mean he disappeared? What did they say happened to him?"

"The curse of Tubu," Jonah said simply.

"What are you talking about?" She needed it straight. "Cannibals or something?"

"Some said evil spirits whisked him away in the dead of the night ..."

"Oh for goodness sake."

"Hey, just tellin' you what I know. These people have a whole different way of thinkin', Vilia, they don't live by our rules."

She sat up in her chair and faced him square on. "What do you think? Really?"

There was an urgency in her tone that he could no longer avoid.

"You really wanna know?"

"Yes! Just tell me!"

"I reckon your dad ran off with another woman."

Vilia blinked several times and slouched into her seat.

"You asked me so I'll stop beatin' about the bush and tell ya. I don't know the details, but I know what the white folk in the area think, and I know what the final police report said. The night your father disappeared, so, too, did a young black woman. I can't recall her name but she and ya dad were said to be ... well, friendly, I guess."

He stopped, tried to monitor her expression, unsure whether to continue. But she was giving nothing away; she didn't even appear to be listening.

"Vil, there are still several old-timers 'round these parts who could tell ya what ya need to know. I'm not the one. I wasn't here. I'm workin' on hearsay."

"Who was the woman? How come they couldn't trace them? You don't just vanish into thin air, surely?"

Jonah shook his head wearily. "If I knew all that, Vilia, I'd tell ya. But as I say, I don't honestly know. I never made any effort to find out, and I think you'd be a fool to. If you start diggin' about, you're setting yourself up for one bloody big fall. Let it be. Go home to your loved ones and just let it lie."

She didn't have any loved ones she wanted to tell him, not really. But she clamped her lips shut.

He stood up. "You okay?"

She didn't answer him.

"I'll give you a few minutes. Be back later for the tour."

Nodding blankly, she watched him walk away. Only then did she notice herself shaking. Her very core was starting to crack where she had recently replastered it. The letter she had discovered in her mother's file, the letter from her father sounding so concerned, so caring, had buoyed Vilia on this trip, had assured her, at least a little, of their love for each other. Now she was being told otherwise, all over again. And it made the journey ahead that bit harder.

Did she really want to search for answers when all it came back to was infidelity and neglect?

Vilia wasn't sure how long she'd been staring out to sea but by the time Jonah returned she had regained control. *I'll sell the damn place,* she thought, *rid myself of it and of her and of him. No more beating myself up over it all.*

"Okay," she said, pulling herself up and straightening out her cotton dress, "let's check this place out and see what we've got."

Jonah's tour of the premises started with the gardens in front of the main house, an unruly collection of herbs, vegetables and fruits. She spotted sweet potato, pumpkin and a stringy green plant he told her tasted a lot like spinach. There were trees, too, some laden with orange-skinned limes, some bearing pudgy bananas, several barely holding on to sagging green pawpaw, aka papaya.

"Plus there's a pig 'round the back," Jonah mentioned matter-of-factly, "some chooks and a duck."

"Good," she said, not quite sure why.

"Tasty, too," he added, his eyes glinting. "And over that way is the tool shed and work room where I fix the equipment and make a few bits and bobs. I'll show ya through that later. First thing first, come an' meet the team. They've been keen to clap eyes on ya. Can't get any work out of them 'til they do."

He led her along a well-worn path away from the house and west along the shoreline to a large clearing containing five small wooden huts. Each one was covered in dried banana leaves and was built up on stilts, and several had small fires burning out the front where billycans were boiling large pots of water, probably for cleaning. Around them small children played in the dirt. One, she noticed, had a machete in hand. The kids jumped up when they approached and scurried inside to alert their elders. Within seconds, the whole village had gathered, the children staring wide-eyed, the women with modest glances, their heads cocked a little to one side.

They were all dressed in fading, ragged clothes, Western hand-me-downs from passing missionaries and expatriates, or mainland trading stores. Their eyes were the deepest brown, like rotting timber, and some of them had yellow tinted hair as though bleached by a relentless sun. Around them six or seven dogs loitered, their thin bodies half turned, waiting for the boot. The dogs were scrawny and covered in mangy patches, and snapped back when Vilia went to pat them, unused to human affection. A small child kicked one in the ribs; it bounced back and then returned, undeterred.

The village leader, an old man with wrinkled limbs and faded blue shorts, stepped forward first and Jonah introduced him as Dabu, the staff boss.

"Dabu is Mary's husband. He's a good man," Jonah told Vilia and she smiled a little uneasily as he took her hand and squeezed it between his own.

His hands were as coarse as the coconut husk from which she had just eaten and she wondered if he was surprised by the softness of hers. He motioned to the other men and three others stepped out from the crowd, all smiling, all anxious to meet her.

"These are the workers," Jonah continued. "That's Lacky over there, and his son Big Tom directly behind him, and that's Boroko to his left."

She greeted them all as best she could, overwhelmed by their enthusiasm, unable to understand it. She had steeled herself for disdain, mournful looks born of disregard and neglect.

The women and girls were introduced next and she later learned that this was not an oversight of Jonah's but an example of PNG hierarchy. Even in their huts, it was the men and boys who slept closest to the fire and the women and girls who hovered around the edges, taking what heat they could. It irritated her.

Lacky's wife, Margaret, was a small, saggy breasted woman with an enormous, toothless smile. Her gums were stained red from betelnut and she had black dotted lines tattooed across her face and along her legs where they poked out from below a faded floral skirt. These turned out to be the symbols of her village, and not unlike the slick tribal patterns Vilia often spotted on the biceps of Sydney and New York folk, as far removed from any tribe as Margaret was from ever ordering a skinny latté.

Beside her was Boroko's young wife, Tia. She approached the white woman upon introduction and reached for her hair, anxious to feel its texture between her fingers. Uneasily, Vilia let her. She guessed that long auburn locks were a novelty around these parts.

"Boroko is Toia's son," Jonah whispered and at first Vilia did not understand why.

Then it clicked. Toia had worked for her dad. Immediately, she wondered what he knew. Didn't these people pass stories down the campfire at night? Or was that some other tribal nation she had read about in *National Geographic*? Perhaps he spoke better English than Mary, who had also known her folks.

There were several small, potbellied children amongst the group who appeared to belong to Boroko and Tia—they all sported the same yellow-tipped hair as their mum. The youngest was dribbling snot into her mouth (if it were not for the bead choker around her neck, the sex would be almost indeterminate) and all of them barely blinking as they stared up at the bemused white woman with the strange green eyes.

Later, Jonah led Vilia and the older men to the large shed where the coconut was stored for de-husking, and as they went about their business, he explained the way it worked, assuming correctly that she didn't have a clue.

"We get all sorts of oil products from the dried, white, coconut meat," he said, leaning one elbow up against a pile of old husks. "The shampoo you wash your hair with? The coconut oil you tan with, or not, as the case may be."

"I hope you are not attempting to insult my fair skin," she said, smirking, and he laughed as he led her back out into the sun and towards the house.

Halfway along he halted and turned up a thin track that lead through the long grass and up a hillside lush with rainforest. She wasn't up for a walk but followed him patiently until he reached a small clearing and stopped.

"In case you're interested, this path here leads up the mountainside to some bloody amazing look-out points. At the top is Kunoo Point which I must say I can't take any credit for. Guess your dad cleared the way before me. Bloody good view looking out northwest across the main house to Samarai."

"Big walk?" she asked, only half interested.

"Not really no. Takes about an hour."

"Hmmm."

"Straight up."

"Ahhh."

"But it's worth it, I'll tell ya that much. Used to go up almost daily at one point, but I'm not the athlete I once was!"

Along the way, he explained, were several other tracks that were worth checking out. She guessed the view would be startling from up there, but didn't want to know. That stinging sensation of time flying by, of a deadline looming with nothing to show for it began to creep up on her.

She didn't care about the island, didn't he see? She wasn't here to sunbake and take in the view. That's what Club Med was for.

When Jonah dawdled to pull away some weeds, Vilia felt her face flush red and she bit on her lower lip furiously. *Why didn't he get it? She just didn't care.* She was here for a higher purpose. She needed to understand why her mother was such a mess, what had happened to her father, what he had been up to all those years ago. And she didn't mean building pretty walkways to look at pretty views. She meant *up to*. His actions thirty years ago left a legacy that she did not understand. Gena had been left a shell of a woman and Vilia, in effect, an orphan. And she intended to find out why.

Fuck the view.

"Oh there's a little frilly, there. See that lizard, Vilia?" Jonah cooed and she could have screamed with impatience.

Instead, she looked where she was told, compliance preferable to confrontation. If she lashed out now, she knew she would never stop.

Eventually, though, her monosyllabic responses hit their mark and Jonah lead her back down the track towards the main house. He had to get back to work, he told her, but there was one place he wanted to show her first. She sighed loudly now but followed without a word, seething within. Under the house Jonah made his way to what appeared to be a small office and, judging by the cobwebs, one that was rarely used. It was mostly full of old bits of furniture, several rusty lamps, boxes of pens and stacks of papers. There were about a dozen boxes stacked along the walls and he tugged at one, at the very bottom, pulling it out and sending dust flying as the other boxes dropped down to take its place. The box was old and stamped Burns Philp with the word Lea scrawled in black, felt pen across every side. Her anger subsided. Now he was getting it.

"This was here when I took over," he told her. "I don't know what's in it, can't really remember. It might have what you're after."

He carried it up into the house and left it by the veranda door.

"Thanks, Jonah," she said guiltily and he waved her off with one hand as he slipped down the veranda stairs and back to work.

She stood staring down at the box for several minutes and then walked away, padding softly into the kitchen for another cuppa. It was hot here, already nudging thirty degrees despite the early hour, but she needed to knock her brain cells into shape and one cup of cheap coffee wasn't going to do it. Mary was back at her post, gently washing up, and she stopped as Vilia entered and offered her another wide smile.

These people are so bloody happy, she thought, smiling weakly.

Back on the veranda, with several gulps of coffee inside her, Vilia pulled the box towards a chair and sat down. For the next hour she went through the contents meticulously. She did not want to miss a thing. The box had been taped shut a long time ago, but broke open easily and scattered dust and dead insects in all directions as she reached one hand inside. It was filled with work log books and account manuals and she soon discovered that every detail involving the sale of the island was in there, including the minutes of the negotiations to the original contract. There were handwritten receipts, too, mostly for the plantation equipment, an inventory of the household items, staff timetables and a mixed bag of correspondence, mostly staff-related (references, job applications, that sort of thing).

Vilia sat back with a thud. Her father had been an excellent bookkeeper. Everything about the island was enclosed in this old box, everything about the plantation, the equipment, the staff, but not one thing about her parents. There was not a personal item anywhere.

Had she really expected a love letter or two? She moaned impatiently beneath her breath and continued rummaging through the box. At the very bottom she found a battered manila folder with the word 'Staff' scrawled across it and an old map ripped around the edges and folded so many times she had to spread it out across the veranda floor to review it properly. It was crudely hand drawn in black ink and titled, "Tubu Island. Visitor's Guide."

She studied it for several minutes, noticing as she did so that something wasn't quite right. Vilia had only been on the island less than a day but it didn't take long to notice a glaring inaccuracy. The path to Kunoo Point, which Jonah had pointed out on the steep hillside behind the copra shed, on the northwestern side of the island, had been marked further southeast, just above the airstrip, right around the other side of the island. It was a totally different route.

She also noticed what she assumed was a worker's hut around that side, too, about halfway down from Kunoo Point. 'WD' was written beside it. She hadn't heard Jonah mention any huts on that side and decided to ask him about it when she got the chance. She folded the map back up and turned her attention to the staff file.

It contained several sheets of paper with what looked like staff lists for the plantation, as well as a range of staff-related correspondence. She picked up one of the pages headed

'Staff, 1975' and looked it over. There were five names in all and, amongst them, she recognized the names Toia and Mary. On another sheet was a list for 1976 and she glanced at it quickly and was about to discard it when a slash of red caught her eye. One of the names on the list had been scribbled out with a red pen and she was unable to tell what the name had been. It wouldn't have mattered to Vilia if it wasn't for the way it had been crossed off—in a kind of frantic, violent manner. The red scribble was more like a series of angry slashes, the pen breaking through the paper in several points. She pulled the page up to the light and turned it around. You could see the indent from the pen on the other side but you could not make out any of the letters clearly. Whoever scratched the name out clearly wanted it gone, for good.

But whose name was it that had evoked such emotion?

Vilia compared it to the list for the preceding year. The two lists were identical except for one name, Veronika Ligaro. On the 1975 page she was listed as "about 19," occupation: "hausgirl." The following year her name was no longer there. Or perhaps it was, thought Vilia, staring hard at the red slashes and then the date: 1976. The year her father disappeared.

Vilia pushed the pages back into the file and slammed it shut, pretending momentarily that it didn't matter. But she couldn't stop Jonah's words from reverberating in her brain: *The night your father disappeared, so, too, did a young, black woman.*

Was it true? Had her father really run off with another woman? A teenage house maid? Had it been as base as that?

The revelation hit Vilia like a punch straight into her stomach. It winded her. She flung the file back into the box, pushed the whole lot towards a corner of the veranda and then ran out of the main house. She continued running, down into the garden, along the grassy path back to the guesthouse, back to her bed. And she lay there, trying not to think, staring at the matted wall and blinking back tears. And all the while the only thing she could think was, "Bastard, bastard, bastard."

March 2: I am bored beyond belief. Why have I come? Chasing dreams, as always. I guess. But I am trying. God knows I am trying.

The afternoon was lingering and Vilia tossed and turned on the thin foam mattress, unable to hide herself in sleep. Above her, the mosquito net had been hooked securely back in place and twisted into a thick knot that she swatted from time to time, watching it sway to and fro, mesmerized by its movement.

She could feel a darkness setting in and it reminded her of the early days, before she left Liam. And of the night when the shadows made their return.

They had been living together just a few months when it happened. She knew even before she woke up. Her dreams had pre-warned her; they were the same dreams she had had so many times before. Vivid. Vibrant. Violent. Too much on her mind.

And so she awoke tired. Exhausted, even. And angry. Very, very angry. She sighed and stomped about the place, enraged at nothing in particular and everything all at once. Her anger was unreasonable, she knew that. She was in love, everything was rosy, but she was bitter nonetheless, and she wanted Liam to understand that, to feel it, somehow.

Yet Liam wasn't interested. He didn't ask a thing, just hid out in his studio all day, plucking away at his guitar. And it made her madder.

Don't give me an inch, Liam, she spat quietly to herself. *Don't give me a friggin' inch.*

She grabbed her keys and made for the door.

"Where are you going?" he said, wandering in.

"What do you care?" she had replied, sullenly.

He shrugged and wandered right back out again, towards the spare room he had decked out in recording equipment and vintage instruments. She slammed the door and fled down the street. It was getting late, everything was closing, but she needed to stay away, to make her point, somehow. She sobbed her way to a dim cafe and sat by the window staring out, forlorn. Hoping he had followed.

An hour passed. No sign of him.

"More coffee, please."

Another hour. Closing time and late enough for him to worry. Yet still no sign.

When Vilia got home Liam was in bed, snoring. So she stood in the bathroom, stared at her sorry face and cried, hot, gasping sobs that wracked her body until it buckled into two, like an old woman bent over with age. Later, when the sobbing subsided, she washed her face down and crawled into bed beside him.

And then one arm reached toward her like an anchor in a stormy sea, and she held on for her life.

"You better now?" he asked softly, and she mumbled that she was.

Neither of them ever mentioned it again. But she remembers now that he had held her hand to his heart until morning.

"Damn it," she hissed aloud and sat straight up in bed, looking around her idly. She was bored and sleep was clearly not forthcoming. She glanced at her watch. 2:15 p.m. She had missed lunch, and she didn't care. For one brief moment she considered another swim but her skin was still smarting from the morning's assault and without a sailboard the water held little allure. She didn't want to be in it. She wanted to be on top of it. Then she had a thought. She pulled herself off the bed, splashed cold water in her face, applied some lip gloss and made her way back to the main house. She had a special invitation to deliver.

Boroko was tall for a Papuan with long, muscular limbs and skin so black, Vilia could barely make out his features as he sat across from her on the veranda, the sun glaring furiously towards them. He could almost be African, she thought, but later learned he was from Buka Island in the North Solomons, north east of Milne Bay, one of the darkest races in the world. He was shy and his black eyes, accentuated by the white sockets in which they sat, could barely meet hers without looking hurriedly, modestly away. She liked him instantly.

Jonah had not objected to Vilia pulling Boroko away from his work and, despite her reservations, insisted that an interpreter would not be necessary. And rightly so, Boroko's English was good, prefixed as it was with Pidgin. He spoke both simultaneously, as though offering up a language lesson along the way.

"How long have you been here?" she asked, handing him a beer, which he took carefully and placed straight to his lips, gulping a quick sip down before answering.

"Aww, a longtaim, Misis," he said. "A long time. Since liklik pikinini—baby."

She offered him a crayfish sandwich, one of two she found waiting for her under plastic wrap in the kitchen. He shook his head no.

"Do you remember my mum and dad?" she asked

"Yes," he said. "A little bit. They gutpela manmeri. Good people."

"Thank you," she replied, surprised. "How old were you when, um, when my dad ...," she recalled Jonah's words and said, "when he left?"

"Awww, me *liklik boi.* Little boy."

"I see."

Old enough, perhaps, to hear the rumors and to understand them, too.

She took a good swig of her own beer before asking, "Do you know what happened? Did you hear what happened?"

As Jonah had done before him, he shifted uneasily in his seat and seemed reluctant to speak.

Finally, not meeting her eyes, he said, "Yes, Misis."

"What did you hear, Boroko?" He hesitated again. "It's very important. I must know. You speak the truth now, okay?"

He swigged his beer again and proceeded to tell his story.

One morning, Genevive had come running into the village unexpectedly. Boroko and his family had all slept in after a big weekend in Samarai and he was waiting with his own mother for the tea to boil when Gena had shown up, hysteria only half hidden across her face.

He knew something was wrong just by her presence. She rarely visited the village. Not like Masta Lea. He came by often, stopping for some tea, imploring them to teach him Pidgin or Motu. He was always bursting with questions, wanting to understand the country he seemed so out of place in. The ghost woman, as the villagers called her, usually kept to herself as though she understood her separateness, and he always wondered if she liked it here, truly liked it like Master Lea clearly did.

That morning she ran straight in and towards his dad who was repairing something beneath their hut and asked where her husband was. Toia's face was blank as he shook his head, not knowing.

"But you must know, Toia," she said a little frantically and the other villagers began to gather around sensing something was amiss.

"He was with you last night. He came around after seven. You worked late?"

Boroko wondered what she was talking about, his dad had been home with him, helping him wind the fishing line to the new reels he'd just bought. Masta Lea had not been around. Toia told all of this to Genevive whose face clouded over and eyes began to dart frantically as though trying to sort something out in her brain.

"That's ridiculous," she had said eventually.

Masta Lea had left her soon after dinner to join Toia at the work shed, she told him. They had some cartons to fill for the cargo boat tomorrow. Didn't they?

There are no boats this week, Toia replied, confused. They weren't due to fill the cartons until the end of the month. He had not seen Masta Lea since the afternoon before.

Boroko watched Gena's face then and it was a look that would stay etched in his brain forever. Her eyes were flooded with fear, like the mongrel dog his father had to put down the year before: unsure, hesitant, hopeful and yet fearful all at once.

A mixed mayhem.

He remembered being surprised by it. *What was the big deal?* he thought to himself. Masta Lea was probably just asleep in the shed. Toia was already leading Gena in that direction and several villagers were following quietly behind. Boroko expected it all to be sorted out in minutes and stayed behind to eat his breakfast.

The look on the groups' faces when they returned from the shed told him otherwise.

Masta Lea was missing.

Toia began putting his boots on to trek around the island, in search of Lea, and that's when one of the other workers, a man called Francis, began shouting.

"No gat bot!"

The boat was missing.

Gena gasped then and dashed round to the side of the bay where Lea's yacht was usually moored. It had disappeared, too. But she seemed relieved by this.

"He's gone to the markets!" she said aloud, turning back to the villagers and laughing nervously at herself. "Never mind," she said, less assuredly. "He's gone to the markets."

But Boroko remembered thinking that it wasn't market day. He hadn't the heart to mention this and neither, it seemed, did anyone else, so they pretended to return to their breakfast while Gena wandered away shaking her head at herself, mumbling at her folly.

"So there were no markets that day?" Vilia asked and Boroko nodded.

She fetched him another beer. She needed to hear more. Eventually his story resumed.

Without Gena knowing, Toia and Francis began searching the island quietly. Francis searched around the airstrip, he was adamant he should do that, he was sure that's where Lea would be, and Toia checked the hills behind the copra shed and the guest house, expecting to find Masta Lea fallen over somewhere with a broken leg, or worse.

But he was nowhere to be found. And his boat did not return. Francis spent a bit of time on the two-way radio to Samarai that afternoon and then took the dinghy across to search for Lea himself, but without success. He eventually radioed back to Gena to tell her the bad news. Lea's boat was not docked at Samarai and no one had spotted him there that day.

Still hopeful, Gena then radioed the mainland but the answers were the same. Lea had not stopped by. He was a friendly man by nature, someone would have remembered him.

Later, as blue gave way to orange in the late afternoon sky, the young Boroko sensed ripples of excitement wash through the village where most of them had remained all day, waiting for word of Masta Lea. Suddenly everyone was talking about the housegirl, Veronika Ligaro.

She, too, was missing.

No one had seen her since their trip to Samarai, and Francis, now back from the port town, said she was nowhere to be seen there, either. Veronika had lived alone in the smallest hut on the other side of the copra shed, and Boroko followed the group who quickly gathered there, fearful of entering, fearful of what they would find. Toia went in first, followed soon after by Mary and Francis. Their wide eyes revealed the awful truth.

All of her things were gone. Nothing remained. And no one had the heart to tell Gena.

But of course someone eventually must have and Boroko wandered along the beach that evening to find Gena sitting with her child in her arms, staring out to sea. He was still young then, but he recognized a woman in mourning, and so he left her there, alone. He didn't know exactly what was going on but he sensed it wasn't good. He knew, even at that young age, that from that day forward everything would be different.

The next few days were long and, he recalled at the time, exciting. Not that he told this to Vilia, of course. Her eyes were too sad for that. As a kid, it was the most thrilling thing that had ever happened in this serene part of the world; even better than the mad dog incident of the year before.

This had the whole region captivated. He remembered a steady stream of visiting boats. The Alotau police chief had sped over with several officers in tow and had interviewed them all separately, asking them what they really knew. *Had they seen anything unusual? Was there some secret they were not revealing?*

Then another policeman, a large expatriate man from Samarai, had taken over the investigation and began a full-scale search of the island and neighboring region. He was gruffer, Boroko recalled, and just as unsuccessful.

Three or four boatloads of white folk sailed over, too, bringing with them food for Gena and the baby and ugly eyes that scanned the villagers suspiciously. Boroko wondered if they blamed them. Wondered if they still did. But still there was no news of Masta Lea and Veronika, and eventually, around the third day, people began to admit aloud what they had been whispering amongst themselves for days.

Masta Lea and Veronika must have run away together.

"I knew they were playing up," someone said one night and soon everyone was recalling certain looks, suspicious incidents that suggested that something was indeed amiss.

By the beginning of the next week, all other options had been discarded. There were no other possibilities. Lea had been having a secret affair with the young housegirl and together they had sailed off into the sunset, deserting a wife and child.

But Boroko felt differently. He didn't understand too much of the talk and couldn't tell whether the white man and woman had been happy or not, but what he did know was that Masta Lea loved the island. As a kid he had watched him working the plantation as though every moment mattered, and as hard as a local, too.

Why would he desert it now?

About ten days after Lea's disappearance, another incident occurred which left the entire region shaken to the core, although Boroko had to admit he wasted no tears over it. Another local man, Dick O'Brien, was discovered dead in his bed one morning and the doctors at Port Moresby General Hospital, where his body was quickly dispatched, could not work out from what. He had all the symptoms of poisoning except any evidence of the substance itself.

It was as though his body had poisoned itself.

"Dick O'Brien?" Vilia interrupted, only half recognizing the name.

"Masta bilong Bado Island," Boroko explained patiently, pointing off into the horizon.

The penny dropped.

"Was he Kyle O'Brien's dad?" she said, recalling her surly pilot from two days before.

Boroko nodded yes. Now it was making more sense. Sort of.

"So what happened to him?" she asked. "Was there a connection to my dad?"

Boroko shrugged. "Me no save," he said in Pidgin. "I don't know. But he nogut, he was no good. He bad man, papa bilong mi say. Not so sad he die."

"Why was he bad?"

"He treat my people no good."

Boroko's furrowed brow loosened a little then and he looked away. Perhaps he'd said too much.

For Vilia, it was all very confusing. What connection could Dick's death have to her father's disappearance? As she pondered this, Boroko shifted a little in his seat and then stood up and declared that he would go. He had work to do.

"Just one more thing," she said quickly.

"Yes, Misis?"

"Does anyone live on the other side of the island, near the airstrip?"

He stared at her oddly and she quickly grabbed the map from the box, untangling it and pointing to the small hut marked 'WD.'

He stepped back abruptly and shook his head. "Me go now," he said sternly, not meeting her eye. "Planti work. Plenty of work to do."

And with that the Pidgin lesson was over.

The roar of the generator broke Vilia's sleep and she looked up and about, unsure for several seconds where she was. The clock said 5:00 p.m. and she was curled up on the sofa inside the main house, one of the paperbacks opened at her side. She didn't recall trying to sleep, but must have drifted off anyway, and she stretched her limbs out and got up. Her head had that fuzzy, overslept feeling, and she shook it a little as she padded outside. She found Jonah forking fresh fish onto the barbecue, several party lights dangling like bright ideas above his head.

"Do you need a hand?" she asked, stifling a yawn, but he shook her off.

"Today's catch—'sweetlip' they call it. Lacky speared you some crayfish last night, too. Mary's boiling it up at the house. You like crayfish, don't ya?"

"I guess so, I've never had it."

"You will."

A crude wooden table and bench seats had been built beside the barbecue and she sat down to watch him cook and to let her brain uncurl and return to the present.

Eventually, she said, "Jonah?"

He stopped his scraping and looked up, alerted by something in her voice.

"Veronika Ligaro," she said simply.

He did not understand at first and opened his mouth to say something when his memory caught up.

"Oh, right," he said. "The missin' housegirl. Of course, that was her name. I remember it now."

"And do you remember the name Dick O'Brien? Kyle O'Brien's dad?"

"Yeah, I do, love. Heard all about it when I got here. Died a horrible death I believe, the color of mildew when they found him. Freaked out all the *dimdims*—the white folk—for a while. His wife ended up movin' back to the mainland. The Highlands, Mendi, I think."

Jonah stopped stirring his food again and turned back to her.

"You don't think the two are connected—"

"My parents' old box contained a map of Tubu," she charged on. "There's a spot marked 'WD' around near the airstrip. Do you know what that is?"

He shook his head. "Work shed maybe?"

"It's not there anymore?"

"Not that I know of."

"Do you have any other maps of the island?"

"Yeah probably, I'd have to have a scrounge around. But—"

"What about staff lists?" Vilia's eyes were imploring.

"What do ya mean?"

She took a deep breath. "I need to know exactly who was employed when you first took the place over from my mum."

Jonah considered this for some time. "Dunno about that. I'll have a look. Vilia, what are you thinkin', what's all this about?"

She let out a laugh, a gulping, girlish laugh that unsettled him.

"I don't know what to think," she said. "I don't know what I'm supposed to think or even what the hell I'm doing here. I'm trying to find connections, I'm trying to find some other reason why he'd go, why he'd leave my mum."

She was now shaking her head slowly from side to side. "Bloody hell, I want to know why he'd leave *me*."

Jonah sat down beside her and placed one skinny arm around her shoulder, his other hand stroking her hair so softly she could barely feel him.

"It doesn't matter, don't ya see? None of it matters now. You have to get on with your own life."

"Oh Jesus!" She sat up, pulling herself away. "Of course it matters. It's who I am. It's why I don't have a fucking life to get on with!"

She stormed off, back up to the house, and grabbed the telephone. She had to dial several times, her hands and mind were shaking so much, but when she finally got through to Alex, she didn't feel any better.

"He's right, Vili," Alex said after hearing her out. "What are you trying to achieve? You never even knew the man. Perhaps it's time to sell the place and come home."

"Home?" She let out a snorting laugh. "*Home?!* Now where exactly is my home, Alex, you tell me?"

"Look, don't get—"

"Don't start telling me what to do," she cut him off. "I'm tired of everyone telling me what to do. None of you understand what it was like to grow up with a loony for a mother and a father who simply vanished. I'm supposed to just pretend it all never happened? Forgive everyone? No harm done, right?"

"Now take it easy."

"I don't want to take it easy," she screamed. "I want to get some bloody answers for the first time in my life and I want people like you to stop telling me to calm down."

There was silence at the other end.

Eventually, he said, "I'm just trying to help."

He sounded sulky. She banged her head quietly against the wall. Took a deep breath.

"I know, Alex, I know you are. I'm sorry." He sniffed a little. "I'm sorry. I'm venting, that's all. I'm just so confused and this whole thing is not working out the way I thought it would."

"So come ho—I mean back here. To Sydney. We'll take a few days off. Have some laughs."

"I've gotta go."

"You can't let this get to you, Vilia. Your parents don't deserve this kind of attention, this kind of care."

"No, you're right."

And then it hit her.

"But you know what, Alex, maybe I do. Maybe I deserve the truth after all this time. I don't care how indulgent it might sound. I have a right to know."

And with that she hung up and returned to the yard and to the plate of food Jonah had dished out for her on the wooden table where he now sat. She chewed quietly on the fish, while he watched her with that look she had seen so many times before. Her neighbor Jane Logan used to look at her like that, and her teachers, and the twin boys, and anyone who *knew*. That's why she fled Cairns and kept everyone at bay.

But then, one day she met Liam and everything was different. He was a Melbourne-born musician, struggling to make it in New York, and had come to polish the floorboards in the Australian consulate's offices, renovating being his day job when music wasn't paying the way. She was mesmerized by him almost instantly. He was so relaxed, so comfortable in his own skin, the way he laughed and swore and seemed completely oblivious to his extraordinary good looks.

They talked for hours that day, he sanding the wood back almost lovingly, she pretending to be busy at a desk nearby, sneaking glances when he wasn't looking. He had so much to say and so many ideas, and none of them were about family or fear or any of the nonsense she had filled her own head with.

At the end of the day, with the floors sparkling and his clothes covered in grime, he had plonked himself on the edge of her desk, glanced down at her through his unruly fringe and asked her out. Just like that. No games, no expectations, he just wanted to keep the conversation going. And for the first time in her life she said yes without so much as a second thought.

A week later they moved in together. It was that simple.

She never could explain what it was Liam saw in her, he just seemed to adore her, warts and all, but she knew exactly what she loved about him. Liam didn't seem to care about her past or pity her with every glance. He just brushed it all aside—that was life, that was love—and she had reveled in that nonchalance, needed it desperately back then. It provided the foundations on which she could rebuild her life.

Eventually, however, his nonchalance began to wear thin. And so she'd walked out on him and the fortress he'd helped her create.

And now this. Now the ugly truth about her father, and not so much as a brick wall in which to buffer her from the pain.

Jonah's voice broke the silence. "Market day tomorra."

As though she were sitting across from him thinking about vegies.

"We leave for Samarai at seven. You'll be wantin' to come, there'll be people there you'll need to speak to." Vilia glanced up at him. "People who can help you. In ya search. See you then."

He took the plates with him and disappeared up into the house while she sat for some time watching the fire in the BBQ fizzle away.

PART 5

SAMARAI ISLAND—WARMING UP

March 7: The harbor is bustling with life. Black men glare at me as they fish between the vessels and young kids gather around to stare at the blonde stranger with the translucent skin. Beyond them men and women, black and white, scurry about busily, loading and unloading, cleaning out their vessels and chatting. It is hot and smelly and crass.

The ocean was like a giant blue sheet with silver beads sparkling in its folds and the wind fluttering it about, creasing it up and then ironing it out again. Jonah's yacht—a thirty-foot ocean-going ketch badly in need of a paint—pierced through the water like scissors, cutting it cleanly into two while seagulls swooped down and pecked at it from time to time. On several occasions, dolphins swam along its seams, zipping in and out as they followed the boat along, and Vilia watched them in awe. Despite decades of sailboarding, she had never seen these creatures up close before.

They had been sailing aboard the *U Beaut* for over an hour but it was not yet 9:00 a.m. and the sun was still half groggy, too weak to scorch Vilia's skin. She felt better this morning, stronger, more assured, and decided it was probably the boat ride, and the fact that she was back on top of things again.

Dressed in blue overalls with a crisp cotton shirt underneath, Vilia had secured her unruly locks with one of her mother's silk scarves but several strands refused to be restrained, breaking loose and slapping her about the face. As her legs dangled over the bow she began screaming a song into the wind, her lungs straining, her voice drowned out. She didn't know if Jonah could hear her but suddenly, surprisingly, she didn't care, she just needed to sing, to release these songs that were swelling out of her now. As a young girl she had always loved singing, but somewhere along the way her voice had stilled. Perhaps it was because it had jarred with her mother's silence, or perhaps she had lost a reason to sing.

Today everything seemed different. She felt light and jubilant, aware (just slightly) that this trip was stirring something in her that she'd long forgotten. And so she went through her schoolgirl repertoire. 'Cats in the Cradle,' 'What About Me?,' 'American Hearts' and 'American Pie,' and was surprised that she remembered all the words. It was as though she were peeling off a layer of skin, one that had become so tight, so numb with pain that it almost hurt to release it. Yet with each song she felt a little of it break away and a little of her old self, the one she had long forgotten, shine through.

As the water crashed around her and the breeze tossed her voice in every direction, Vilia sang as though she had never sung before. She felt young and giddy and careless and alive.

For the first time since she could remember she was enjoying the journey.

Samarai was just a dot on the horizon when they started out, but eventually its craggy hillside came into view and then the splotched white of houses and the bustling port with its fishing boats, yachts and dinghies, tied two to a dock so that, when they eventually arrived, they had to clamber over others to make their way to land. There can be no sailboat snobbery when an old fisherman helps you across, his creaky vessel your savior from the writhing sea below, while everyone else stops to watch.

Jonah brought Big Tom with him for the journey and issued orders in Pidgin English so that the young worker ran off ambitiously.

"What now?" Vilia asked Jonah and he smiled as he straightened his hat, last night's outburst now just a fading memory.

"It's market day!" he announced. "Let's go and shop."

He led her away from the wharf and along the dirt road that hugged the coastline to an enormous arena buzzing with fruit and vegetable stalls and lone traders sitting cross-legged, their wares on display before them. There was a large crowd, a few white faces amongst them.

"I've got a lot to get," Jonah said, "so why don't ya just take a wander and we'll meet back at the boat in a few hours. Might be worth your while to go look in on the local police station. They might still have a file on your dad. They're just east of the markets, can't miss 'em. Let's meet at noon back at the boat."

Vilia barely had a chance to object before he disappeared into the crowd. Feeling conspicuous, she feigned a smile and began wandering along, keeping pace with the throng and pretending she had a purpose. The sense of liberation she felt earlier had rapidly dissipated. She usually liked marketplaces, relished their anonymity and marveled at their myriad colors, smells and tastes—a flash of silver here, a swirl of cloth there, white buckets bursting with flowers, fresh food scattered in all directions, a palm reader's tasseled table, a blushing young girl sitting to portrait for a beaming young boy. People stopping, turning, ploughing strollers through. And everywhere a bargain, everywhere the contents of tomorrow's garage sale.

This market was altogether different.

It was miserable and dirty and desperate. It reeked of old fish and rotting fruit and there was no shade from the strengthening sun. At one stall she spotted a giant turtle, belly up as several locals prodded it unceremoniously, and at another, what looked like smoked pig covered in flies. There were dusty bunches of peanuts and, in every direction, small neat mats lined up with rows and rows of *buai*, neatly clumped together with some *daka* and lime. Hands reached out for her at very glance and eager eyes implored her to buy.

"Just looking," she murmured as though window-shopping in a mall, and she tried to avoid the vendors' eyes as she shuffled past, wishing she was elsewhere.

At one stand a large white woman with a heaving breast and sweating brow was haggling for tomatoes like her life depended on it and, both embarrassed and intrigued by her, Vilia stopped to watch.

"Nogut!" she spat as the seller held his tomatoes out for her to see. "Noooooo good. Ten for two kina. Pinis." The end.

He shook his head, disgusted, and dropped three tomatoes from his palm. But the white woman wasn't having it, she hissed and looked about dramatically as though set to storm off to another stall, her scraggly gray hair tossing about her defiantly. Reluctantly, he took one tomato back up again and thrust it in her face. She looked a little placated, picked another up and handed the man two kina while shoveling the tomatoes into her string bag.

"Tenkyu!" she said happily and took off to haggle for pumpkin one stall down, while the vendor smiled his own gap-toothed victory and hid the cash away.

Vilia looked around and noticed several other expatriates playing the same game with lively vegetable sellers rising to the challenge. There was much shaking of head and furrowing of brow as buyer fought with seller for the middle ground somewhere. And there right in the middle was Jonah, a bag of sweet potatoes in one hand, his other raised in a fist to the heavens.

Oh no, this wasn't a breezy, Sunday stroll, a chance to blow ten bucks on a string bag you don't need. This was the real deal. These people were filling their kerosene fridges so that in their seclusion they did not starve, while the little men and women with their legs crossed lithely and the flies buzzing up their noses could clothe their kids and light their lanterns at night.

This wasn't pocket money, it was survival at its most basic, and it terrified Vilia suddenly because it wasn't wrapped in plastic with a price fixed to its breast.

This was island living, haggling on hope and helping each other out.

A young woman with her hair squished up like tufts of steel wool beckoned Vilia to her mat and she looked down to see the bananas she had before her. They were small and fat, like plump, yellow cigars, and she opened one, eager for the white woman to try. Instinctively Vilia nodded no, but something made her take the fruit and eat its sweet flesh. She had to admit it tasted good. She bought a clump of six and told herself they'd be perfect for the boat trip back.

By the end of the hour Vilia had haggled for avocado, mangoes and a large hat, made of dried palm fronds—in memory of her youth—and, stuffing the food in her bag and the hat on her head, made her way to the police station. It was housed in a two-story gray concrete besser-block building with louvers at the front and a makeshift washing line strapped to coconut trees to one side. Several locals loitered near the doorway flirting with a policewoman in a faded uniform, and another sat chewing betelnut as though he hadn't a care in the world.

Inside, a younger policeman with a timid smile greeted her at the front bench. Behind him the room was almost empty. Several desks had been deserted and an old upright fan was whirring loudly and vibrating so violently, it threatened to topple over.

"Hello, my name is Vilia Lea," she said. "I'm from Australia, and I am looking into the disappearance of my father near here in May, 1976."

His gaze was blank and she took this as an indication to continue.

"I was wondering if you still have records of the investigation which was carried out ..." she rummaged through her handbag, "by ..." she located the piece of paper and brought it out, placing it on the bench before her, "by a Provincial Police Commander Riley."

He took up the piece of paper and scrutinized it carefully, then he put it back down and looked blankly towards her again.

"Your father, he go missing?"

"Yes."

"Today?"

"No," she said. "In 1976. Thirty years ago."

"Awwww." He started shaking his head skittishly. "1976?!"

"Yes, well it was a long time ago."

"Too long!"

"Yes, that's why I'm here. I was hoping you still had the old files."

"Fire?"

"Fire? No, no, files ... fiiieeels."

He was clearly confused and Vilia wondered if his training had extended beyond theft and assault complaints to weird white women digging into their pasts.

"Look," she said, trying to stay calm. "Is your boss around? Is the Commander here?"

"Commander Giwi," he proclaimed and smiled back at her.

Perhaps he's just stupid, she thought.

"Right, Commander Giwi. Is he here? Is he inside?" She motioned behind him, to the empty office and its rickety fan, expecting him to say no. But he raced out the back door, reappearing seconds later with another young policeman in tow.

"Commander Giwi?" she asked, doubtfully.

"Yes, ma'am," he said, waving the junior officer aside. "How can I help you?"

Vilia repeated her request, showing him the letter from Commander Riley and he read it through carefully, his eyes squinting beneath thick glasses patched up with a Band-Aid on one side.

"Oooh, dear, dear, dear," he said, shaking his head sadly. "Long, long time ago."

Yes, I am aware of that. "Do you still have the old files?"

His eyes squeezed shut for several seconds and he pursed his lips together thoughtfully.

"Now let me think. 1976 ... wait here, please."

The woman watched as he wandered off out the back and hoped that luck would be with her, that they had not been destroyed over time. She waited, and she waited. Ten minutes passed and the Commander had not returned. The young policeman smiled at Vilia from time to time as he studied a *Phantom* comic at his desk, and the fan kept right on whirring, defying gravity all the while. She was about to give up hope when Giwi returned with a wide smile across his face that belied his empty hands.

"No file?" she suggested and he shook his head happily.

"You must go to Alotau. The old files are stored at main station in Alotau."

Her heart sank. It seemed like hard work.

"Do you know if that particular file is still there?"

"Maybe," he replied.

Back at the boat, Jonah was placing his purchases down below the deck and in the large eskies he had brought with him. He added her goods to the pile.

"How'd you go at the coppers?"

"No luck. The file, if they still have it, would be at the main station in Alotau. Looks like I'll have to pay another visit."

"Or you could try hunting down the original investigator, see if he still lives on Samarai."

"Got any ideas?" she asked.

"You've got the old investigating officer's name?"

"His surname, yes."

"Rightio then, stop at the post office. See if he's listed. I'll join you, then we'll head to the club for some lunch. There's some people there you might want to see."

Her mood darkened. *Great,* she thought. *Now the Samarai expats get their chance to feel superior.*

It was just after midday when they entered the small post office and headed to a booth where some tatty old phone books were stored. Jonah grabbed the Samarai one, a skinny white manual dating several years back, and handed it to her.

"They don't update it often," he said. "But if he's here he should be in it."

She scanned the pages slowly, searching for Riley, and located two numbers for a G. and a V. She picked up the receiver and dialed the first. It had been disconnected and she smiled at Jonah, two fingers crossed as she dialed the second. It rang out. She waited a few minutes and dialed again. Still nothing.

"Never mind," Jonah said. "Jot the number down and try again from home. If he's still around—and to be honest you'd be bloody lucky if he was, love—he'd probably be down at the market. You're unlikely to catch him today."

The Paradise Bar was bustling as they approached, spilling its beer-guzzling patrons out every door and onto the veranda out the back. She gathered this was the Mecca of the market day, where the locals paid homage to a small brown beer bottle after the weekly purchasing pilgrimage. She was composing herself for the walk through, eyes straight ahead, blank and disinterested, when she heard her name called out. She spun around to see Roger coming in behind her, several bags full of fruit and vegetables in each hand.

"I was hoping I'd see you here," he said with a laugh and she almost leapt into his arms, thrilled to recognize a face amongst the leering onlookers.

Jonah and Roger greeted each other like old friends and then the former fetched them drinks while Roger steered Vilia away from the crowd to a quieter corner to chat.

"How are you going? Was the flight with Kyle okay?"

"Oh fine, if you like your journey swift and quiet. He barely said a word. Got me there, though, so thanks for that. I appreciate it."

Roger blushed a little and she noticed sweat forming on his upper lip. He'd ironed his shirt today and smelled faintly of aftershave, his three-day growth shaven off to reveal the face of a much younger man, his thick, curly hair tied neatly behind his back. She wondered who it was he had dressed to see and stepped back several inches, straightening up her smile.

"So how are you going?" she asked. "What brings you over here?"

"Oh I come every now and then—just for a change from the Alotau markets and to catch up with mates."

"And how's the bottle shop holding up?"

"Oh yeah, no probs. Well, bit of a brawl on payday yesterday but, well, that's nothing new, eh? Anyway," he said, "that's all boring to you. How's Tubu?"

"Good," she replied, not sure what to say.

Roger cleared his throat awkwardly and said, "I'm sorry about what happened ... you know ... to your dad and all."

"Oh. Thanks."

"Not that I actually know what happened ... exactly."

"Yeah, well, I guess nobody really does." She was starting to feel a little prickly again.

"Aw, there's gotta be some old-timers here that'd remember."

Suddenly a loud roar of laughter erupted from a nearby table. Vilia turned to see the large white lady from the tomato stand holding court over a group of expatriates, all listening intently as she chatted away, roles of loose fat wobbling like dough beneath her arms as she flung them about to emphasize her point. Her cheeks were flushed red and Vilia noticed she had tied her thinning, gray hair into a loose bun behind her neck so that she looked older than before, in her seventies, perhaps.

"Martje Hindricks," Roger said, following her stare. "Been here as long as I can remember and a good many years before that. Now, she probably would have known your dad, certainly would have been around at the time."

"Well I can hardly go up and ask her."

"Why not?" His expression was deadpan. "Go on."

But before she had a chance to consider, Mrs. Hindricks was already calling out Roger's name and motioning for them to join her. Warily, Vilia followed him over, applying a strained smile and nodding at the crowd now staring inquisitively towards her.

"How you going, Mr. Roger?" she said in a thick, Dutch accent. "I saw your father earlier, looking pritty good zees days, huh?!"

She shrieked with laughter and the rest of the table laughed along too, some a little nervously. Vilia wondered whether she terrified everyone or if it was just her.

"Who iz zees, then?" she demanded, looking the younger woman over liberally.

"Hey, don't you pick on my guest!"

Jonah cut in suddenly from behind, handing them their drinks and then swooping down to peck the Dutch woman on the cheek.

"How ya goin', Margie?"

"Jonah jolly Johnson!" she exclaimed and slapped him on the bum, plunging him towards the table and nearly sending his drink flying. "Now vere have you been? Huh? Ve have not seen you for zo long time!"

"Working like a trooper, Margie, you know me. Anyway, let me introduce young Vilia Lea, her family owns Tubu."

Martje's smile dropped like a lead zeppelin. She was dumbstruck and Vilia wondered if she'd ever been speechless before. The group looked anxiously towards her as though waiting for some signal, unsure how to react. And then, in a flurry, the older woman's voice returned.

"Oh my Lordie, Lordie!"

She motioned Vilia closer, grabbing her hands to her heaving bosom, her mouth agape, her eyes wide.

"De baby of Jamison and Gena?!"

Vilia nodded uneasily. "Just back for a week or two."

"Back indeed! I haven't seen you since you were ze little baby in ze nappies, changed you once or twice myself, ya know!"

This brought the laughter back and then Jonah and Roger pulled some chairs up so they could join the table while Martje signaled for more drinks from the man at the bar.

"So how iz Genevive, poor dear, she'z all right, no?"

"No," Vilia replied. "She's dead."

She hadn't meant to sound so melodramatic but the Dutch woman was unperturbed.

"Yah, poor dear," she said, shaking her head tragically, as if there could be no other outcome. "Always so sad. She never like it here anyway, you know? Maybe towards the end … but then, well, it happened. And such a beautiful lady, too."

Vilia had her own opinion about that but kept her mouth shut and accepted her second beer.

"Vilia's here to find out what happened to her father," Roger blurted before she had a chance to stop him and once again every eye turned towards her.

"What iz ze problem?" Marge asked. "Ze truth is pritty plain, eh?"

"Careful, Martje," an elderly man at her right said, placing one frail hand on her enormous knee and Vilia suspected this was the poor, long-suffering husband.

Jonah waved him off. "Vilia's heard the rumors, guys, so don't get too excited. She's just here to look up a few *facts*, that's all."

"But I'm also here to check out the island," Vilia added, desperate to change the subject.

She didn't need sympathy from anyone, certainly not a bunch of small-towners with big opinions. "I'm really here to see how Jonah's been keeping it."

"Well where have you been, huh? He az been keeping it for thirty-five years, ya?"

"Thirty, Margie," Jonah said, smiling warmly at Vilia who was looking increasingly uncomfortable. "Anyway, give the girl a break. It's been a rough month or so, okay?"

"Oh no worry," Martje boomed, grabbing Vilia's pale hand back up and squeezing it tightly. "I am just havin' ze fun, you know? So, iz Jonah showing you ze good time?"

And with that the inquisition ended and the mood lightened up as the group began chatting amongst themselves.

"Did you see old Tommo's new tractor?" one woman wanted to know. "And where did he get the money for that?!"

"Oh and poor young Jillie had a miscarriage!" came the cries of another.

And what an awful tragedy, they all agreed, but no use crying. Oh no, they chirped between mouthfuls of beer and chips, you just pick yourself up and get on with it. That's the important thing.

Vilia wondered if that's what they told her mother when the news finally broke, if that's how they consoled her in her darkest hour. *Chin up, dear, she'll be right!*

It was no wonder she fled down south.

As the group chatted away, Vilia only half listened, smiling when they laughed and accepting the food and drink that was being offered her way. But she was smarting a little at the Dutch woman's words, her flippant disregard of her feelings and motives. She wondered how Martje Hindricks would have coped being deserted as a child by her dad and in slow increments for the rest of her life by her despairing mum. She wondered if they took all that into account as they sized her up with their churlish glances between gobs full of gossip and advice. It was just like small-town Australia, she decided, and it was everything she had ever avoided. She understood that the second she stepped out of ear shot, she too would be up for discussion, to be dissected and deliberated upon. As if any of their opinions mattered. And yet she wanted to explain herself, to make them understand. But how could she when she didn't understand it herself?

She remembered her ninth-grade report card and the angst it ignited in her.

"Vilia doesn't try hard enough. She has to stop making excuses and start making grades."

Mrs. Bev Walton, Vilia's teacher. Despite being tall and scrawny, the kids called her 'Bev the Heav' and Vilia had always assumed it was just because it rhymed. But later on she wondered if it had more to do with the stronghold she seemed to have over them all. It was as though she could read their minds, could tell what they were up to even before they got up to it. No one seemed to get away with anything on her watch. Or so it seemed back then.

"What does she mean?" Gena had asked, half interested. "'Stop making excuses.' Excuses for what?"

Vilia shrugged as she always did and mumbled, "She's just an anorexic freak," before wandering off to fetch her sailboard.

But she knew exactly what the bitch meant, and she knew what she was doing. Well she could mind her own bloody business. And she could try walking in her shoes.

Jonah shifted restlessly in his seat and, as the locals gossiped away, Vilia realized that he was as eager to be out of there as she was. Even Roger was looking ill of sorts. These were pretty basic blokes, she realized, and gossip was probably something they had little time for. They stayed for a quick bite—a stringy steak sandwich in a stale white bun— and then made their excuses to leave. That's when Martje pulled Vilia aside conspiratorially, her giant brow furrowed like a series of sand dunes, rippling with each change of emotion, and as easily washed away. Vilia noticed that she smelled like the local villagers, of cheap soap and talcum powder, and wondered if she knew.

"Now, Vilia, I veckon if you are lookin' for ze answers you should talk to old McCafferty. He was here back then, yes? And a good friend of your daddy. He vill set you straight. You can find him at ze dock yards. Good luck, little Vili, you will be okay."

Vilia thanked her, nodded good-bye to the table and hurried outside, eager for some fresh air.

"I'll leave you to it then," Roger said, shifting his bags between hands. "Gotta get some kero and then I'll be off. Give us a call if you're ever back in Alotau ... maybe we can, you know, go and get a beer or something."

His eyes darted across her face and he blushed then. Vilia smiled warmly and said good-bye.

"You need to get going?" she asked Jonah later as they walked back towards the harbor.

"Not really, love, just keen to get out of there. Martje can be a handful, eh? You wanna go see McCafferty?"

"You don't mind?"

"No sweat. It's only two o'clock, and we're not due to set sail 'til four. There's someone else I think you should see, too, figured she might be at the pub but she wasn't. We'll try McCafferty first. The other one's a bit trickier."

The sun was strong and furious when they strolled back along the main road towards the harbor. Many of the boats had departed by now but Vilia noticed the same fisherman still at their posts, and marveled at their patience, wondering if it was paying off. At the furthest dock, Jonah marched towards a rusty old houseboat with faded floral curtains and a plethora of pot plants covering its entire upper surface like a fluffy green carpet. The name *Mathilda* was just visible in old scroll across one side, and small fairy lights were strung along its entire length.

It must look quite magical at night, Vilia thought.

Jonah called McCafferty's name but it was some time before an elderly man with a wild mop of white hair poked his head out of a side window.

"Jonah Johnson!" he barked happily. "Fancy a visit from you. Come aboard, come aboard."

This was the standard greeting Jonah got in these parts. He seemed very popular but it was clear he wasn't a regular. And she was beginning to see why. Cocooned in his island haven, Samarai must seem a bustling metropolis by comparison, and its lively inhabitants more like hard work than play.

As they clambered aboard, Mitch McCafferty emerged on deck and dwarfed the boat with his enormous size. He was not tall exactly, just wider than he should be with thick hairy arms, a quivering double chin and a beer belly that protruded over his tiny, faded blue shorts. He clenched Jonah's hand happily and nodded quickly at Vilia. As the old pals exchanged local news for several minutes, she wiped bird droppings from an old plastic chair and took a seat. There were several kerosene lamps, cigarette packets and mozzie coils strewn about and nothing appeared to be bolted down so she doubted the old girl had seen open ocean in a very long time. A giant fern poked at her from its home in one corner, reminding Vilia who was boss, and its mates spilt all the way down the small wooden stairs that led into the hull and the heart of McCafferty's home. She strained her eyes to see inside and sensed a cool, calm haven from the crazy world outside. Ordinarily she'd be put off by its dark, musty interior but today there was something oddly comforting in its solitude, like a mother's womb, muffled and compact, ebbing to and fro on its watery tide and tempting you to curl up and stay awhile.

"So you're the Leas' kid?" Mitch said after Jonah had filled him in, and Vilia nodded yes.

"I believe you knew my parents?"

"Knew em!? I was one of your dad's best mates."

"Mitch used to be the main realtor in these parts," Jonah explained. "Sold your dad Tubu."

Vilia wondered why a man who sold entire islands couldn't find a small patch of earth for himself.

"Well, I negotiated the lease," he was saying, "although that was a difficult enough task in itself. Nobody wanted to touch the place."

"Evil spirits, I know."

"Huh? Nah, the white folk didn't give a shit about that hocus pocus. No, it was a lot of factors. Too rugged, if I recall. It's got a mighty great mountain in the middle of it. There's also no fresh water—the real reason the locals didn't want the place if you ask me. Of course a bore was put in which sorted that out. And then there were those damn sandflies."

As if on cue, Vilia's skin began itching, but she resisted the urge to scratch. McCafferty was already eyeing her splotches and shrugged his head towards her legs.

"As I see you've discovered."

"Yeah," she said sullenly. *The stupid tourist girl.*

"Fancy a drink, Jonah? I'll fetch us some lolly water, eh?"

As he shuffled downstairs, Jonah turned to Vilia and said, "Mitch was the first person your mother called when she found your dad missing. He called the cops."

"Well what else is a man to do?" Mitch called out from below and then made his way back up, three small bottles of Fanta in hand.

"You lookin' for answers my dear?"

"If they can be found."

"Oh I reckon they always can be if you look hard enough. How long you hanging around for?"

"As long as it takes." Vilia surprised herself with the answer but McCafferty simply nodded his head, as if there could be no other course.

He downed his drink in one long gulp and placed it with other bottles in a large plastic bag dangling over the side of the boat. It looked like recycling had found its way to the tropics.

Mitch McCafferty hadn't always lived in PNG, he explained, his voice raspy from old age and the tobacco he was now rolling carefully as he spoke. He looked as though he was in his late seventies, but for a man who was obviously in the sun a lot, it was hard to tell.

He'd been in the Australian navy, he explained, gently working the paper around his tobacco. He'd jumped ship at Samarai and there he'd stayed setting up one business or another before eventually settling in real estate.

"There was quite a call for islands back then," he said. "Your dad came in one day all green and gushing about his own little place. I didn't fancy he'd take to Tubu, nobody else had, but he loved the place instantly. Didn't want to know about anything else after that. So I organized the sale of the lease and we were mates from then on.

"I don't know if you know much about your dad's folks," he continued, pausing to light his smoke and then dragging on it long and hard. "They sounded like tough people. Wealthy as all hell."

"Really?" *Of course she didn't know.*

"Yeah. Your granddad was in shipping or something like that, in Sydney I believe. He expected Jamison to join him. Jamie had other ideas. I believe they cut him off completely when he married your mum and that's part of the reason they came up here."

That certainly explained her grandparents' absence during her youth, but it only clouded the issue of her father's infidelity further. *If Dad loved Mum enough to alienate his family*, she thought, *why would he walk away from her so easily just a few years later?*

A spark of hope was reignited.

Gena and Jamie had been living on Tubu for three years when she fell pregnant with Vilia and traveled to Cairns for the birth, Mitch explained.

"And your dad was overjoyed. All he bloody talked about. Your birth, your first tooth, your first words. Christ, he even had a group of us over for your first couple of birthday parties if I recall rightly."

His words were like a blanket offering warmth in the cold light of day, and Vilia couldn't help smiling. She had waited thirty years to hear this, to be told how much he cared, but now as the white-haired man spoke, so full of fervor, so determined to make her see, her alarm bells began to ring and her smile began to fade. She wasn't sure she believed him. He was probably just trying to console her, she thought, like he must have consoled Gena all those years ago.

Did he really think that a few words of grace would wipe the slate clean? Your best mate still left me, she wanted to say, still took the sailboat and with it my sense of self. One or two birthday parties weren't going to cut it when he'd stood me up for the other thirty.

"Sounds like a happy man," she said, more coldly than she should. "So why run off with the housegirl?"

"Bullshit!" Mitch boomed, his double chin quivering and she blinked, startled. "He didn't run off, Vilia, and he didn't leave poor Genevive. And he certainly didn't have an affair with any bloody housegirl. Okay, I don't know all of that for a fact, mind you. But I know it as a friend. And I was one of your father's best."

"So what do you think happened?"

He dragged on his cigarette awhile and collected his thoughts.

"Dunno, but I've had a lot of years to think about it, and I got me theories."

Vilia's eyebrows shot up. "Such as?"

"Something bad happened, that's for sure. Either a bloody awful accident—his bones'll be found years from now down some crevice—or he met with foul play."

"What do you mean?"

Mitch looked away, clearly he'd said more than he intended. He glanced at Jonah but Jonah was looking out to sea, his expression inscrutable.

"Did it have something to do with Dick O'Brien?" Vilia continued prodding.

Mitch shot his eyes back towards her. "Been doing your homework, I see. You're smarter than your mother. She didn't want to know."

"She died last month. Drowned, actually."

Mitch looked shocked by this, gulped hard, sat back a little dazed.

Eventually he said, "Bloody hell, what a waste. Suicide was it?"

"Probably." It amazed her how quickly the assumption was made.

"I'm truly sorry. Gena was a good woman, Vilia, but she just didn't want to hear the truth. She was happier to believe that he took off with another woman than anything else."

Vilia stared at him angrily. *How could she possibly want to think that?*

As if reading her thoughts, Mitch said, "He might come back, then, you see? Might wake up to himself and come back. Better than thinking he's dead. It took Sebastian Cone and me three months to convince her to stop waiting. Three months."

"She waited thirty years," Vilia said softly.

He dropped his head and shook it slowly, sadly. She wondered if he would cry, and what a bloke like him would look like in tears.

"So what about Dick O'Brien?" she asked, her voice hoarse. "How was he involved?"

"Oh I don't honestly know," he said. "All I know is that he wanted that island badly."

"But why? What about the sandflies, the—"

"Because of the Bird of Paradise, of course."

When she looked at him blankly, he glanced at Jonah again.

"The country's national bird? They're truly beautiful birds, amazing feathers. The locals use them for their ceremonies, traditional dress."

"Yes, I've seen pictures." *But what did birds have to do with anything?*

"The strange sound you've been hearin' in the mornin's," Jonah added, "you know, the 'kwa kwa'? That's the birds. We still have a small population, mostly of the Raggiana but a few of the lesser-known Goldie's. Not nearly as many as before, though. Sadly."

"But what's all this got to do with Dick O'Brien?"

Mitch dragged on his smoke. "Well, the birds are usually found inland, in the Highlands, so their presence on Tubu was pretty remarkable. Your dad wanted to keep them there. Dick was more interested in hunting them for sale and export. They fetched a high price in Europe and Asia back then, even though they were supposed to be protected. Wouldn'ta stopped the likes of Dick. He kept suggesting Jamie sell him the place, offered quite a bit I believe. But your dad wasn't budging." He shook his head. "Seemed mighty convenient when Jamie suddenly just disappeared."

"But Dick never bought Tubu after my dad disappeared."

"No but I'll bet me boat that he was about to when he finally got his own justice. You can count your lucky stars there. Look, I wish few people in this world ill, but Dick was a bad seed. Greedy as all hell. If he was alive today he'd be Lord of Tubu and probably half the region. And he'd be hunting and pilfering and doing what he bloody well liked. I hate to speak ill of the dead, Jonah you know that, and I've got a soft spot for young Kyle, he's not as bad as people think. But Dick O'Brien was a mongrel. Whatever he died of, and I can tell you it wasn't suicide—he was too ambitious for that—it was a blessing from above."

"That still doesn't explain the missing yacht," she said.

"Huh? Oh, that's right, the yacht went AWOL, too."

"It was never recovered, right?"

"Nah, don't believe it was."

He considered this for a few moments, dragging deeply on his smoke.

"Maybe Dick took it," he said eventually. "Maybe the housegirl and some fellow she'd got involved with sailed off on it. Maybe it was all a bloody coincidence, who knows, love. But you count my words: your dad did not run off anywhere with anyone. Not without you and your mum."

They all sat contemplating this for some minutes when Mitch pulled himself up.

"I know ..."

He disappeared below deck again, this time returning with a faded timber picture frame. Clumsily he unhooked the back fastening and pulled a black and white photo from its hold, handing it to Vilia.

She read the scribbled inscription on the back first: "Jamie and me, Samarai Sept '72' Her heart did a somersault. She glanced up at the men who were watching her closely. Mitch nodded reassuringly and she turned it over, holding her other hand to her heart, lest it leap outside.

The picture was a little blurry and featured two men peering into the lens, chins held high, smiles as wide as wild corn. Vilia recognized Mitch instantly. He had the same head of white hair, thicker though, and was leaning against a revolver, as though it were a walking stick. His other arm was slung loosely around another man who stood straight-backed beside him, eyes beaming, with a pair of binoculars around his neck and big, baggy clothes belted in at the waist. It was obviously her dad and she was shocked to realize that she recognized him.

She had seen that face before. It was one of the faces that had been plastered to her mother's cabinet for all those years. His closely cropped black hair and small, trim moustache had been the red herring that had led her to look at the other shots, the lighter-haired shots, imagining they were related to her.

But as she studied the picture now she saw her eyes in his, and recognized his smile, his full red lips, his cluttered teeth. There was no mistaking the likeness, except this man looked happy and carefree.

"You can have that if you like," Mitch said and then sighed heavily. "I won't be around much longer and I'm sure it'll go down with the ship."

Vilia still had so much she wanted to ask him, but she could see that he had grown weary, even a little melancholy.

So they left him to his boathouse, bobbing gently to and fro, like a giant pot plant floating on the sea.

"You okay?" Jonah asked and Vilia shrugged him off. "Then I reckon there's one more stop you need before we go. I think it'll be worth it."

Jonah led her back to the main road in the opposite direction of the club where most of the traffic was now heading and past the post office and police station to an old Queenslander with 'Lawyer' painted on a sign out the front.

"This was Gena's lawyer Sebastian Cone's place before he died."

"I thought Cone was in Alotau."

"He was. Moved here some years ago. His replacement took it over soon after. Her name's Angela Robinson. Let me do all the talking."

Angela was a large black woman with a full afro of hair and a fluorescent white smile that lit up when they entered. She was sitting behind her desk in the front room, and stayed there to greet them, extending one arm for a strong handshake and scattering the papers about in front of her as she did so. Unperturbed, she motioned them to take the two mismatched arm chairs in front of her.

"What can I do for you, Mr. Johnson?" she asked, rubbing her hands together and winking playfully at Vilia. "Haven't had another brawl with the Copra Cargo Company I hope."

He laughed her off. "Just here for some old records, love. This is Vilia Lea. Her folks owned Tubu and it's been left to her now. She'd like copies of any files old Conesy might have had on the place when he was helping Gena out back in the '70s."

"Oh," she looked inquisitively towards the white stranger. "So you are going to sell up, Miss Lea?"

Vilia wasn't sure what she was going to do but before she had a chance to answer, Jonah chirped in.

"Not necessarily, Ang', just lookin' at all our options, aren't we, Vil?"

She nodded and the lawyer seemed placated by this, motioning behind them to an old rusty filing cabinet leaning against the back wall.

"Help yourself, Jonah. I have barely touched Sebastian's stuff since I moved in. Should be under L for Lea, or maybe T for Tubu. God knows he was a messy old bugger!"

"Thanks, Angela." He jumped up and began foraging through the drawers.

"So we haven't seen you here at Samarai before, am I right?"

"That's right. It's my first trip."

"Why you take so long to come?" She bat her enormous eye lashes innocently enough but there was something accusatory within them and Vilia just shrugged. "And why sell? Don't you like Tubu?"

Again, Vilia felt uneasy and again Jonah came to her defense. "Oh she's lovin' the place. We're just keepin' all our options open, right, love?"

Vilia nodded yes.

"Well, if you need a good lawyer ..." Angela began scribbling her details onto the back of a blank card. "It always helps to have someone looking into your legal rights when selling. Especially when it comes to islands in this country. Are you aware, for instance, that the government can always claim the land back if it feels entitled?"

Vilia shook her head. "But I have a lease."

She scoffed. "This means nothing to them. They can void it in five seconds. It's always a possibility, Miss Lea. That's why it helps to have good legal representation. You just never know."

"Got it," Jonah announced. "Got a copy machine or something?"

"Awww, I trust you Jonah," she said as though she didn't. "Get it back to me next time you're in town."

"Thanks Ang, you're a sport."

As they heard the door click shut behind them, Jonah turned to Vilia.

"Can't stand lawyers. Bloody busy bodies the lot of them!"

Then he began marching back down the road towards the harbor.

"Home!" he declared happily, waving the folder above his head like bait.

And, feeling every bit the prey, she quickly followed.

That night, Vilia dreamt of a shadowy sandstone mansion with an enormous fig tree looming out the front. As she wandered towards it, she heard a piercing scream that stopped her in her tracks and sent prickles of fear racing down her spine. She crept closer, edging her way up the stairs to a foreboding oak door. It creaked open at her touch and she slipped through. There was deathly silence inside. She stood there for some time, waiting, watching, filling with dread. Then she heard it again. Her mother's scream. She started running, frantically throwing open doors, trying to find her. Trying to help. But the scream was getting louder and she didn't know where to turn.

Suddenly she was in a spacious white room and her mother was sitting in the middle, sobbing quietly to herself. Vilia tried to reach out but she did not see her. She cried, "Mother!" but she could not hear. Gena just sobbed away endlessly, wrapping her ribs in her arms and rocking back and forth on a rickety stool, saying "Why? Why? Why?"

Then she saw him, standing in the corner, leaning on a gun, sniggering to himself. How could he laugh? How could he be happy? She ran up to him, she hit him, pinched him, bit into his thick, mousse-like flesh. But he didn't feel her. She tore at the skin and slashed at his eyes, but he just laughed. And laughed. And laughed. While her mother kept right on sobbing, hiding her face deeper between her knees.

They had been walking for two hours and seemed no closer to the top. Vilia's legs were starting to shake and she was swimming in rivers of sweat and white RID. She asked Boroko to stop and he obliged, standing perfectly still while she grappled for her water bottle and sipped from it greedily. Vilia held it out to him but the notion seemed too absurd and he tried to contain a giggle as he looked away meekly. They shared an island together, but that was as close as it was going to get.

Vilia leant down, her palms against her knees and breathed deeply and slowly, reminding herself why she had embarked on this merciless little adventure in the first place. "Your dad built this trail, Vilia," she told herself. "Show a little interest. It'll be worth it, just wait and see."

They had not returned from their Samarai jaunt until late, and it was past midnight by the time she had digested the contents of Sebastian Cone's file and finally drifted off to sleep. The next morning, Vilia awoke not to the shrill cry of the Raggiana but hours later to the soothing sounds of the ocean beyond. At breakfast, Jonah suggested she check out Kunoo Point and, feeling rested and revived, she had readily agreed.

Hundreds of feet up and barely able to catch her breath she regretted her burst of enthusiasm and glared irritably at Boroko who looked about as weary as a pup. From time to time he had halted her step and plunged into the thick forest to check on the pig traps, and she had been left standing in the thickness, swatting at mosquitoes and darting her eyes around furiously, lest a wild pig suddenly appear. And it did feel like a herd of wild pigs were about to break through. The forest was a writhing, rustling organism, alive with sounds and movement she did not recognize or understand. The wind came in gushes, rustling through and stirring up the branches while birds constantly tweeted and fluttered, as though having a party way above her head. Butterflies darted in front of her face and a sudden crunch forced her heart into her mouth. It was Boroko returning to the trail where he smiled and waved her on.

He broke branches as he went and slashed at vines with his machete, clearing the path for the frightened white woman. At one point he stopped to inspect an unfamiliar rustling in the undergrowth, whispering, "Python," before continuing on his way. As if she wanted to know.

"How much further?" she asked, her nerves now on edge.

"Not long. Ten minutes." He had said that half an hour ago.

"Let's get it over and done with then." She returned the bottle to her backpack. "See if it doesn't kill me."

He ex-boyfriend Liam had a fetish for heights. He always managed to find his way to the top floor of whatever building they happened to be in, and would peer down at the world below with utter awe. He loved that view, of sprawling streets and messy, unpainted rooftops that were not meant to be seen, and of people scurrying about busily below.

"Look at the view," he would say. "Really look at it. Manhattan seems different from this angle, don't you think?"

"Yes," she said and he was right.

It looked more ominous, more frightening, less appealing to her. She preferred looking up at the impressive buildings, at their neon signage and neat design. Crusty roof gardens and air conditioning vents were not her thing.

"They don't encourage the tourists to come up here," he told her. "Prefer it if we all just went to the Empire State and looked out from there. But I like this view. It's more honest, you know?"

Uglier, too, she wanted to tell him, but he seemed so earnest all of a sudden so she kept her mouth shut and kept right on staring. If there was one thing she could count on, Liam was no cliché.

"Nilly there!" Boroko announced and Vilia groaned beneath her breath.

Sure, sure, she thought. *I've heard that before.*

"Hey, Boroko," she called out a few minutes later. "You are taking me on the right path, aren't you?"

He turned around looking confused.

"I saw an old map. There was a different route to Kunoo Point, on the other side of the island, near the airstrip."

Very slowly, comprehension began to cross his face.

"Oh yes, Misis, that's right. It change, longpela taim—long ago. That path he too steep, too hard for the *dimdims*, for the white tourists!"

He sniggered at this and she was about to protest when she looked up to see the most magnificent view appear. Spread out below her was the entire northern half of Tubu and the island-littered sea beyond. This view was indeed a cliché—your typical Pacific island cliché—vivid greens and blues set against a painfully bright sky.

Liam would scoff at that, she thought. But he would have loved it, too.

She dropped her backpack on to a wooden bench that had been cleverly positioned to catch the weary walker, and stepped closer to the edge to embrace the scene. She spotted the main house, the guesthouse, the plantation shed and the village. Jonah's yacht was a tiny speck in the bay in front of the guesthouse, and she could see Samarai, small and seemingly insignificant on the horizon.

"Where is Kyle O'Brien's island?" she asked Boroko.

"Bado behind us," he said pointing back in the direction of the forest. "Other side, you see from airstrip."

Out of sight, out of mind, she thought and then collapsed onto the bench to rest her legs and to mull over what she had learned the day before. Her conversation with Mitch McCafferty was certainly interesting but she wondered how much was based on his friendship with her father and how much on fact. He had all but accused Dick O'Brien of murdering her father in order to buy Tubu Island from under her mourning mother's nose. But if it was evidence of this she was hoping to locate in Sebastian Cone's file, she was sorely disappointed.

The file contained a disorderly collection of notes and letters and all sorts of suggestions about 'how best to get rid of it,' dated after Lea's death. Whether Gena actually saw these, Vilia was not sure. In any case, the O'Brien name did not appear in the documentation, not even once.

She was particularly baffled, however, by the names that *did* appear in the file, amongst them Mitch McCafferty's. He had made an offer for the place just three weeks after Lea's disappearance and, although her mother had refused, it sent a tiny shudder down Vilia's spine. *Why hadn't he mentioned it?* And why would he want the island? He had already criticized its rugged terrain and sandfly-infested beaches. He was the local realtor back then, surely he had his pick of a better spots elsewhere?

Perhaps she couldn't trust him after all.

More intriguingly was a purchase bid made in writing by a Walter S. Mosley, sent to Sebastian Cone just one week after her dad's disappearance. The expediency of the bid was damning enough at a time when most locals were still out looking for the lost landowner. But it was the name that really caught Vilia's eye.

Who was this new player in the game?

The final oddity in the file was a hand scribbled note addressed to Sebastian and signed by Gena herself.

"Sebastian,

Francis is acting strangely. Disappears for long intervals. Rarely shows up for work. Love him dearly but cannot have it. Not now, when we need to be strong. Seems particularly worried about Hettie for some reason. What to do? Any more news from Riley?

Gena"

Below her name, someone, Sebastian she assumed, had scribbled the words: *"Under control."*

Under whose control, she wanted to know? *And who the hell was Hettie?* She didn't think she'd seen the name on the staff lists, yet it rang a bell. She began scrounging through the papers she brought with her from Cairns to discover why: her father had mentioned a Hettie in his letter to her mother.

"The coconuts are coming along nicely … Old Hettie has blessed the crop … So we should be in for a winner (or so the workers think).

Vilia looked up at young Boroko, Toia's son, and wondered what he really knew. The young man was squatting down in the clearing beside her, carving something out of a small piece of wood, and he seemed content, a world away from the troubles of Toia's time.

"Boroko?" she said, startling him.

He dropped the wood and stood up, assuming she was ready to go.

"What happened to your father? To Toia?"

The young man swallowed hard and sat down again. "He get killed by bush pig. Two years ago."

"I'm sorry," she said. "And Francis?"

Boroko thought about this for some time. "He get new job or someting. He go away."

"When?"

"Longpela taim. Long ago."

"Can you remember when exactly?"

He thought for some time. "Soon after Masta Lea go. Then Francis go."

Interesting, she thought.

"How did he get the job?" Boroko did not understand. "Who give him new job?"

Boroko paused again and eventually shrugged. "Me no save," he said at last. "I do not know."

She had just one more question and she could not have predicted his reaction.

"Who was Hettie?"

The young man jumped up with a start, as though he'd just been stung, and shook his head furiously. It was not dissimilar to his reaction that day she mentioned 'WD', Were the two linked, somehow?

"Me no save," he said again, this time more vehemently. "We go. Yes."

She stared at him, hard, but he was no longer meeting her eyes. Earlier she had asked the same question of Jonah but he seemed genuinely not to know. Boroko was less convincing. Was he trembling, she wondered?

"Fine," she said at last, and followed him back down the trail for the long trek home.

March 29: After just ten minutes of this, a low rumble heralded the end of the tempest and, like a turned tap, the rain suddenly stopped and the sun reappeared on its perch so that I had to cover my eyes for the glare. Only the dripping trees and the air still bristling with electricity reminded me of what had just passed. I was strangely, oddly exhilarated.

"Hello?" an older woman's voice answered the phone.

"Um, hello, I'm looking for Commander, I mean, Mr. Riley," Vilia said. "Is he around?"

It was later that same day. Vilia had returned, wearily, from her walk with one thing on her mind. She had to clear up some of the conflicting rumors and unanswered questions, starting with the investigating officer's whereabouts. If she could get in touch with Commander Riley, she might make some headway at last.

"Who's this please?"

"My name's Vilia Lea. I'm trying to locate some information on a case Commander Riley investigated quite a few years ago. Is he available at all?"

"Vernon died of a heart attack, dear, almost twenty-seven years ago," the woman said, her accent thickly Australian. "I'm his widow, Muriel. Is there anything I can help ya with?"

She should have guessed. "I don't s'pose you know anything about a case involving a man who disappeared from Tubu Island back in 1976, do you?"

There was a long silence at the other end of the phone and Vilia wondered whether the line had dropped out altogether. Eventually the woman spoke, her voice higher now, more strained.

"Who did you say this is?"

"I'm Vilia Lea, my father—"

"Yes, your father," the woman spat back, her tone startling Vilia. "Your father caused a lot of grief to a lot of people around here. I've got nothin' to say to you."

"But ... I ..."

"Don't call back. D'ya hear? I can't help you."

And then the line went dead.

Vilia turned to Jonah who had been listening intently and he took the phone from her grasp and placed it back on the receiver.

"What is going on?" she said, more to herself than him.

She had arrived on this island three days ago expecting to find some quick answers, put the place up for sale and return to her comfortable life in New York a little wiser and a lot more content. What she hadn't expected was getting caught up in the middle of a bad murder mystery— *Death on Tubu*— complete with shady characters and more red herrings than the North Atlantic. If it weren't so serious it would be farcical.

She didn't know what that phone call was all about but she knew one thing for certain, she couldn't let it go now. Not now.

"I need to get back to Alotau," she told Jonah. "I need to get hold of Commander Riley's case notes. As soon as possible."

"Mail boat comes by on Wensdy," he replied.

"Wednesday?! No, I need to go now. I want to get on with this!"

"Well it's not gonna happen, so just relax, love. Your dad's been missin' thirty years. Another two days won't hurt anyone."

He picked up his battered old hat and placed it firmly on his head.

"I've gotta get back to the plantation. Why don't you take a stroll, have a swim. Enjoy yourself."

Enjoy myself?

Vilia wanted to scream. That was easy for him to say. This was his home, the place he had chosen to live. She was here by default, thousands of miles away from the world she knew, the world she had constructed so carefully back in the US. Suddenly, Vilia longed for her little brownstone apartment, looking out at its sea of glittering lights, with its comfy furniture and twenty-four-hour electricity. She longed for her microwave oven and her favorite café and the weatherman who almost always got it right. But most of all, she longed for that New York sensibility, of telling it like it is. Ten minutes means ten minutes, not an hour down the track.

In contrast, Tubu was a riddle, a mystery she couldn't unlock. Everything about it was strange and unfamiliar: the weather, the forest, the natives, the neighbors. Time was erratic, inconsequential even. And truth? Well, what was that in this superstitious land? What was real and what was mere fantasy or local folklore or simple idle gossip? She simply couldn't tell and it drove her to distraction. She needed a sense of control, to get some kind of order, and so she picked up the phone again and dialed Alex. His answering machine clicked in, so she put the phone back down angrily and glanced around.

What was she going to do now? How would she fill her time?

Never one for idle holidays, Vilia hated free time. She loathed not knowing what was next, and so she set herself a plan. She would attempt another swim. See if she couldn't conquer this sea.

She trudged back to her hut and put her swimming costume on, lathering herself in sunscreen and RID this time. Then she grabbed a sarong and hat and made her way back to the small bay where she had swum two days before. She was damned if she was going to let it defeat her.

This time the sandflies hovered around her without landing and she smiled at this, feeling better already. At the ocean's edge she peered out to sea for any sign of fins. Nothing. She melted slowly into the water, warmer than a long bath and just as transparent. Despite her surliness, she had to admit it was heavenly. She waded out so that the cooler, deeper water could slither around her toes and then floated on her back, letting the ocean's heartbeat bob her about. This time she was careful to keep herself in line with the beach, swimming against the tide from time to time to ensure she didn't stray far before flipping onto her back again, and just floating.

Vilia must have been in this semi-comatose state for some time because she never noticed the surly storm approaching, reflecting its bad mood on the water around her. The first flicker of lightning startled her and she dropped her legs down beneath her. A clap of thunder quickly followed and within seconds she was splashing back to shore, grabbing her things and scrambling up the rocks again as the sky released its anger in strong, steady sobs.

Vilia ran for cover, first under a bread fruit tree and then on to the guest house where she stood entranced, watching the tropical thunderstorm whiplash the coast and fling the coconut trees about as though they were made of rubber. Rain pelted against the hut, spitting in at her and drumming away at the roof above, and she wondered just how waterproof palm fronds could be.

The storm had taken her totally by surprise, reminding her of those sudden afternoon drenchings from her childhood days in Cairns. She'd forgotten how exhilarating they could be, and how everything else faded away. Human concerns seemed of little consequence when Mother Nature was having a spat.

"Enjoy the breeze?" Jonah asked Vilia as she climbed the sundrenched stairs of the main house just ten minutes later.

She still had her wet sarong wrapped around her limbs and had neglected to tie back her hair so that it hung in wild, curly strands around her face.

The rain had halted work and Jonah was sipping a beer, his hat resting on the table in front of him. He offered her a beer but she declined, leaning against the veranda railing and smoothing her sarong out to help it dry.

"Breeze?!" she echoed.

"Yeah, well, the winds get a lot angrier than that 'round here. Tore an entire fig tree from the front of the house one year. Enjoy it?"

Enjoy seemed an odd choice of verb and she laughed. "Once I got under cover," she replied.

"I like a good storm. Sorts things out."

Washes away your bad mood, too, she thought, feeling oddly content. Perhaps it was also the swim, the cooling effects of the water, but she was less agitated now, calmer and more positive.

Perhaps that's why she finally asked about her grandmother.

"Ahhh, well, Miriam was a lot like you actually," Jonah said. "Had your green eyes and reddish brown hair."

"But what was she *like*? As a person?"

He considered this for a few moments, scratching at his shaggy hair with one hand while he swigged his beer with the other.

"Dunno. Guess you could say she was pretty down-to-earth, a no-nonsense kind of woman. Miriam wasn't much big on emotion. She believed in gettin' on with it."

"The complete opposite of my mother then?"

"Yeah, I suppose she was," he said, thinking it over carefully, smiling at the idea, as if it had never occurred to him.

"Was she married? Was there a Grandpa lurking around that I also didn't get to meet?"

He shook his head. "If there was I never met him either." He paused. "Nah, I always got the impression Miriam was flying solo. Certainly acted like she didn't need a bloke. And good on her! She came out every coupla years after Gena left. Always on her own."

"For a holiday?"

"Ohhh, maybe more to see how I was runnin' the place, you know? She was hardly the banana chair-and-daiquiri type. She'd only stay a week or so, but she'd be checking out the work sheds and goin' through the books. I gathered ya mum put her in charge of the place because Gena never came back."

"Really? Never?"

"Nope, not once after I took over. Surprised me to be honest. I got the feeling ya mum didn't want to leave ..."

"I'm not surprised at all," countered Vilia. "From what I'm hearing, she didn't exactly fit in."

He shrugged. "Who knows. Anyway, I reported to Miriam or Sebastian. And then, of course, Angela. Miriam stopped comin' out about four, five years ago. Guess it got too hard, all that travelin'."

"So when did Miriam die?"

"Last May. Angela informed me. I gather nobody bothered to tell you?"

"I didn't even know she existed until last week." Vilia inspected her sarong, it was almost dry. She smoothed it down around her legs and sat down. Her hair, too, had dried quickly and was now hanging in ringlets around her face. "Were they estranged? My mum and grandma?"

"Bloody looks like it. You clearly didn't know her or you wouldn't be askin' all these questions."

"No, I didn't. But why would they be estranged, do you know?"

He thought about this, patting down his hair where he had roughed it up. "Maybe it was 'cause Miriam forced ya mum back to Cairns after ya dad vanished. I reckon if it'd been up to Gena, she'd still be here, searching for Jamie."

"But there must have been more to it than that. They must have had a big fall out over something."

"Dunno, love, no one ever told me. From what I could tell, they'd barely exchanged more than about five words in twenty years."

Like mother, like daughter, she thought. The Lea legacy.

"Did you ever find that staff list and old map I asked you about?" Interest in her grandmother was fading fast. Hating her parents was all she could muster for now. Grandma Miriam could wait.

"Yeah I did. Left 'em in the bloody shed. Can I get 'em for you later?"

"Sure."

She smiled, helping herself to some coconut that Mary had just placed on the table beside Jonah's empty beer bottle. Then, settling back in the seat, she turned her attention to the marine park that was spread out before her eyes.

And that's the way they remained for the next hour or so. Not talking, just sitting, chewing, watching. She saw mackerel that evening, flipping in and out like silver slithers in the seaspray, teasing the sea gulls that swooped down to try their luck, and after them dolphins diving and dancing in a rhythm all their own. As the sun slowly checked out it left behind a fiery red and orange coat that lit up the sky like a corny velvet print, the sort you see in doctors' surgeries, too bright to be real, too stunning to believe. And when the colors gradually faded, and Vilia thought the show was through, the moon made an appearance, shining her fluorescent sliver across the ocean below so that the revelry could continue.

"God, it's beautiful," Vilia whispered into the darkness but Jonah had long disappeared.

Feeling suddenly alone, she wandered through the kerosene-lit corridor to the kitchen where she found him peeling potatoes for dinner.

"Potatoes au gratin," he announced, handing her a bottle of red wine and an opener, "just like my mother used to make."

"Sounds good to me."

She extracted the cork and poured them both a glass, then pulled herself up onto a bench by the fridge and sipped slowly, enjoying the warm, woody liquid as it coated her tongue and slithered down her throat.

Eventually, she asked, "Do you ever get bored here?"

"Not now," he replied. "But Jesus I used to."

"Yeah?"

"Well, when you're brought up with plenty of company around—I come from a giant family remember—you grow to expect other people to keep you amused all the time. It takes a bit to learn how to amuse yourself, you know."

She nodded, knowing only too well.

"The trick is not to try too hard. Just relax. Go with it. Feel your way instead."

Vilia frowned. She had learned to do away with feelings and that had been her salvation. Doing was her deliverance, activity her release. When her mother's eyes glazed over, she didn't stop to wonder how that made her feel. Too painful. Instead, it was off to the beach she went, playing and digging and searching for shells. If she could just find enough shells, everything would be okay. That's why she took to windsurfing and made straw hats and shorts.

And why she walked out on Liam before she got in too deep.

And wasn't it the very act of doing that lured her to this foreign land on a few letters and a whim? Surely if she had stopped to think about her feelings, she would never have left home.

As Vilia watched the old man stir his sauce with memories of his mother spurring his spoon on, she decided that feelings were just fine for a simple man like Jonah, but she had bigger issues to contend with. Feelings would only swallow her alive.

That night they ate on the veranda out the front and Jonah told Vilia tales of the early days on Tubu, when the generator broke down daily and he was sometimes stranded without supplies for weeks. And the time he taught young Tom to sail and they were caught in a sudden squall, ripping the sail apart and surviving by sheer good luck. He laughed a lot as he spoke, letting his small gray head bob back with glee, and he wiped away tears of joy as though longing for those days all over again. Those days of hardship and hard work.

But it was the story of the skull caves that had her intrigued.

"Thought I told you about them?" he said.

"No," she replied. "You told me the island was inhabited with evil spirits, that cannibals used to live here, but you never mentioned a cave."

"Ahh, well, it's all linked, see."

"How so?"

"Well, it's all folklore, of course, but the villagers—the ones who've been here longer than ya dad—they say there's a cave somewhere on this island and it's crammed with skulls. Cannibal skulls. And missionaries, too, perhaps."

"Seriously?"

"Seriously."

"So where is it, this mysterious skull cave?"

He shrugged his shoulders. "Well, that's why I call it folklore. No one knows or at least, if they do, they're not telling."

"A *hidden* skull cave? Even better!"

The red wine was working its magic now, chiseling away the edges, helping her relax.

"Well, word is it's somewhere up near Kunoo Point. At least I'm sure that's what Toia, Boroko's dad, told me once. Others say it never existed."

"What did my mum say?"

"Didn't know of it as far as I can tell. Certainly didn't tell me about it if she did."

Vilia crossed her legs beneath her and spotted a glimmer of light dancing on the sea. A flying fish, perhaps.

"You haven't thought to go searching for it?"

"Oh, bloody oath I have," he laughed. "I've had plenty of time to kill here—no pun intended. But no luck. And of course I couldn't get the blokes to come and help me."

"Why not?"

"'Cause just mentioning the place sends shivers down their spines. Freaks 'em out."

Vilia scoffed at this. "That's ridiculous."

"That's Papua New Guinea," he replied, his tone more earnest now. "I reckon it's still around and I reckon Boroko knows where it is. Reckon he's just not tellin'. Scared stiff of the place."

"Why?"

"Dunno, maybe the fact that it's full of dead people might have somethin' to do with it. You'd have to ask him yourself. Although good luck with that one. In case you haven't noticed, when Boroko doesn't wanna talk about something, that's the end of it. Can't get another word out of 'im. The bugger." And then he smiled. "So, no, there's nothing boring about this place, not if you start listening to the folklore."

"I'm not sure I'm too big on folklore," she replied, finishing off her drink. "So tell me about you. Ever wanted to get married, have kids, a place of your own?"

"I'm married to this place, the workers, they're my family."

"And if you had to leave?"

"Well I'd be disappointed, sure, but I'd move on, Vilia. It's a big world out there, this isn't the only island in the sea." He drank his wine. "Why? You really thinkin' of sellin'?"

"Oh I don't know, Jonah. I was just talking hypothetically."

"Just promise me one thing, then. Promise me you'll give it a good long think before you make any major decisions. You've been given a gift here, Vilia, don't throw it away." And then he laughed uproariously. "Crikey, I sound just like ya bloody mum!"

When Vilia awoke the following morning, she realized she was listening to the strange squawking sound of the Bird of Paradise. She snuck out of bed and gently opened her window wider but couldn't see them through the thick foliage, and she frowned. She knew they'd be a sight. As she padded to the bathroom, she noticed Jonah had placed an old manila folder just inside the hut door. On the front he'd scribbled: "From Sebastian Cone, the week I moved in."

She opened it to find a poorly typed staff list and several maps including a large surveyor's sketch of the island that almost shredded to pieces in her hands. It was dated 1965 and showed few of the structures now standing. She put it carefully aside and turned her attention to the staff list instead. This one was marked 'Sept 1976' and had a list of initials typed down the page with job titles beside each one and a list of their weekly provisions.

Vilia already knew what most of the initials stood for and noticed that 'VL' (for Veronika Ligaro, the infamous missing housegirl), was now absent. But there was one initial she did not recognize: 'H'. Beside it was an empty space where the job title should have been.

The mysterious Hettie, she wondered?

She picked up the remaining map. This was smaller than the other map and hand-drawn by an amateur. But this amateur got it right. All the original structures, the house, the guesthouse and the workstation were in the correct place and the path to Kunoo Point was on the northwest side of the mountain, where it should be. She was about to discard the map when she saw it, a tiny 'H' scribbled into the forested area on the other side of the mountain, the side that no one used, the side where she had spotted the initials 'WD' on the original map, near the grass airstrip.

Did 'WD' stand for Hettie? None of it seemed to make any sense and she chewed at her lower lip mercilessly trying to get it clear in her mind. Whoever Hettie was, she obviously used to live or work right around the other side of the mountain, on her own, away from everybody else. *But why?*

Now more than ever, Vilia needed to find out exactly who or what 'WD' was. Turning the map over, she saw the words, "As promised. Please pass on to Mr. Johnson," neatly handwritten on the back.

Goose bumps tingled across her body. It was her mother's handwriting.

That morning, as Vilia lolled about in the ocean and watched the seagulls swoop around her, she realized that she was no longer just searching for her father but for the missing links in between. She was looking for Veronika, the housegirl who had disappeared that same night, the 'stupid fool of a girl' who may or may not have wooed his heart away. She was looking for the yacht that they were said to have fled in. What had happened to that? And she was looking for the local staffer Francis who had departed soon after, accepting work a long way away.

And just who was Walter Mosley? A man so desperate to own Tubu he didn't have the decorum to wait until her mother's mourning had started to make his purchasing bid. There was also Muriel Riley, so distraught by Vilia's call she could barely speak. What did she have to hide?

And finally, there was Hettie, the elusive inhabitant whom no one seemed to remember but who was clearly mentioned in her father's correspondence.

As she stared out at the horizon, like the edge of a bath full to the brim, it was clear to Vilia that it wasn't just Gena and herself who were affected by her father's vanishing, but a whole stream of people one after the other, quietly dropping off the face of the earth: Veronika, Francis, Hettie, Dick, Vernon. And yet nobody had stopped to ask why.

Back in the guesthouse, refreshed and showered—she was starting to get used to the shock of cold water against warm skin—Vilia tugged a comb through her hair, placed it in a neat ponytail, then thought better of it and released it again. It might be her way in, she thought, spreading the coppery curls out around her. She stepped into a red, cotton sundress and flat sandals, then slipped out, past the main house, towards the village.

Stray dogs shifted begrudgingly from their place of rest along the pathway, and small children appeared again, rushing up to the white woman now, thrilled by her mere presence.

"Is your mum here?" she asked one of the redheaded kids, and he stared at her blankly, smiling his wide, white-toothed smile.

"Mama bilong yu I stap?" she tried in the little Pidgin she had picked up.

He nodded his head fervently and pointed away from the village and northwards along the coast.

"Felix Cove," he announced. "You come!"

Before she could stop him, the young boy—nine, maybe ten years of age—was storming off towards the beach, a gaggle of small children and mangy dogs in his wake. She glanced around uncertainly and then joined them, looking back from time to time to see if anyone had spotted them. There was no one else around.

The young boy stopped just short of the beach and waited for Vilia to catch up, then pointed to a thin, grassy trail that lead through the thick forest and west along the island.

"Felix Cove," he said again, clipping each word carefully as though he were reading the news.

"Okay," she told him. "Take me."

Why the hell not?

He waved her on ahead.

"No, no," she said, "You go."

But he shook his head. This might be his island, but she was the white woman. She would always be first.

And so they set off, her following the overgrown road ahead, he issuing instructions whenever it looked like she would lead them astray. The boy was clearly the leader of this gang and his dog, a mutt he called Easter because that's when he got it, was the only dog allowed to walk alongside him. The other dogs, four or five with mangy fur and ribs that stuck out painfully, were kicked and punched and pushed away by the children and yet, unperturbed, they always returned to the path and followed right along.

"What's your name?" Vilia called back to the boy.

"Jonah," he cried and she smiled at his obvious pride. Named after the boss.

"I'm Vilia," she said.

"Yes," he said. "Plaua."

"Sorry?"

"Bougainvillea," he replied. "You bougainvillea."

She stopped, stunned, and looked at him as he pointed at the thick, spiky ground cover they were passing. Perhaps he was right. She had long hated her name, her silly, nonsensical name. And now, looking around her, at the magnificent magenta colored plant that was everywhere on this island, clinging to fences and trees, and growing in lush patches around the house, it was all so obvious. Her name must have been derived from bougainvillea . And yet she had never twigged.

They continued walking for some time, silently now, except for the breaking of branches and the crashing of the ocean, which followed them on one side. And she wondered then of all the things she didn't know or was never told. And she wanted to be angry at her mother but couldn't muster the strength today. She was tired of being angry. And besides, she had to admit, she suddenly liked her name. It didn't seem so idiotic after all. She liked the idea of being named after a vibrant plant with fluttery petal-like bracts, tiny white flowers, and sturdy black thorns. Both soft and strong.

For the first time since she could remember, she was proud of her mother.

At several points Jonah Junior steered them from the shady path, onto the sand and into that ocean, Vilia hitching up her dress to wade around an overhanging mangrove, and back onto the beach and the grassy path again. She hadn't thought to wear her hat, and the sun, when it found her in these deviations from the path, was like a blowtorch against her skin. She wished she had brought sunblock. And RID, too. The sandflies near the beach were rife.

Along the way she spotted a small child paddling a wooden canoe out towards the deeper China Strait.

"Who is that?" she asked Jonah and he turned to squint into the sun and out across the glaring sea.

"Nemo," he said, "brada bilong me." His brother.

"Wow, like the clownfish?"

The young boy stared at her blankly. Maybe Disney hadn't reached the outer echelons of the Milne Bay yet.

"So what's he doing all the way out there? Where he go?"

"He hukim pis for kaikai," he said matter-of-factly.

He was fishing for their dinner.

"Really? How old is he?"

Jonah Jr. shrugged. He did not know. Age was irrelevant here.

Much later, as she sipped a cold drink up at the main house, Vilia would see Nemo return, several buckets brimming with Red Emperor, Reef Shark and a myriad of other fish. He had been out all alone in those deep, dark waters for almost five hours, and, she had discovered, was around eight years of age. It put a whole different spin on her own childhood.

She would never complain again about her mother not watching her flapping about in the shallows of Sunside Bay.

Eventually the children steered Vilia away from the coast and inland where the road was now wider and a little muddy where the tractor had recently ploughed through. As she slipped about in her sandals, grabbing stray branches for support, Vilia noticed that they were heading to higher ground and she began to lose her patience.

"Your mama up here? Really?" she asked Jonah and he nodded, yes. "This is the way to Felix Cove?" He nodded yes again. "Then you lead the way!"

This time she insisted and so he did, proudly stepping in front of her and continuing along. Within minutes they were detouring away from the road and began clambering up a steep, grassy pathway. Vilia struggled to keep up, gulping in giant gusts of air, but when she reached the top she was heartened by a magnificent view of a tiny inlet several meters below. The kids were already scrambling down the other side but she stopped to catch her breath and survey her surrounds. She was standing on the edge of a cliff face, looking down at what was obviously Felix Cove, a black sandy beach with azure waters that crashed surprisingly large waves into shore. It was bordered on three sides by almost-sheer, volcanic rock with all manner of lush ferns, coconut trees and breadfruit clinging on for dear life, and on the other by the ocean that was crashing into the surrounding rock face. Later she would learn from the giggling children that these waters were infested with sharks. No wonder they never strayed far from the shore.

"You come!" screamed Jonah Junior below and she watched as he pointed along the shoreline to a craggy outlet at the farthest end. There, she spotted several women hunched over, string bags or *bilums* on head, hard at work at something.

"You come!" he screamed again and she waved, then slipped off her shoes.

The children had gone down barefoot and it seemed like a good idea. She trusted her toes more than she did the smooth, slippery soles of her new sandals, and she began making her way carefully, tenuously down the slope. The kids met her at the bottom and then ran off ahead again, towards the women who had now noticed them and stood tall against the waves that were crashing close by.

As she closed in on them, Vilia realised they were collecting what looked like mussels from the shallow rock pools, scooping the fleshy meat from the shells and placing them in a bucket.

She huffed as she reached them and could barely find words, hunched over now and struggling for breath. The women smiled meekly at her and waited, one of them turning to grab hold of a small child who had strayed on to a distant rock, pulling him out of reach just as a wave crashed inches from his feet.

"Tia?" she said at last to the woman she remembered as Boroko's wife.

The orange-haired local stepped forward. "Yes, Misis," she replied.

"Do you speak English? Can we talk?"

"Oh yes, Misis," she said again and turned back to the other women who, on her nod, turned away and continued their work.

Vilia lead Tia back towards the safety of the sand and splashed a little water on herself as she went, trying to cool down from the long walk. They sat down under the shade of a reclining breadfruit tree.

"Jonah, he bring you here?" Tia asked.

"Yes. He's a great kid. Good boy."

Tia snorted. "He cheeky bugger tru! But yes, he good boy, too."

She spoke in a kind of singsong manner, also pronouncing each word carefully and Vilia recognized who had been giving the young Jonah his English lessons.

"I need to find out something," she said, cutting to the chase. "About the island."

"Yes?"

"Do you know about the skull caves?"

Vilia expected a look of apprehension or fear but the other woman simply shrugged.

"Yes, I know."

"Oh. Did Boroko tell you?"

She laughed at this. "No, my daddy he tell me, long time ago. He from here, lived over on Sideia."

Her head indicated an island off the horizon. "He doctor over there."

"Really?"

"Yes, what you want to know?"

Vilia wasn't exactly sure. Even if the skull cave really did exist, she couldn't see how it was connected to her father, and yet she felt an urge to know, as if it were important she leave no stone unturned.

"Is it real?" Tia looked at her blankly. "Does the skull cave really exist?"

The village woman shrugged again. "Yes, but nobody see it for long time. We let it …," she struggled to find the word, "sleep."

"Sleep?"

"We leave it alone. No good to go there."

"Why?"

She continued shaking her head, a scowl crinkling her forehead. "No good," was all she would say.

"So you haven't seen it?"

Tia's eyes widened. "Nooo, me no like!"

And she 'tsked' the foolish white woman, as if she could not imagine for one moment why anyone would want to check it out.

"So whose skulls are they?" Vilia asked, brushing some sand off her dress and licking her dry, chapped lips.

"They bilong to the people from Tubu."

"The original people? Were they cannibals?"

"Mm, maybe."

Again, she sounded blasé, as though the question were insignificant somehow. And then, brushing her own skirt down, she turned her eyes towards the children who were splashing about in the shallows and began to tell Vilia the story of the skull caves.

Back in the days when headhunting was an ordinary Papua New Guinea pastime and missionaries had not yet managed to get a stronghold, the people of Tubu practiced a macabre burial ritual. Upon a villager's death, their bodies were taken to the edge of the beach and then buried vertically in a deep pit (where, exactly, Tia could not say). It was as though they were standing upright in the sandy soil, only their heads remaining above ground, not so much to look at the lapping waters nearby as to allow the gathering crabs to pick their flesh clean. And all the while, the locals went about their daily lives, fishing, spearing crayfish, tending the vegetable gardens, seemingly unperturbed by this open-air mortuary. Later, after the crabs had done their job, the heads were chopped off and the skulls carried up into the mountain beyond. There they were placed in the ceremonial caves and there they would stay, sitting amongst their forefathers and looking out over the living for centuries to come.

"Maybe they still there," said Tia, her tone now hushed and reverent. "Nobody knows. But we don't want to find them. They are not our people. We must leave them in peace."

Vilia looked across at the woman, wondering if that was a warning, a way of telling her to back off, but Tia's thickly lashed eyes were giving nothing away.

"I must go back to work now. Okay, Misis?"

"Okay," Vilia said, "and thank you."

Tia shrugged, smiled and walked swiftly away while Vilia sat for some time looking out at the waves and then up past the craggy cliffs to that lush mountain above.

She wondered if the skulls of past headhunters were watching her now.

PART 6

ALOTAU—CLOSING IN

April 11: Who am I? Really? I don't know anymore and I wonder if I ever did. What I do know is that I never really liked her, not really. She wasn't interesting or courageous and she certainly never went out on a limb like I am doing now. The old me would have deserted long ago, given up, pretended to get on with her life. And left it all behind.

The man with the missing ear was starting to piss her off. Vilia was wedged awkwardly between his desk and another, in the dingy old corrugated iron building that housed the Alotau police station, and he was asking questions of no relevancy.

"What do you do for work?"

What's that got to do with anything? "I work for the Australian High Commissioner in New York."

"I see." He scribbled something down on the form in front of him. "And where do you live?"

She sighed heavily. "Well, surprisingly, New York city. Look," *Vincent,* "I can't see how this is relevant. I'm just after some information on my father's disappearance back in June, 1976. A Provincial Police Commander—"

"Address and date of birth?"

She wanted to scream, but told him anyway, followed by her nationality. No use upsetting him, she thought patiently. She'd come all this way, she didn't want to blow it now.

The mail boat, really just a large fibreglass dinghy with a makeshift shelter and smoky outboard motor, had arrived at Tubu just after noon and she'd hopped aboard with two Samarai locals for the wet and bumpy ride back to the mainland. By the time they reached Alotau she was covered in salt spray, her backside aching and eardrums shattered, but she made a beeline for the police station anyway. She had less than an hour before the boat was due to return to Samarai and didn't intend to stay. But she hadn't counted on Vincent and his copious questions.

"Okeydokey," he said happily, scratching where his ear should have been. "We are ready to get down to the business at hand."

He spoke methodically, accentuating every word like it was a gift from God. It was clear he had all the time in the world.

"Tell me from the start what happened to your father."

"Actually," she said, shifting in her seat, impatiently, "I don't have a lot of time and that's what I'm here to find out."

"Yes?"

"I was told by Commander Giwi, I think it was, over at Samarai, that you would have old files dating back to 1976. June 1976, that's when he disappeared."

"Hmmm?"

"He owned Tubu Island, east of here. My mother woke up one morning and he was missing. They never found him."

"And what is your mother's name?"

"Genevive Lea. Look, Sir," her temper was taking over, she was tired of being a sheep, "that is not really the point." She tried to lower her voice, could tell people were watching. "I've come a long way. I've only got twenty minutes now to catch the boat back and I'm asking for your assistance in releasing an old file which you may or may not still have here somewhere in storage. Can you possibly go and see if it's there? If not I'll leave because I'm wasting my bloody time."

The police officer blinked several times, clearly unsure how to respond to her outburst—he probably didn't see too many cranky white women around these parts—and then slowly got up, strolled down the corridor, turned a corner and disappeared from view. Vilia took several deep breaths and tried to stop shaking. Confrontation wasn't her cup of tea, either. A minute later another, older officer came over and held out his hand.

"How do you do, Miss Lea, my name is Commander Wanton. I believe you are looking for information on the Jamison Lea case?"

"Yes," she said, a little relieved.

"That was your father, yes?"

"Yes it was. He disappeared when I was three."

"Okay, then follow me and we will see what we can find."

Calmer now, she let Commander Wanton lead her into his office and towards a seat, but when he inquired if she'd like some tea she felt her exasperation rapidly return.

"Don't worry, Miss Lea," he said softly. "My people are looking through the files for you now."

She lowered her shoulders a little. "Thanks. I'll have a coffee."

Wanton called out instructions in an obscure local language to somebody and then turned back to her.

"Please, tell me, what brings you back, all these years later?"

"I only just learned about the island," she said. "My mother recently died. That's when I found out about my father."

"Yes, of course. I met your mother, you know?"

Her heart skipped a beat. "Really?"

"Yes. I was with Commander Chimu when we questioned the islanders. I think that was a day or so after your father vanished. I was just a young policeman then."

"And what did you find? What do you think happened?"

"Very mysterious, indeed."

And that was all he could say before Vincent walked in, a box of files in his hands, beaming from ear to missing ear. He said something incomprehensible to his chief and then dropped the lot on his desk and promptly departed. Behind him a local woman appeared wearing a bright, floral shirt over a clashing floral *laplap* and placed a cup of steaming coffee in front of Vilia. It smelled percolated and she smiled her appreciation as she attempted a scolding sip.

"It appears we have located the files you were after," Wanton said. "But I am afraid you can not take them with you. They are still police property. I hope you understand."

"Oh."

She glanced at her watch. Time was flying by. She took another, more tentative sip of her coffee.

"To go through the contents you must be in the company of a police officer and we must register your details—which I believe Officer Harry has already done?"

"Yes, he's certainly done that."

Exasperation was returning like a ball of heat. What was she to do? All of the formalities would take longer than the ten minutes she had left to return to the wharf. If she didn't catch the mail boat back, how would she return to Tubu?

She placed her cup down and sighed. Relenting.

"Let's go through it then," she told the police commander, and settled into her chair.

Clouds were fast forming in the sky above Vilia as she trudged her way up the hill to Top Town, the leafy suburb high above Alotau's town center. She'd been assured by Commander Wanton that she would have no trouble finding a roof for the night and at the sight of the encroaching clouds, she hoped he was right.

The police files had taken a good deal longer than ten minutes to peruse and, having missed her boat, she had little choice but to stay. There would be another boat heading her way tomorrow, she was assured, but she'd given up caring. Vilia was suddenly not so adverse to a stopover in this town, somewhere quiet and comfortable to collect her thoughts. She considered contacting Roger for a bed, but decided against it. He probably didn't need the encouragement.

The Mala Mala Guest Lodge was a sturdy timber building with no air-conditioning but a cool sea breeze. A friendly Papuan couple greeted her at the front desk and proudly informed her that tonight was BBQ night: "All you can eat for just twenty kina!" All she really wanted was a cool shower and a bed, but she feigned interest anyway and signed up for the banquet.

Vilia's room, tiny and cluttered with white wicker furniture and local wooden artifacts, didn't face the ocean but had an enchanting view of thick rainforest out the back. She pulled up a chair and dropped down wearily just in time for nature's next installment of a tropical thunderstorm. As the rain roared down, shrouding the forest in a misty veil, she considered the notes she had read in the police chief's file and felt that they, too, were cloaked in a veil, one of unanswered questions and contradictory "truths."

According to the file, the first week of the investigation was carried out by a local Alotau team headed by Police Commander Chimu and including Wanton. There were streams of badly typed notes and it took Vilia some time to wade through them, most appearing to be of little value. Every now and then, however, she came across a paragraph or a sentence that caught her by surprise, and she noted it down as best she could, her mind racing all the while.

In the end, there were five key pieces of evidence that, to Vilia at least, seemed to suggest foul play:

1) Scuffle marks at the entrance of the copra shed (heel indents, broken doorframe, etc) and in the far right corner of the shed (heel indents).

2) Blood splatter (untested) in copra shed, various spots including far right corner.

3) Cut rope belonging to missing yacht.

4) Personal items belonging to Miss Veronika Ligaro missing.

5) Personal items belonging to Mr. Jamison Lea all present except small backpack, water bottle and watch.

Yet it was the final sentence in the file that left her in shock. It had been scribbled, as though nonchalantly, across the final page: "*No incriminating factors. Case closed.*"

Beneath it was the signature of Commander Vernon Riley.

"That is pretty standard practice," Wanton had assured her, quickly sensing her indignation. "We cannot keep investigating forever. We must decide one way or the other. Commander Riley was brought in to decide."

"But what about the blood?" she cried. "How can you ignore that?"

"It was a working shed, Miss Lea. Workers would have cut themselves on a daily basis, including your father. Yes?"

"And the scuffle marks?"

"We did not get there until days after he vanished. They could have happened at any time in between. It was not a fresh scene you understand? The villagers had all been through it. It could not be considered reliable evidence."

"Well surely the cut rope from Dad's boat? You can't tell me that's not suspect?"

"Cut, perhaps, by your father in his hurry to be away? How are we to know? Who is to say?"

He turned the file over then and showed her a small, aging newspaper clipping from the Port Moresby *Post Courier*. It was a simple two-paragraph piece:

"Parts of a shipwreck were discovered off the coast of Ahloma early yesterday morning by locals fishing in the area. There are no identifying marks although they are believed to belong to a white yacht possibly manufactured circa 1965. Maritime Emergency Services Chief Wally Wintago said they would scan the area for further debris."

It was dated three months after Jamison Lea's disappearance and slashed in red ink with the word: "Lea?"

The police had assumed the answer was yes.

Vilia moaned. *Not that, please, not that.* She stood up and pulled her clothes off, then stood for some time under a tepid shower, trying not to imagine his body becoming fodder for the fish below. Somehow the thought of her father falling prey to the ocean's grip seemed too much to bear. She wondered, too, if her mother had been told, and if that's why she joined him in his watery grave.

Vilia hadn't had a good piece of steak in a very long time and as she sucked into the juicy flesh, she tried to enjoy her meal, to calm down, to get some control. But her mind was darting in every direction and she barely tasted the meat as she ate.

It amazed her how quickly her emotions had chopped and changed over the past week, from surprise and hurt to anger and betrayal, and now, after today's findings, a wallowing sense of irrepressible despair. Two little words had sealed her father's fate: "Case closed."

We've given up. We really don't care.

In the light of today's evidence, she was beginning to understand her mother's woe, and why she kept a vigil looking out to sea. Even when the search parties were called off and the rumors became the easiest option to believe, her mother had stayed faithful to her father, assuring him (or was it more for her?) that he hadn't been deserted.

But it didn't change the fact that little Vilia got lost along the way. She had become the next casualty, as cut off as her father's sailboat, drifting alone at sea. And she wondered now if her mother ever realized this.

The next morning Vilia awoke with one clear thought in mind. She had to find the missing housegirl. It was as simple as that. The fact that Veronika might also be making the fish a nice little playground underwater did not occur to Vilia. Just as she did not—would not—believe that her father set sail that night on some merry escapade. Instead she was beginning to suspect that he met with foul play and his boat was cast adrift. It was an ugly thought but it was better than digging her head in the sand, or looking out to sea.

She decided to pay Commander Wanton another visit.

The police chief smiled widely when she entered the station and waved the brightly clad receptionist off, ushering her straight into his office.

"So how are you today, Miss Lea? I see you are still with us."

"'Fraid so. But I won't start screaming this time, I promise."

He laughed. "That is a relief. What can I do for you?"

Vilia asked him about Veronika Ligaro and whether they had any leads on her whereabouts. It had occurred to her as she had wandered back down the hill to the city center, that her father may have been the priority and that Veronika may have got lost in all the confusion. Wanton retrieved the file and began flipping through the pages.

"That is a good question, Miss Lea," he said. "I think we assumed that our search for your father would reveal her whereabouts, too. But if you suspect foul play, she may have been involved, and living somewhere else today."

"Or she might be an innocent party who simply took off at the wrong time?"

"Perhaps, now let me see ..." He stopped at a page of notes and quickly scanned them. It contained Veronika's original address, Komunive village, near a place called Goroka in the Eastern Highlands.

"Did anyone ever contact her family? Check out the village?"

He shrugged his shoulders. "Probably not."

And, to her raised eyebrows, he added, "We do not have the money and resources you have in Australia. Or New York city, yes?"

"I guess not," she replied.

Vilia jotted down the village name and other details, noting as she did so that Veronika's date of birth was rather vague. It said simply, "20+."

"Birthdays are not such a big thing in my country. Anything else I can help you with?"

He appeared to be enjoying himself and she guessed he didn't get a lot of chances to help solve age-old mysteries.

"Yes," she replied, closing the file and handing it back to him. "You can tell me how to get to Goroka."

The mountainside was too close for comfort and Vilia wondered, momentarily, if the pilot had dozed off up there in the cockpit. She had done enough flying in this country by now to know that getting about it was an exercise in nerve control so she tried to ignore the jagged ridges and looked out the other side instead. The mist there was thick and ominous, explaining why they were forced to hug the hillside so formidably. It was the only line of visibility.

She was strapped into a tiny six-seater, twin-engined piper, with only the pilot (white) and some important documents (classified) for company. Commander Wanton had made a few phone calls and discovered that, due to low visibility, the airport at Goroka was temporarily closed but he managed to find her this seat, which would get her into the coastal city of Lae by the afternoon. Wanton assured Vilia she could find her way northeast to Goroka easily from there.

In between, she phoned Jonah to alert him of her plans and then stopped at one of the local stores for fresh underwear and a shirt. Her khaki trousers would hold out for another day or two. She also bought a toothbrush and some deodorant, and quickly repaired herself in the policewomen's toilet block, wondering all the while what on earth she was doing.

Chasing ghosts again, Vil? she asked, staring at her reflection in the mirror.

Vilia stared for some time, surprised by the woman who looked back at her. This one seemed almost foreign to her. Her hair was loose and unruly, with sun-kissed streaks she had not seen in years, and her lips were dry and chapped, not a shred of make-up on her sunburned face. But she looked good, healthy even, and less out of place somehow. Perhaps it was the sunburn.

Still, Vilia rustled through her bag and retrieved some lip balm, quickly applied it and then scratched about for a brush. Not finding one, she pulled her fingers through her hair and then, meeting nothing but knots, gave up, scooped it into a ponytail behind her and returned outside. She had ten minutes to catch her bus back to Gurney airport and the pilot would be waiting.

"You're a lucky woman," the pilot yelled over the roaring of the engine.

If Wanton had called about the flight one minute later, he explained, she would have missed the plane.

"I was just about to leave."

"That is lucky!" she cried back and then released a slow smile.

Deep down inside, in the part she rarely dared to linger, Vilia felt a gentle strengthening and she smirked at the mountainside now as it teased her with its proximity. She knew this decision to fly to Lae—to try to find her way to a remote village in the middle of nowhere—was bordering on the insane, but she felt emboldened by it.

"I'm on the right path," she told herself. "I just have to be."

"You going the wong way!" screamed a middle-aged Chinese woman with spiky black hair and bright red spectacles.

Vilia was standing on a battered bitumen road, attempting to hitchhike. The young pilot had dropped her on the outskirts of Lae and, according to Wanton's scribbled directions, she now needed to head north on the Highlands Highway which would take her all the way to Goroka and to the village which, Wanton assured her, was close by.

"Take that road," the pilot told her, "and it should get you on to the highway. You can probably catch a PMV along the way."

But Mrs. Wong had other ideas.

"Oh no, no, no, no, no!" she squealed, flinging open her small Mazda door and ushering the younger woman inside. "You get the bum steer! Highway is this way. If you not in huwy, I must stop first for food, then we go to Kainantu. Goroka not far fwom there. Okay? Okay?"

Unsure, but feeling short on options, she agreed and jumped in beside her. No sooner had she closed the door when the Chinese woman began chastising her again.

"Hitching no good now!" she said, propping her specs into place. "Vewy dangerous. Many, many wascals. You listen to me, my name Mrs. Wong. You vely lucky to get me!"

"Well I'm feeling lucky today, Mrs. Wong," she replied, surprisingly cheerfully, and they both burst into giggles as they sputtered along the highway.

As they left the coastal jungle of Lae and emerged into the grassy flat of the Markham Valley, Mrs. Wong wound up her window and pushed her door lock down, insisting Vilia do the same.

"Wascals," she explained. "Vewy bad—okay? Many people get attacked here. But we be okay."

Vilia admired her optimism and marveled at her courage, especially when she learned later that she made this journey every week. Mrs. Wong's family had a small trading store in Lae but two days a week she helped out at her uncle's restaurant, two hundred kilometers away.

"He wife die last year," she told her, "and he go' no help. He kids they go away, back to China, so he need help, you know?"

Not really, Vilia thought, and envied her this familial bond, so strong she risked her life each week with barely a second thought.

Leanne Wong and her husband, Chau, had fled China twenty years before and settled in Lae's Chinatown where they opened their small store and raised three daughters, two of whom still worked for their parents in town. The third, just out of school had recently moved away.

"She no like Lae," Mrs. Wong said, shaking her head deliberately. "She like the big lights of the biiig city. Like you, huh?"

"Yeah I suppose."

Vilia wasn't so sure what she liked anymore.

"She live in Sidanee, Austwalia now. You fwom Sidanee?"

"Cairns, actually. In far North Queensland."

"Ohh, Gweat Bawier Weef?"

"Yep, that's the place." It seemed a world away.

"Me? I like Lae. It's quiet, sure. But it vewy beautiful. And not so many people. But beware of the wascals, hey?!"

And she crinkled her small face as she giggled with glee. She seemed happier in this one moment than Vilia had ever been.

They drove for several hours through the hot, dull stretch at the base of the Kassam Pass and from there up into the Central Highlands. Mrs. Wong maneuvered her Mazda like a pro, chatting away about her children and her uncle and her wonderful life in Lae, both fists clenched around the steering wheel, one hand occasionally breaking free to reposition her glasses at the top of her nose.

She asked about Vilia, too, and Vilia was surprised to find herself opening up in way she hadn't done in such a long time. She told this woman everything, from her father's disappearance to her mother's recent death. She told her of Liam and the love she gave away and Leanne shook her head then and poked her shoulder adamantly.

"You silly girl," she said scowling. "You find nice boy, you keep him. You no wun away."

"I didn't run."

"Vely, vely silly. No' many love in this world. You vely lucky but you thwo i' away."

They stopped talking for a while then and Vilia watched the road ahead, zigzagging along the hillside where the view over the valley and across to the Sarawaget mountains beyond was breathtaking. And she smarted at the woman's comments because she knew she was right, and she tried to pry Liam's face—his beautiful, carefree face—from her mind.

The day they broke up was a normal New York day. He went to his day job, renovating old brownstones for young rich folk, while she headed off to her office at the Australian consulate.

Yet it turned pear-shaped fairly quickly. Trivial now, thinking back on it, but it had seemed so important at the time—she'd faxed the wrong document to the wrong person and her boss had been irate. So she'd returned home furious with him and herself and the world at large, and had proceeded to rant and rave to Liam who was busily cooking Atlantic snapper in their tiny kitchenette.

"Shit happens, Vilia, don't let it get to you," was all he had to say and suddenly she wanted to smash his face in.

"No, Liam," she'd snapped. "Shit just happens to me!"

When he turned from the stove to look at her there was something new in his eyes. It was the first time he'd ever looked at her with pity, and she shrank back.

That night she packed her bags and walked out.

Eventually Mrs. Wong's car made its way back down the mountain and pulled into the small village of Ukarumpa south of Kainantu in the Aiyura Valley. As the headquarters for a linguistics institute, it was teaming with international expatriates, mostly missionaries, and had an impressive supermarket into which Mrs. Wong scurried to fetch some groceries for her uncle. Vilia took the opportunity to visit the local post office where she penned a quick note to Alex.

It had been several days since they had spoken and she knew he'd be worried. She knew, too, that this postcard—if it ever made its way out of the country—would probably take weeks to reach him, and would be meagre compensation to a phone call. But she was running out of cash, and she didn't have the stomach for Alex today. He seemed part of another world now.

From Ukarumpa, it was just eleven kilometers through the rolling green hills blanketed in Kunai grass, past pine trees and causarina to Kainantu, a small, bustling town 1600 meters above sea level and right on the dirt highway. It was the main support town to the many coffee plantations and produce growers in the region and even had a small share of gold which, Mrs. Wong informed Vilia, had lured her uncle to the area many, many years ago. Bad luck and a bothersome back had forced him to give up the search and start up a restaurant instead.

Night was falling fast and there was a chill in the air as the car finally came to rest outside the Chow Down Chinese restaurant with its crudely painted sign and its dusty hanging lanterns. Mrs. Wong had already invited Vilia to overnight with her that evening and resume the last leg of her journey, fresh, in the morning, and Vilia had willingly accepted.

It was nearly 7:00 p.m. and the place was empty but Mr. Zhang was in high spirits. He was decked out in white robes, with a red bandanna around his head and black slippers on his feet, and had a merry face that lit up when they arrived. He greeted Vilia like an old friend and quickly ushered her to a wobbly table where he poured some green tea.

"You don't have any coffee, do you?" she asked but he just beamed and continued pouring the tea.

Then he disappeared out the back where Mrs. Wong was strapping on an apron and preparing to take over the cooking duties. The feast, when it came, was magnificent. There was sweetcorn soup with crab meat and crispy chicken wontons to start with, followed by a mixed platter of twice-cooked pork, ginger beef, Combination Chow Mein and Peking duck.

"Too much food!" she told Mr. Zhang as he handed her a bowl of candied banana fritters for dessert and he just smiled again, bobbed his head and shuffled back into the kitchen.

By 8:00 p.m. several patrons, including a Chinese family and a Dutch couple, had come in and one takeaway order had been serviced but it was clear Zhang was not doing good business and Vilia hoped it was not always like this. She took her plates to the kitchen and helped him clean up, the smile firmly planted on his face as he chatted with his niece. A skinny local boy with mismatching thongs and an oversized apron was on sink duty but by 9:00 p.m. Zhang had to let him go.

"Quiet night?" Vilia asked the old man as he rung up the till, and he nodded yet the dazzling smile was still there, as though he hadn't a care in the world. He stopped and reached for a basket on one side, holding it out to her. It was overflowing with fortune cookies.

"Why not?" she said, laughing as she plucked one out.

Cracking it open, she pulled out a thin white strip of paper on which something in bright red had been typed. She laughed again. It bore the words: *"Your failures will lead you to your success."*

"Here's hoping," she said, placing the paper in her pocket and popping the cookie in her mouth. As she began crunching, she took the broom from Mrs. Wong and finished sweeping the floor.

"Vely sad," Mrs. Wong whispered when her uncle was out of earshot. "Once best westwant in weigion. Now, vely hard to ge' people come."

"Why? The food's delicious!"

"Oh no' so many people in this town now. Many expats they leave after the cwime start. No' so many go out a' nights now, too."

"Why doesn't he close down? He must be old enough to retire?"

"Westwant is his life now, you know? I' all he go'."

In fact, Mr. Zhang also had a breezy weatherboard and besser block house behind the premises with a bamboo garden that swept down to a small creek below and it was here that Vilia retreated while Mrs. Wong and her uncle finished up for the night. Zhang had also nurtured lush ferns and tropical flowers—hibiscus, spider orchids and rhododendrons—and a tiny pebble pathway meandered its way through with handcrafted benches and birdbaths and chimes.

It was no wonder he didn't want to leave, she thought, he had his own slice of heaven carved discreetly out of the wilderness around him.

Dressed in one of Mrs. Wong's sweaters because it was late and surprisingly cold, Vilia followed the path along to where a lantern had been lit, and took a seat on the bench, staring up at the sky. She could not recall a clearer night. The stars all sparkled like Sirius, strong and nearby, and the moon, now fuller, glowed like a torch through a keyhole. She wondered if Liam was peering up at the same time as he rehearsed a riff on his Rickenbacker. And she wondered if he ever gave her a thought or wanted to call.

With self-pity threatening to close in, she returned to the house and to the futon Mrs. Wong had prepared for her in the lounge room. And she swiftly fell asleep to the foreign sounds and smells of a pit stop along the way.

The next day Vilia discovered that Goroka was a good deal easier to get to than she had been expecting, and her good fortune was beginning to scare her.

Bad luck must be close by.

Mrs. Wong had fed her well that morning and packed some mini spring rolls and bananas for lunch, as well as a bag of salted plums (dried red plums that tasted both bitter and sweet and were surprisingly addictive) to snack on along the way. Then she dropped her back on the highway at a small bus stop where Mrs. Wong insisted a PMV would soon come by.

Vilia had given her a long, firm hug before she hopped out. She'd bonded with the small Chinese woman so quickly, something she never normally did, and she promised to keep in touch, exchanging addresses by the roadside.

"You go find twoo love," Mrs Wong had instructed, "I know i' waiting for you!"

"I'll just settle for a comfy bus at this stage, thanks," Vilia had laughed, and the older woman frowned.

"Oh no, no, this one harder to find!" Then she, too, shrieked with laughter.

As usual, Mrs Wong was spot on. After just ten minutes, a rusty white minibus bursting with locals creaked to a halt and spat open its doors beside her.

"Six kina," the large man behind the wheel yelled above the roar of conversation, crying babies and, if she was not mistaken, the crooning of caged poultry. The stench—sweat, animal droppings, tobacco—was overwhelming and she tried not to inhale deeply as she paid the fare and stumbled to a seat, every curious face upon her.

But it didn't dampen her spirits this time. She was happy today, almost exhilarant, and she wondered, excitedly, whether Veronika might be here on the bus, too, staring up at her, unknowingly.

The journey between Kainantu and Goroka once took several days to complete but, thanks to the Highlands Highway, could now be achieved in just a few hours. The region had been settled by Europeans long ago, and the road was in a serious state of disrepair. Vilia felt every bump and pothole as they plotted their way slowly past vivid green valleys and through the rugged mountains that formed the spine of this seemingly impenetrable country.

The thick morning mist gradually dissipated as they drove and she smiled defiantly at the cliff faces that were becoming such a normality on this journey. Along the way they came across orderly villages of low, circular huts with two peaks at the top in which a tuft of grass protruded, and she learned later that each tuft represented the owner's area and that of its neighbor, and that the villagers believed that the tufts talked to each other through the night so as to hear each other's secrets.

Vilia wondered if Veronika's hut had such tufts and what, if anything, they had to say.

Eventually, the tidy little city of Goroka came into view with its shady, green streets and friendly inhabitants who waved enthusiastically at the bus as they passed. A minor outpost station in the 1950s, Goroka had flourished to become the provincial capital with an eclectic population of missionaries and miners, students, shopkeepers and plantation workers and, plumping it up from time to time, a stream of adventurous tourists keen to trek the neighboring mountains or explore the nearby prehistoric caves. Vilia noted that the people were smaller here than on the coast and the men bore enormous protruding leg muscles, their feet thick, naked and wide. They looked almost comical, like miniature Incredible Hulks.

The bus finally screeched to a halt outside the market center and as she got off, Vilia noted that it was not yet midday. She had all afternoon to find her way to Veronika's home village, Komunive. But she was a seasoned traveler now and wasn't taking any chances, so she stopped at the information center and asked for directions.

The middle-aged white woman inside barely bat an eyelid at Vilia's presence or her request and simply turned to a stack of regional maps, opened one to where Komunive Village had already been circled in red pen and handed it to her.

"Popular place?" Vilia asked, surprised.

"Ooh yes," the woman replied, the faint hint of a New Zealand accent. "The mudmen are a big attraction."

"Mudmen? Sounds interesting. How can I get there from here?"

"You can walk. Takes about an hour."

"That's the only option?"

"Or ..." she fiddled in a drawer beneath her and produced a small brochure for a Goroka motel.

"The Happy Guest House on McNicholl Street runs tours. You can always stay there tonight. The tour is expensive but if you stay you get it for free."

Vilia hadn't considered staying over, would certainly have balked at it a few days earlier, but she realized now that it was the smartest option. The village was a good distance away and even if Veronika was there and easily found, Vilia would hardly be back in time to catch the 3:00 p.m. bus which, the driver had informed her, made the 330 kilometers journey all the way directly to Lae.

Getting from Lae back to Alotau and then on to Tubu was a whole other matter but she assumed it would be easier done if she set off first thing the next day, and so she turned back to the information officer with a smile.

"Where's this guest house then?"

The town of Goroka is nestled around a small, busy airport, yet the environment was almost serene as Vilia strolled through, finding her way easily to McNicholl Street east of the PMV stop. The *Happy Guest Haus* was a surprisingly beautiful, colonial era, timber home with large shuttered windows and lavish verandas and was situated near an equally sprightly church and a forest of soaring pine trees. As soon as she checked in, she inquired about the village tours and was informed one departed at 1:00 p.m. that afternoon. She had an hour up her sleeve so returned to the town center and to a store called Steamships where she bought a lined exercise book, pen and the first decent sweater she could find. Like the evening before, she knew that upon sunset the temperature would drop dramatically again and she wanted to be prepared this time. Then she returned to the guesthouse, took a seat outside reception and waited.

The tour bus was running late, but she expected this, and she polished off the food Mrs. Wong had given her and began to scribble away in her new makeshift journal. It had been a long time since she'd found the desire to write and she couldn't get the words down fast enough as she attempted to describe just a portion of the events that had happened over the past few days. She recalled unexpected generosities and openhearted strangers, exotic Chinese food and rattling road journeys. But when she thought of the next leg, the one to Veronika's village, her mind was filled with apprehension and her pen was suddenly still. Her trepidation, she knew, was understandable. She was there, after all, to confront a woman about running off with her father, or, worse, playing a part in some dreadful deed. Every possible scenario began playing her stomach like a soccer ball, bouncing about, unsettling her deep within.

She could be dead, Vil, she told herself sternly, hitting the thought around for some minutes before considering the prospect that she might also be alive.

Certainly a relative would be, and they must know something.

But what if they don't?

Then at least you tried.

And spent a good deal of time and money for nothing.

For an adventure, Vilia, for the adventure of your life.

That final voice was not hers. It seemed more like Liam talking through her. Or Jonah. Or Mrs Wong. Or anyone but the Vilia of old.

She put her journal away and looked around at the gathering group. There were only five others but she felt comforted by the thought that she would not be completely alone. She had help should things turn sour. There was an elderly white couple who appeared to be speaking something foreign and guttural (German, perhaps?), a young black woman and a middle-aged mixed-race couple. They all seemed as blasé about the delay as Vilia, but when the small van drove up to the motel reception, one of them called out

"Yee-ha" and they all climbed quickly inside. Vilia hopped in last and was pleased to find that the seats were cushioned and the bus air-conditioned. Mrs Wong would be most surprised!

She smiled at the others as she took a seat up the back.

"Hello peoples!" came a hearty cry from the front and Vilia looked up to see a large black woman waddling into the passenger seat, frangipanis in her hair, motioning to the young male driver to start.

"My name is Wendy," she continued, adjusting her hefty bosom within an enormous floral top, "and I am your tour guide for today."

She flashed them a confident smile, clapped her hands and then turned to face the road ahead. No sooner had they spurted their way out of the motel driveway than her voice began to boom loudly from the front.

"Goroka has a population of around 25,000 people," she announced as they wound their way through the city past the Raun Raun Theater—"internationally known"—and the small police station to the J.K. McCarthy Museum.

"That was named after the legendary patrol officer McCarthy. It has one of PNG's best collections of photographs showing first contact between the local highlanders and Europeans."

Vilia tried to concentrate but her mind kept galloping in every direction, ahead of her to the elusive housegirl, and backwards to the early days of Tubu. The idea of coming face to face with Veronika was exciting, upsetting and nerve-wracking all at once and she felt a kind of hollow in the pit of her stomach.

Wendy continued her rant and the bus slowly left town and began the bumpy drive north, across the Zokizoi River on the road to Veronika's village. Before long, they were turning into a thin, muddy road sign-posted 'Komunive.' Vilia's heart beat double time.

What if she isn't here?
What if she is?

What if she won't talk to me?

What if she will?

They soon stopped beside a cluster of small huts sitting snugly on the hillside. A dozen giggling children had raced up to meet the bus and began grabbing the passengers' hands as they disembarked.

"Plis do not give the children any kina," Wendy warned loudly. "Begging is a bad habit we try to stop."

And then, more quietly, she added, "It is white man's habit."

But it was hard to ignore their tattered clothing and wide, inquiring eyes and Vilia found herself warming to them as they pulled her along the dirt trail to the village center where a group had gathered.

The villagers were a friendly lot, offering flowers and reaching to shake their hands, except for a small group of elders lingering on the sidelines. Their eyes were not so wide, their lips held tightly shut, their expressions deadpan. After meeting the chief, a gray-bearded man called Walli, the tourists were ushered to straw mats in front of a small arena where the crowd suddenly dispersed. Some minutes passed and Vilia took the opportunity to glance around, taking in the village layout and scrutinizing the few women who stood, quietly watching them from behind.

Suddenly the bushes behind the clearing began to shake, slowly at first and then more violently, and Vilia snapped her attention back to the front. Abruptly, the shaking stopped and a man appeared, his muscular body coated completely in a thick gray-white substance that looked like dried mud and which was cracking as mud does around his elbows, knees and joints. He was wearing a small, bamboo *laplap*, decorated with green leaves and, over his head, had placed an enormous clay mask that was grotesque and garish, with oversized ears and nose, protruding lips and a sorrowful smile.

Gradually more masked men appeared behind him, one after the after, treading slowly, silently towards the wide-eyed tourists. They didn't utter a word or wave a single weapon, just a few palm fronds, yet their presence was eerie and threatening, and Vilia felt a small shiver rush up her spine.

All thought of Veronika disappeared as the villagers re-enacted the tale of the Asaro mudmen who had donned gray paint and frightened their enemies away.

As the revelry began to wind up, Vilia shook herself from her own trance and glanced around again. She needed to find Veronika before they were ushered back to the bus. She slipped to the back of the crowd and made her way quickly to the sullen looking elders standing to one side.

They straightened up as she approached and she greeted them in what little Pidgin she had picked up: "Moning." Good morning.

She did not know if they spoke Pidgin—Wendy had already boasted that there were scores of languages in this region alone—but she had to try.

They simply stared at her silently and she tried to maintain her smile.

"Um, anyone speak English?" she asked and they continued staring, unblinkingly.

She turned to the oldest in the group, a short, scrawny man well into his seventies.

"I am looking for another villager, um *wantok*, Veronika Ligaro?"

But the man didn't appear to understand and Vilia wondered what to do when she felt a tap on her shoulder. It was Wendy.

"You are missing the show, Miss," she said, waving at her large face with an elaborately decorated, bamboo Chinese fan.

"Oh, yes, sorry, I just thought I'd say hello to the locals."

Wendy laughed richly at this.

"Oh dear, most of these people do not speak very good English. Not like Walli!"

She turned, waving in the direction of the village chief who was standing watching them from one side.

"You must wait until the show is over and talk with him. He will show you around."

Vilia assured her she would and smiled weakly at the old man who was still watching her, a bemused expression on his well-worn face.

Within minutes, the dancing came to an end and the tourists began clapping heartily. Vilia joined in the applause and followed them as they were led around the village and shown the set-up of the huts and told the story of the grass tufts which sat bent in the wind above each one.

They were then led to a shady area where several villagers were selling artefacts, mostly course, hand-woven baskets, rugs and placemats. They were treated to some fresh pawpaw and bananas, too, and ate heartily while Walli waxed lyrical on the importance of pigs to the region and their significance in the wedding ceremony.

"The pig is very important for bride price," he declared and the couples chuckled, making obvious jokes about their own net worth in pork.

Vilia discreetly scanned the black faces watching idly from the sidelines. They were mostly very old or very young and she guessed the strong men and women were working the gardens or had been employed by the neighboring trout farm, tobacco factory or on one of the many coffee plantations that Wendy had told them about. That had her worried. By her estimate, Veronika would be in her fifties now, and probably still able to work.

That's when she spotted a young boy motioning towards her from a distant hut. She looked around and then back again. His head nodded, *yes you*, and she glanced quickly at Wendy. The guide was enthralled by Walli's words and it occurred to Vilia then that the two were probably in on it together. They probably lived in a brick house back in Goroka and enjoyed taking the dumb tourists for a ride.

Discreetly, she slipped to the back of the crowd and then wandered slowly, casually towards the young boy. He grinned wickedly as she approached and motioned for her to follow him behind the hut.

She did as instructed and as soon as they were out of sight, he hissed excitedly, "You look for Veronika?"

Vilia stared at him, aghast. "Yes!"

"I show you Veronika."

"Veronika Ligaro?"

"Yes, Ligaro, yes."

"Great, where is she?"

"Five kina."

"Huh?"

He smiled, his eyes twinkling cheekily. "Five kina," he repeated.

The little bugger, she thought. He must have overheard her talking to the elders. She wondered if he even knew Veronika, if she was being taken for another ride.

"Forget it," she said and turned to leave.

"Okay, two kina."

Vilia squinted at the boy who was still smiling like a devil. He had all the trademarks of a rascal in the making, from his shifty little eyes to the woolen beanie on his head. But what choice did she have? She nodded slowly and produced two one kina coins. As his hand went out to grab them, she closed her fist tight and shook her head no.

"Veronika first."

His smile quickly deflated and was replaced by a tiny frown. But he soon nodded his head and led her away from the group and down a thin track through the thick, green grass. Again her alarm bells began to sound. Was he leading her astray? Would a vicious rascal gang appear to mug her, or worse? Suddenly all the warnings she had received about these violent people began circling her brain and she hesitated. He turned back then to give her a smile, a small reassuring smile, and she sighed and continued on. She had come all this way. She could not stop now.

After a few minutes the path came out onto a large clearing with vegetable gardens that had been fenced in with pickets and barbed wire. Several women were tending these, large baskets of what looked like sweet potato nearby, and the young boy pointed at the group, saying, "Veronika, Veronika."

Then he held out his hand for the coins.

Vilia eyed him suspiciously.

"You take me," she said but his head shook violently from side to side.

"Veronika! Veronika!" he hissed, pointing again, and she had little choice but to take him at his word.

No sooner had she handed him the money than he scurried back up the track and vanished from view. She made her way over to the women, some of whom could well be in their fifties, and smiled as she approached, terrified of scaring them off. They stopped their work and stared at her oddly, the weird white woman with the funny hair.

"Um, good morning," she said.

"Hello!" they choroused and smiled sheepishly through long lashes.

"Speak English?"

Two of them raised their hands halfway, again sheepish, polite, not used to being addressed by visiting tourists.

"I am looking for a friend—*wantok*—of my father, um, papa bilong me. Veronika Ligaro?"

One of the women's faces lit up and she smiled widely as she stepped forward. Vilia held her breath.

"Veronika?" she managed to stammer.

"Theresa," the woman replied. "I am cousin of Veronika."

She exhaled. Of course, that would have been too easy. But it was close enough.

"Is Veronika here? At village?"

Theresa shook her head no. "She work at the Paradise Guest Lodge, in Lake Kutubu."

"Lake what?"

"Kutubu, Southern Highlands."

Vilia was only just registering this when a shrill cry came from behind her.

"Miss! Miss!"

It was Wendy, waddling angrily towards her.

"Thank you," Vilia told the woman and shook her hand.

Then she dashed back in the direction of the tour guide who was standing hands on hips, shaking her head impatiently.

As she relaxed in the bus on the way back to Goroka, Vilia could barely contain her excitement. Sure, she had been defeated yet again but there was some victory in there, too. She now knew that Veronika had not perished in the ocean as the police had presumed.

Perhaps that meant her father had also not died out there?

Vilia sat straight up at the thought. Was he also still alive? And living in the Southern Highlands? It was too much to bear and she shook her head, releasing her wild curls from their cuff and smiling broadly, involuntarily.

She took a deep breath, calmed her rattled nerves, and then studied her regional map for the road to Lake Kutubu.

*May 1: Today I feel a twinge of strength, a flutter of hope that I fear will fly away. I have the skeleton of renewed strength encased in a trembling skin. I need to shed the skin, I know that now.
If only I could work out how...*

"Air Niugini from Goroka to Mt. Hagan is sixty-seven kina and from Hagan to Mendi is fifty-eight kina. You can get a bus to Lake Kutubu from Mendi."

Vilia stared at the Air Niugini desk clerk and quickly did her maths. She had just under K100 and change in her purse. Not nearly enough. And they did not take VISA.

"Machine no work today," he said matter-of-factly. "But you can catch a bus, a PMV."

She tried not to laugh. She was in a fine mood but eight hours was more than she could stand on a smelly, rattling public bus with no air-conditioning and bad suspension, so she thanked him anyway and stepped back out on to the streets of Goroka.

It was almost 3:00 p.m. She didn't know what to do. Then a small *kai bar* caught her eye and she crossed the street to take a table on the dusty road outside. There were several other people sipping cool drinks in the sun, and, much to the waiter's surprise, she ordered a coffee.

"Strong and black," she told him.

She needed to think.

Several minutes later, when the coffee (too weak and too hot) had arrived and she was contemplating her next move, she got a surprise. Kyle O'Brien was stepping out of a bank and walking directly towards her. Vilia's first instinct was to duck but her curiosity got the better of her and she waved her hand and smiled.

Kyle stared blankly at Vilia for several seconds and looked ready to walk right by, then his memory must have kicked in and his face lightened up.

"Oh, hi. Lea, isn't it?"

"Yeah, hi, Kyle. Vilia Lea. Fancy meeting you here."

It sounded a little vacuous considering that she was the stray tourist.

"Just here on business," he explained, scooping his hat from his head to fan himself with it. "I'm on my way to Mendi."

You could have knocked her over with a feather.

"So, you just travelin' around? Checking out the Highlands?"

"Yes," she said, eventually reclaiming her tongue. "Actually, what a coincidence, I'm also on my way to Mendi."

He shifted uneasily. "Oh?"

"Yeah, but it seems like a really long bus ride." He didn't say a word. "How are you getting there?"

"I've got the plane." His voice was clearly tense.

"Really?" She couldn't let him get away. "You don't fancy my wonderful company again do you?"

Kyle put is hat back on quickly and shook his head.

"I'd help you out, but I'm kinda full up, you know? Plane's overweight as it is."

"Oh, pity." Her heart dropped.

"But no need to take the bus," he said. "There's regular commercial flights from here. You should inquire at MBA, sometimes they have cheapies."

"MBA?"

"Milne Bay Air. Coupla blocks up."

"Oh, I see."

"I really gotta go." He glanced quickly at his watch. "Have a good trip, eh?"

As she watched lost opportunity walk hastily away, Vilia consoled herself that it would have been an agonizing flight anyway, and quickly slurped the remainder of her coffee, grimacing as she did so.

As it turned out, Kyle O'Brien proved more help than Vilia had realized. Not only did MBA have a cheap flight to Mendi, they had an even cheaper one to a place called Moro, the closest strip to Lake Kutubu, and it was leaving within the hour. Better yet, they took VISA. She booked herself aboard and then dashed back to her hotel to pay the room bill. She hadn't needed to stay over after all and she felt a pang of regret. The rooms here looked comfortable and she liked Goroka, had already spotted an open-air restaurant that would be perfect for dinner.

Still, regret was quickly replaced with anticipation as she scurried down Edwards Street to the airport, and thanked her lucky stars that it was located so close to the city center. Then she laughed aloud at this because until this week, she never knew such stars existed.

By 5:00 p.m., Vilia was winging her way to Moro, at the west end of the Lake and just a boat ride away from the mysterious Veronika.

There is a lake they call Kutubu in the very heart of Papua New Guinea that is vast by PNG standards—about twenty kilometers in length and three kilometers wide. Legend has it the lake was formed when a giant fig tree was cut down by a woman seeking water. As the tree fell, everything it touched, from its roots to its trunk, turned to liquid.

Today, in the grassy hill behind the glassy lake sits the Paradise Guest Lodge, a magnificent wooden structure set on stilts. There are wide glass windows looking out at the view of the lake and, beyond it, of towering limestone peaks and lush rainforest, and it caught Vilia's breath as she entered the main foyer. It was magnificent.

She stood entranced for several minutes, watching someone splashing about in the shallows just below her and, despite the cool alpine air, she felt a sudden urge to join them, to simply forget everything and plunge into that silky water.

She shook the thought away and, noticing that there was no one at reception, wandered around the sparse foyer, admiring the variously painted artwork that adorned every wall.

So that's why they call this place the Paradise Guest Lodge.

Each painting featured the magnificent Bird of Paradise. She hadn't yet had the good fortune to spot one on Tubu so she took some time to study the pictures, delighted by their flamboyant beauty. There seemed to be a wide variety of the birds with a showy array of plumes, fans, crests and tail ribbons in every imaginable color, from metallic blues and greens to the deepest of blacks and the most vivid reds and whites she had ever seen. Some of these tails were almost twice as long as the birds themselves.

A large plaque in the center of the room announced that this was a national park and safe haven for the country's feathered mascot, and if she looked very carefully she might just see one strutting its stuff in the treetops above.

Vilia peered out the windows to the canopy but could see nothing, so she turned back to admire the painting nearest to her. It was done in oils and the colors were dazzling: iridescent golds and greens and velvety maroons with silky orange plumes.

"Stunning, yes?" came a British accent behind her and Vilia turned to find a woman in her forties, with long black hair and bright green eyes standing smiling towards her. She had the highest cheekbones Vilia had ever seen, and her eyes were almost feline. She was as stunning as the painting Vilia was perusing.

"Gorgeous," Vilia said, turning back to it.

"That's the Raggiana Bird of Paradise."

"She's beautiful."

"She's a he, actually. The females, I'm afraid, are rather dull. The men get all the glory. Not unlike the men of Papua New Guinea."

"Men everywhere," Vilia said and they both broke into laughter.

"I'm Annalise Horton."

The woman extended a long, lean hand and Vilia shook it warmly.

"Hi, Annalise, Vilia Lea."

"Just arrived?"

"Yes, I was about to book in. I hope they've got a room."

"I'm sure we can find you something," she laughed, leading her towards the reception desk. "My husband and I run the place. Welcome to Lake Kutubu."

That night Vilia dined with Annalise and her husband, Thomas, on the restaurant's veranda looking out at the moonlit lake below. There were several other couples staying, all foreigners, as well as a few young backpackers who looked delighted to be in such plush surrounds, glancing around and beaming from ear to ear. The rooms were expensive so Vilia wondered how they could afford it, but eventually learned that there were cheaper digs at the back of the lodge for just such guests.

As they devoured freshwater barramundi, crayfish and sago served in huge portions with white wine to wash it down, the Horton couple told Vilia of their quest.

"We came here, initially, about eight years ago," Annalise began.

"To help put a stop to the slaughter of the birds," added her husband, a smallish man at least ten years her senior with a mop of gray hair and a long reddish-gray beard.

"It was still legal to kill the birds back then?"

"No, of course not," Anna said. "But the law was not enforced."

"We heard about it on a BBC documentary," Thomas said. "We were appalled."

"So we packed up everything and never looked back."

They spoke in this ping pong way throughout the meal, finishing each other's sentences and holding hands from time to time, and Vilia envied their devotion almost as much as their sense of purpose. Once she would have scoffed at such blind obsession, but she was a different woman now. And she was hardly one to talk.

"And what brings you out here?" Thomas asked, as though reading her mind.

"Just traveling," she said, not willing to reveal herself just yet. "So how did the lodge come about?"

They told her of their work with the national wildlife foundation, which took them from the Varirata National Park in Port Moresby to this very region. As crime took a turn for the worse and government funding all but dried up, they decided to build the lodge and continue their work from here.

"The lodge serves two purposes," Anna told her, brushing long black hair from her face and then sweeping it up into an impromptu bun. "The first to give us money to continue patrolling the area—"

"You actually patrol?"

"Oh yes," Thomas said. "We do random patrols of the various parts of the park and neighboring areas to make sure no one is hunting illegally."

"And we get around to the neighboring villages to educate the people about the birds near extinction," Anna added. "It's not just that they hunt the birds, but they also destroy their habitat. Logging has been such an enemy of our feathered friends."

She took a sip of her wine. "But we also use this lodge to protect the privacy of the surrounding people from the passing tourists and backpackers."

Vilia looked at her blankly so Thomas explained.

"That's why we have a range of accommodation to suit every budget. If backpackers stay here they will not harass the villagers so much for a cheap bed and spoil their serenity. They're *fiercely* private people, you see. And we respect that privacy."

Vilia's heart sank. *How could she inquire after Veronika with that kind of attitude?* As she considered her next move, a young local waiter announced that Thomas had a phone call, so he excused himself and disappeared inside. When he returned, a few minutes later, he was clearly distracted and motioned for Annalise to join him, apologizing for the disruption.

"We must get back to work," she said knowingly. "Enjoy the rest of your evening and have a good night's sleep."

Vilia wandered back into the lodge to take a seat by the giant fireplace and work out her next move. Over dinner she had not spotted a single staff member who would fit Veronika's description. The employees in the main bar, the reception and the restaurant were all young, barely out of their teens, so she decided to wait until morning to check out the cleaning staff. Perhaps she would be amongst them.

But daybreak brought with it bitter disappointment. Or at least it should have. Not only was Veronika Ligaro nowhere in the building, none of the room staff had even heard of her. As Mrs. Wong would say, it looked like cousin Theresa had given her the bum steer.

Despite this, Vilia didn't despair. Instead, she made her way back to the restaurant for breakfast and, as she took her seat, was startled by the sight of sailboards bobbing about on the lake below.

"So what's on the agenda today?" Annalise asked bouncing up to her table, fresh rolls in her hand. "It's a beautiful day for a swim."

"Actually, I was thinking of a sail," Vilia replied. "But I didn't bring my swimming costume."

"Oh, you have to cover up when you swim around here. Very important to be discreet. We advise *laplaps* and a T-shirt. You can buy a souvenir *laplap* at reception or you can hire one, along with a sailboard, down at the lake store. Just ask for Joe or Ronnie. They'll help you out."

Vilia thanked her and sat back in her chair nibbling a roll and enjoying the view, excitement bubbling gently just below the surface. It seemed like a lifetime ago when she'd taken her last sail, but really it had been less than a fortnight, in Cairns, the day after her mother's funeral.

So much had happened since then and she knew she was a different person now. She wasn't sure exactly how, but she understood that everything was suddenly, irrevocably altered.

It was only a little later, after she had bought her *laplap* and was threading her way down the steep pathway to the lapping waters of the lake's edge, that it occurred to her.

The dread and fear had dissipated, and in their place she felt a kind of calm acceptance. The answer, while still eluding her, seemed suddenly unimportant, and she knew then that it was simply *the asking* that mattered. That she had come all this way and tried, that she had stopped closing her ears and turning her head away and, instead, had leapt towards the truth, come what may.

It was so completely unlike the old Vilia.

Vilia's mother, in one of her rare talkative moods, once told her a tale of an old woman with a snake on her face. It just lived there all the woman's life, entwined around her forehead, across her chin, down around her neck and back up one cheek.

"It was striped black and white," she told Vilia, a small child then, wide-eyed with anticipation and the fact that her mother was actually addressing her. "With the longest tongue you ever saw."

The old woman did not like her slithery companion but there was nothing she could do. Despite all her efforts, it stayed firmly planted on her head. She tried going to a doctor but that did not work. She tried voodoo and black magic and ointments and creams. But the snake did not budge.

"And then one night, before going to sleep, she kissed the snake long and hard on the mouth. 'Rightio, then,' she said. 'If you're going to hang around, let's become friends.' The following morning the snake was gone."

Vilia remembered being exasperated by the tale. Typical of her mother, her infuriating mother!

What do you mean, Mum? she probably asked. And her mother had probably just offered one of her whimsical smiles and wandered off and back into her own world again.

Thinking of it now, as she stopped, staring at the magnificent lake, Vilia understood it at last. She, too, had accepted the chains around her neck and by doing so, had been released of their burden.

She smiled the same smile as her mother had.

There was a young black man tending the lake shop when Vilia entered and he greeted her politely. It was a small shop, crammed with a collection of pottery, artefacts, baskets, postcards, T-shirts and *laplaps*, all for sale and many featuring the Bird of Paradise logo of the guest lodge. Small signs dotted around the place informed buyers that the proceeds went to the preservation of the national bird.

Vilia asked the shopkeeper about sailing and he explained apologetically that their two boards were already hired out, but if she hung around for ten minutes, one would be back.

Vilia thanked him and wandered around the shop, stopping to flip through a box of illustrated cards featuring the bird in all its glory.

"All done by local artists," he sang out. "Just K2 each."

But she wasn't listening. Something else had caught Vilia's eye and she replaced the cards and walked over to a small cabinet with an intriguing collection of figurines that seemed out of place amongst the wild life. They were made out of clay and featured small pointy faced women decorated with miniature grass skirts and tribal paint.

"Ahhh the little witches," the man said with a laugh. "Ronnie does those."

"Ronnie?" She didn't dare to breathe.

"She comes in soon."

And then, suddenly, she did, a small black woman in her fifties, with closely cropped hair, graying a little at the front.

It couldn't be anybody else.

"Veronika Ligaro," Vilia said and the woman looked up at her, surprised.

Vilia waited while she smiled uncertainly, clearly trying to place the face.

"I'm Vilia Lea. Jamison and Genevive's daughter. From Tubu."

Familiarity struck a chord with Veronika's face and it lit up like a Christmas tree. She dropped her small knapsack at the entrance and rushed over to grasp her in her arms.

"Ahhhh little Bougainvillea! From Tubu?"

"Yes," she laughed, "I guess that's me. All the way from Tubu."

If Veronika had anything to hide or fear or regret she wasn't showing signs of it. There was no trace of guilt or remorse on her beaming face, and her next question only served to confirm this.

"Masta Lea and Misis they okay? Still at Tubu?"

Vilia's jaw dropped. Veronika hadn't heard. She had nothing to do with any of it. Vilia took hold of the older woman's hands and walked her to one side.

"No, sadly, they both passed away," she said, hoping she would understand.

Veronika looked momentarily surprised and then shook her head sadly, not saying anything, and Vilia was glad for her silence. She didn't want to elaborate. After all this time, after all that had happened, Veronika did not need to know the details.

"Do you have a few minutes? Can we talk?"

Veronika nodded and said something to her colleague before leading Vilia out of the shop and down a small slope to a wooden bench that was perfectly positioned to stare out at the lake. They sat down.

"Veronika," Vilia said before pausing and preparing herself for the question of her life. "You disappeared from Tubu one night. Where did you go? Who were you with?"

The woman looked confused.

"May, 1976. You had been to Samarai and then you didn't come back to Tubu. Why?"

A flicker of comprehension crossed Veronika's face, followed fast by apprehension, a little guilt perhaps.

"Yes I go away, Misis. It was problem?" she asked.

You might say that.

Vilia just nodded, giving nothing away.

"Sorry, Misis. I no realize."

"Why did you go, Veronika, who were you with?"

"Big man of island."

Vilia's heart sank. "My dad?"

"No, no, Big man of Samarai…"

"Dick O'Brien?"

Veronika shook her head again. "Polis man."

Vilia's heart skipped a beat. "Commander Riley?!"

Veronika considered this for a few seconds and then nodded, yes.

"I stay at Samarai and Francis he come and find me—"

"Huh? Francis? From Tubu?"

"Yes, he come back to Samarai and find me and say Commander Riley have big job for me. In Mendi, plenty kina, but I must go fast, no time to muck around. I say, what about Masta Lea and Misis Lea, and Francis he say they tell me to take job. They happy for me. So I give him message to say good-bye to your family and thank you and then I go with Riley in boat to Alotau."

A frown crinkled her face. "You not know?! Your parents, not know?!"

"No. They had no idea."

Veronika looked mortified. "I so sorry, Misis! There no time to tell. I thought it be okay."

Vilia couldn't believe what she was hearing. Why would Francis lie about not seeing Veronika in Samarai that day? And what were he and Riley playing at?

"What was the job?" she asked at last.

"Housegirl for Misis O'Brien. At Melview in Mendi."

"Mrs. O'Brien? Mrs. Dick O'Brien?!"

Yes, she said emphatically, Mrs. Dick O'Brien.

That bit made sense; Jonah mentioned that she lived around here. The O'Briens had obviously been in cahoots with Vernon Riley. And with Francis. There could be no other explanation.

"So you still work with Mrs. O'Brien?"

"Ohhh, no, no!" she squealed insistently. "She go finish down south. Then I get job here. Much better job. I so sorry, Vilia! Masta Lea he angry?"

She wished he had been around to be, but she just shook her head no. Veronika didn't need to know the rest. It was clear she was just a pawn in the Riley/O'Brien game. Whatever that was.

"It's not a problem," Vilia said at last. "I was just wondering. Now, you'd better get back to work before I get you into trouble. Just tell me one thing, though, before you do."

"Yes?"

"Was Mrs. O'Brien selling Bird of Paradise feathers?"

Veronika hesitated for a moment before crinkling her nose up again. "Yes, she no good. Misis Horton say she bad woman, tru."

As Vilia watched Veronika return to her work, the male shop assistant called out to her from the store. The sailboard was in. Did she want to have a sail?

"Um, no, maybe a little later," she replied and started back up the trail.

She didn't need to lose herself right now, not when everything was finally starting to become clear. What she did need, however, was to have a serious conversation with Annalise Horton.

Back at the lodge, the owners were nowhere to be found and Vilia was considering her next move when a familiar voice caught her by surprise. Again.

"Hello Vilia."

It was Kyle O'Brien, sitting in the lounge area, his legs up, an icy drink by his side.

She stared hard at him, unsure how to react.

"You're staying here, too?" she eventually blurted.

"Oh no, just dropping by."

Anger began to well up inside her, and she glanced away, not trusting herself to look at him.

"Actually I'm heading back to the Milne Bay tonight," he continued, unperturbed, "and I've now got an empty plane. If you need a lift, I'd welcome the company."

She took a deep breath, barely concealing the scowl that had now hijacked her face.

"I don't think so."

He looked a little surprised. "Everything okay?"

"Fine, thanks, Kyle."

She turned her back on him and walked away. What she really wanted to do was stand there and howl abuse at this man but she wasn't exactly sure why, or even if it was warranted. She needed to get everything straight, her brain was starting to cloud up. There were now so many snippets of information and she hadn't yet had a chance to put them in order, to get them under some kind of control.

She fled to her room, a spacious bed of luxury overlooking the lake, and she grabbed her journal and began to write, scribbling the names Riley and O'Brien and then the word 'Tubu.'

What was their connection? And why did they plot to get Veronika away from the island so fast?

She thought of Kyle, probably still relaxing in the lounge below, and wondered whether she should alert the Hortons to this man. Was he here at Lake Kutubu to pilfer their healthy bird stock? Was he a chip off the old block?

After an hour or so, tired and frustrated, Vilia decided it was time for that sail and made her way back to reception. As she descended the staircase, she noticed that Kyle was still sitting in the lounge area and beside him sat the Hortons, laughing at something he had just said. She tried to slip past discreetly but Annalise spotted her and waved her over.

"Come join us, Vilia! You have to meet the magnificent Kyle O'Brien."

Warily, she walked over and tried to keep her tone civil.

"Actually, we've already met."

"Oh great!" Anna glanced across at Kyle who nodded, smiling tentatively.

"And have you also been to Melview, his wonderful property just north of here?"

"No I haven't. But I have heard of it."

Kyle's eyebrows shot up, surprised.

Feeling a little more composed now, she added, "In fact, Kyle, I just ran into an old friend of ours."

"Oh?"

"Yes, Veronika Ligaro. You know Veronika don't you, Kyle? She worked for your mother, I believe."

Kyle blinked a few times and something flickered across his face. Was it fear? Guilt? He maintained eye contact with Vilia but his smile had disappeared.

"Yes, I know Ronnie well."

"Ronnie? *Our* Ronnie?" Anna was saying. "Well, of course he knows Ronnie, that's how we scored her. She's a darling! Ronnie used to be your housegirl at Melview, isn't that right?"

Kyle nodded and Thomas, who seemed a little confused by the banter, turned to Vilia and asked, "But how do you know Ronnie?"

"She used to work on the island I lease, Tubu, in the Milne Bay."

And then, staring pointedly at Kyle, Vilia added, "She used to work for my dad."

Kyle didn't seem surprised to hear this but the Hortons did and Anna began scratching her forehead.

"Tubu ... Tubu, now why does that name ring a bell?"

"It's near—"

"Actually," Vilia interrupted Kyle, "you've probably heard of it because it's also a safe haven for the Bird of Paradise. I didn't mention it last night but my dad was also a big fan of the bird. Despite the efforts of his neighbors."

Vilia knew she was treading on thin ice now but she was tired of being polite.

"Of course!" Anna was saying. "I read about that. Some of the finest species in the country I believe, particularly the Goldie's Bird of Paradise. I'm yet to see one. Are there still many there?"

"A few," she replied, wanting to add, *No thanks to Dick O'Brien*, but instinct shut her up.

Being bold was one thing, being a bitch quite another. Kyle had been just a boy then, probably no older than five or six. He could not be blamed for the sins of his father, anymore than she could.

"Now, Kyle, isn't your island down in the Milne Bay?" Thomas asked and Kyle nodded, turning to Vilia.

"My island, Bado, is now a safe haven too."

Vilia was caught off guard. She swung her head towards Kyle and then at Anna, not sure whether to believe him or not. Anna was nodding, smiling, and Kyle glanced away, out of the window towards the lush forest and the beautiful secrets hidden within.

"Both my parents used to hunt the bird."

He addressed the comment to no one in particular but judging by the Horton's relaxed expressions it was clear they already knew.

"After my mother got in a bit of trouble a while back I was given control of both Bado and Melview. I turned them into safe havens for the bird. My own little way of making amends."

He looked directly at Vilia then, his milky blue eyes boring into hers, and she wanted to crawl under the sofa and hide. She had pre-judged Kyle just as she had been pre-judged all her life.

"If you get a chance, Vilia, you must go take a look at Melview," Anna added. "It really is a superb bit of land, and some wonderful breeding ground for the King of Saxony bird. It's a beauty, all yellows and blues. Magnificent."

"I'd like that," Vilia stammered, blushing red.

Late that afternoon, before Kyle's plane took off, Vilia returned to the lake shop to bid Veronika farewell.

"Come visit us at Tubu any time you like," she said. "Kyle can always give you a lift across."

"Oh, Vilia. Good idea tru!"

They embraced warmly and then Veronika plucked a small witch from its shelf, handing it to her proudly.

"Tubu Witch doctor," she said. "Gift for you."

As Vilia thanked her and placed it safely in her bag, the penny finally dropped.

"Good witch or bad witch?" she asked and the older woman giggled like a schoolgirl, covering her mouth shyly with one hand.

"She very good witch, you know that! She look over Masta Lea."

When Kyle's plane finally lifted off from the airstrip at Mendi and they weaved their way back through the mountainous highlands, Vilia realized there was only one person still left to speak to, one person who could tie up all the loose ends.

But she had to get through this journey first.

Thomas Horton had given them a lift to the airstrip and chatted breezily along the way, not reading the mood between his two passengers who could barely meet each other's eyes. Vilia was embarrassed by her earlier outbreak and her rush to judgment, and hoped her island neighbor could forgive her. Kyle was giving nothing away, clenching and unclenching his jaw as they drove.

Once his plane was mid-air, they both visibly relaxed, Vilia staring out the window, mesmerized by the mist suddenly swirling around them, and Kyle shifting back in his seat, one hand on the wheel.

"Everything okay?" he called out eventually and she nodded.

"I'm sorry about your mum," she said. "I didn't realize."

He shrugged it off. "You've got nothing to apologize for. My parents were rat-bags. I'm not. That's all there is to it."

"It's hard to escape the past, though."

He shrugged again. "Better to face it, I reckon. Head on."

Then he turned to face her, and in those startling blue eyes she saw a softness that she hadn't noticed before, and a vulnerability, too. They were more alike than she'd realized, two children trying to overcome a devastating past. Unlike him, however, she had been removed from the evils of that time and, once again, she had her mother to thank for that.

How would it have been, she wondered now, growing up in this region with gossip and innuendo following your every move, and people never quite trusting you? Perhaps living in ignorance in Cairns wasn't so bad after all.

The scorecard was beginning to even out.

"Why don't you stop over for the night, when we get to Tubu," she suggested and, noticing his look of surprise, quickly added, "It's just that it'll be late, you know, and you'll be tired. I'm sure Jonah won't mind."

He gave it some thought, scratching the stubble on his chin with one large, rough hand.

Eventually he said, "Sure, why not? Haven't done that since I was seven."

"Seven! Really? You went to Tubu as a kid?"

He laughed. "God yeah, spent a bit of time there. In fact, you and I were thick as thieves once, you don't recall?"

She looked flummoxed and he laughed again. "It's okay, you were a tiny tyke back then—no more than three, there's no way you'd remember. But I remember it clear as day. We used to hang out for hours on the beach, out the front of the main house. Got eaten alive by the sandflies, of course. Your mum was always unimpressed but your dad just laughed it off. So did you."

"Me?" she scoffed. "Doesn't sound like me."

He flashed her a cheeky grin. "You were a pretty cool little kid back then if I recall. Sad you had to go down south. Weren't many littlies around in those days, I enjoyed my trips to Tubu."

Now it was his turn to look embarrassed and he cleared his throat and returned to concentrating on the wheel. They settled into a comfortable silence then but Vilia couldn't help wondering what might have been.

As the small plane made its journey home to the Milne Bay, Vilia's guilt began to creep back in. She knew that her search was not over yet, and that one or both of Kyle's parents were clearly involved. No childhood friendship or bird sanctuary was going to change that.

May 5: A trip to Samarai: The market place is a delight today,
brimming with odors and oddities too numerous to mention. There is
succulent, smoked pork fresh from the burning earth, and raw coconuts
still dripping with their juices. And men and women and dogs and hens
and a lively menagerie of fish and crayfish and turtle meat and clams.
I can only wonder why I have never noticed it before. And marvel
that he saw it all along. Of course he did!

Vilia slowly weaved her way through the maze of vegetable stalls and fish vendors, waving off the sellers with a warm smile. Earlier, she had paid old Mitch McCafferty a visit and told him everything she had learned, from her union with Veronika to the contents of Sebastian Cone's files, including the two bids for Tubu.

"Why didn't you tell me you tried to buy Tubu?" she asked.

"It was hardly a sincere attempt, Vilia," he replied, wiping one giant hand through his thick, white hair. "Did you read the pitiful figure I offered? Couldn't afford the place but wanted ya mum outta there, and I hoped money was the only thing standing in her way. Besides," he added unapologetically, "I couldn't stand the thought of Dick O'Brien ending up with it, profiting from his crimes."

"And yet Dick never put a bid in."

He dragged on his rollie awhile, just looking out to sea.

"Walter S. Mosley, you say? Gee that sounds familiar. If only I could place it ... hang on a minute ... now it's coming to me. Wasn't he that fancy lawyer fella who spent some time in Alotau before it got the better of him?"

He plucked some tobacco from his tongue and contemplated for a while.

"Yeah, I reckon it just might be. He had an initialed name like that. I remember thinking, 'S stands for stupid'—he wasn't altogether bright."

And he laughed at that as though it were the funniest thing in the world.

"I've got to go, Mitch, but thanks for everything, you've been a big help."

"Ahhhh, it's nothing your dad wouldn't've done for a daughter of mine."

As she climbed back off the Mathilda, he added, "You come visit me again, you hear? Don't be a stranger."

"I will, Mitch, I promise."

And this time she believed herself.

Eventually Vilia found the pathway leading away from the market, back towards the police station. She passed dogs sleeping in the middle of the narrow roads and children who had stopped their idle play to watch her. The houses here were quite large and made of good timber with spacious verandas and neat gardens, all except for one. This house was badly in need of a paint and its garden had been neglected long ago, but there were thick security bars on every window and across the front flyscreened door. Vilia marched boldly up to it and knocked.

Several seconds later a shadowy figure appeared behind the screen and asked, "Who is it?"

She hesitated before answering.

"It's Vilia Lea, Mrs. Riley. I called you last week."

The woman moved back from the light.

"Mrs. Riley?"

"What do you want? Told you I got nothing to say."

"Yes, well, I have plenty to ask so if you could let me in I'd really appreciate it."

Still nothing.

"Mrs. Riley, I've come all this way. Please."

The woman hesitated for some time before unlocking the gate and waving the younger woman through.

"I don't know what I can do for you," she said, leading Vilia through a large lounge room crowded with beaten-up leather lounges that looked out of place in the tropics, and numerous chests of drawers cluttered with photos, and out to a small kitchen at the back.

A half-eaten bowl of cereal was crusting up in the sink and she pushed it to one side to fill the kettle. The place was dusty and dank. It smelt vacant, devoid of life, and sadly familiar.

"Mrs. Riley, you obviously know about my father and his disappearance."

"'Course I do," she snapped, staring at the kettle.

"Well I'm trying to put the pieces together. Find out what happened."

"Why don't you just let it go?"

Her mouth was set in an angry downward grin and her eyes would not meet Vilia's, so she stepped into her line of vision, forcing her to focus. Mrs. Riley blinked, trying to look away, trying to look aloof.

"My father went missing when I was just a toddler, Mrs. Riley. And my mother eventually killed herself—dead of a broken heart thirty years later. I can't just let it go."

The older woman shook her head, unwilling to hear.

"Mrs. Riley, I know about Walter Mosley. He was your lawyer or realtor or something, wasn't he? He put your bid in for Tubu barely a week after my dad disappeared. Before he was even officially missing."

The older woman's shoulders twitched but still she remained silent.

"And I know your husband was involved. I've just seen the missing housegirl, Veronika Ligaro. Your husband was in it with the O'Briens. I know that."

Mrs. Riley met Vilia's eyes then and she saw that anger and pride were shrouding her fear. And there was sorrow etched into her face, in the deep furrow of her brow and around her mouth where it was chiseled in sharp downward strokes. Her face was a portrait of misery, and of the agony of holding a secret for too long.

Not unlike Genevive Lea.

"I'm not here for vengeance, Mrs. Riley," Vilia said gently. "I just need to know."

Mrs. Riley sighed deeply, motioned for Vilia to take a seat at the kitchen table and then slowly made them some tea. She said nothing as she waited for the kettle to boil and this time Vilia did not push her. She was near the end now, she knew that, and she could wait a few minutes more.

Mrs. Riley placed two cups on the old laminated kitchen table, retrieved two teaspoons from a drawer and placed them down too, along with some milk and raw sugar, some *Paradise Kokonas* biscuits and, finally, a pot of steaming Bushells tea. She slowly poured them a cup and sat down and, again, Vilia did not prod, simply waited for the widow to find the courage to dig up the dirt she thought she had buried forever all those years ago.

Eventually Mrs. Riley cleared her throat and spoke.

"I don't know what you know or what you think you know," she said in a voice barely audible. "But my husband was a good man, deep down, he had been a good man."

Vilia took a tentative sip of her tea.

"But, well, you see what I live in here?"

The older woman motioned to the house around her, a look of contempt curling up her top lip.

"The government all but forgot my poor Vernon in the lead up to Independence. Tossed him aside as if he was nothin', as if all his hard work meant squat."

She fiddled with her teacup, turning it around and around in the saucer as though unsure how to stop.

"We used to live on a fine bit of land in Alotau, you know? Had our own staff and everything. Then they decide that Vernon ain't black, see, so he can't be running the main police station. All politics, you understand? So they demote him over here. Suddenly he has to answer to a *kanaka* with no brains. It was the ultimate humiliation."

Vilia wondered why Mrs. Riley was still hanging around and guessed she didn't have the strength or courage to leave.

"And Dick O'Brien?"

"So he gets himself involved with that blasted O'Brien."

"And the illegal bird hunting."

She looked up at Vilia then quickly away.

"For a while there I thought the old Vernon had returned—comin' home every day sayin' he's gonna make good. We'll get our own island just like the Leas he used to say. Just like the Leas."

This surprised the younger woman. She had never heard her name used as an object of envy before. She decided she didn't like it.

"So he needed my father out of the way?"

"Yes ... I mean, no!" Mrs. Riley grabbed her cup in both hands, steadying it at last.

"Not directly you understand? Okay, sure Vernon was involved with the birds— everybody knew that's how Dick O'Brien made his money, selling illegal Paradise feathers and whatnot—and Vernon had always turned a blind eye but this time he figured if he was puttin' his job on the line for a mate, he might as well get in on the action."

"But why then? Why Tubu?"

"Tubu was different. Big money. The place was packed with birds, more than even your dumb dad knew."

Vilia flinched at this but stayed silent.

"But Francis knew," she continued.

"Francis, from Tubu?"

"'Course. He was workin' for Dick. That's how they got in. He told Dick when the coast was clear. They only worked at night, or when your folks were away."

Like the cowards they were, she wanted to say but instead she asked about that fateful night, thirty years ago.

Mrs. Riley's lips began to slump downwards again. She was clearly uncomfortable with this topic.

"Vernon didn't tell me the details," she said eventually before taking a long, slow sip of her tea.

Vilia glared at her. *She wasn't getting away that easily.*

"What happened that night Mrs. Riley? I need the truth."

The teacup was placed back down carefully and another sigh released before the woman finally spoke.

"What I know is this: My husband went off with Dick the night your dad disappeared and every single minute of every single day I wish to God he hadn't. Vernon was never the same again after that."

"What happened?"

Vilia's tone was tougher this time. She wasn't interested in this woman's rue, she needed answers and she needed them now.

"I honestly don't know, you gotta believe me on that one. What I do know is that Vernon came home very early the next mornin' with Dick O'Brien and they both looked sore as a cut snake. Vern said something had gone horribly wrong, that I was to shut me big mouth and say he and Dick had been here with me all night. They were really in a fluster. They talked for a bit, spoke with Francis by radio and then took off again. Next thing I know he and Dick are off to Alotau with some local girl. God knows what that was about. Vern came home a day later and that was that."

"And the boat? My dad's boat? What did they do with that?"

She shrugged. "Maybe they cut it loose, to give the impression your dad took off. I can't tell you. Don't know."

Vilia thought about this for a while.

"So what do you think happened? On the island that night?"

This was something Mrs. Riley could tell her. It was clear she'd been thinking about this ever since that fateful night, and she didn't hesitate this time.

"I reckon they went to do some innocent huntin' and, well, somethin' bad obviously happened, somethin' Vernon couldn't stop. Obviously your dad caught them in the act, maybe a fight started. Maybe it was self-defense. Dunno, but I don't reckon anyone was meant to get hurt, honestly I don't. Not my Vernon. He wasn't that type."

"But at the very least he helped cover it up, after the fact," Vilia said and Mrs. Riley looked away. "And it didn't stop him from trying to buy the island."

"Oh, that was Dick O'Brien's idea. They were gonna go halves ..."

"But then Dick died."

The widow sniffed, swallowed hard. "Vern had to spend some time on Tubu, investigatin' you understand? Well, he came home one evening and was all hysterical, screamin' about some bloody curse, how some witch doctor on Tubu had seen the whole thing, had put a curse on them or some such nonsense. That they would soon be dead."

"But surely your husband didn't believe it?"

"'Course he believed it! Any other white folk would just laugh it off. But Vernon was a copper, see, he'd seen how it worked in the villages. How the people dropped like flies. Then of course when Dick carked it with that weird bloody virus or poisoning or whatever the hell it was, well that marked the end for poor Vernon. He all but begged his heart to give way after that. Oh no, if he'd just laughed them off he'd still be alive today."

"And living on Tubu?"

Mrs. Riley looked down into her lap. Vilia finished off her tea, tried to quell the tears that were now rising in her eyes.

"What you gonna do now?" the woman asked, her voice trembling. "He died a good man. No one knew ... if they did it would only kill me, too."

"It's okay, Mrs. Riley," she said, standing to leave. "In this country it's called payback and by the sounds of things, the check has already cleared. I'm not here to destroy anybody else's life."

And so she left the old woman sitting all alone in her grubby little kitchen. And she understood then, why this woman hadn't fled to whiter shores long ago. She was paying her own kind of penance, just like Genevive had done.

Another woman wasted in the name of greed.

As Vilia strode back through the markets and towards Jonah and his yacht, she knew that there was only one thing left to do.

"Come on, Jonah," she told him as he stood waiting on the pier. "Let's go home. I've got some hiking to do."

PART 7

KUNOO POINT—FIRST STROKE

The path to Kunoo Point was unusually arduous. Early morning rain had turned the under scrub into a slippery mat teeming with nests of red bull ants and leeches, and the man was careful to tread with assurance, checking the stability before applying his full weight and moving on.

Droplets from the low-lying branches trickled down his neck and teased the sweat beneath his shirt, occasionally splattering his face along the way, and he licked up any lingering drops to wet his throat from time to time. The cicadas, previously hushed by the downpour, had resumed their symphony and all manner of creatures slithered and scratched and fluttered about, reminding him that in this forest he was never alone.

His journey had begun at daybreak, he had plenty to think about and Kunoo was a good spot to do it in, but the muddy pathway up the mountain and through the strangling scrub was taking longer than he expected. The month before he had done the trek in an hour, winding easily along the cleared pathway until he reached the top, rewarded as always with a stunning ocean view. Today he had been at it nearly two hours and still had some distance to go. Weary, despite his youth, he laid his small backpack down, wiped one hand through his sweaty black hair and across his moist moustache, and leaned against a red cedar tree to catch his breath.

Suddenly a small clearing caught his eye. He moved steadily towards it, wondering why the boys hadn't mentioned that they'd been up here lately. The remains of a campfire were still in place newly soaked by the rain but showing none of the cobwebs or coverage that would suggest it was built longer than a day or so earlier.

This surprised him. As far as he knew, they had all been over at Samarai for the past two days, for the annual Pearl Festival. In fact, he and Gena were due to stay longer except little Villy had fallen ill, and so they had returned with most of the villagers that day.

Vilia's illness was the reason he was storming his way up to Kunoo Point now. He needed to get away, to think. To persuade himself, somehow, that it was time for them to leave. Enough was enough. This island was too remote, too rugged for his wife and child. He was being selfish, he knew that now. But with every step he took, he wondered how he could possibly pull himself away and return Down Under.

Tubu was in his blood now. It was inevitable.

And he was beginning to suspect that it was leaching into Gena's blood, too. Vilia's recent illness had upset him more than her, she had shrugged it off, suggested they stay on Samarai. That was surprising.

He looked about keenly. Perhaps Hettie had made this clearing? He fossicked through his pockets, tried to recollect what he had brought in his backpack. He didn't see the witch doctor often but when he did he always liked to give her something, some gum, some *buai*, some cream chocolate biscuits from Samarai. It seemed to please her and she would smile her crinkly smile and nod her tiny gray head, clasping his hands strongly in hers, almost prayer-like. Sure, the other *dimdims* laughed the old woman off, but he could understand why the local people so revered her.

Hettie didn't speak a word of English but when she looked into your eyes, she could read you like a book.

He noticed that the camp extended further into the scrub, an oddity considering the likelihood of snakes and other creatures, and he began to doubt that it was Hettie's. She had her own little hut not far away, why clear a patch here? He pushed his way through the scrub and saw that a pathway had been scratched out into the brush, leading deeper into the forest and away from the main trail.

Perplexed, the man returned for his backpack and began to follow it. He had not heard of a second trail up here and his mind raced with possibilities while his feet worked overtime to prevent him from slipping. This trail lead deep into the mountain side, away from the cliff view and, while barely used, was not as fresh as he thought. Between the newly torn branches were older limbs broken some time before. These were covered with moss and other foliage, and animals had already nested and re-nested beneath their shelter. They could be months old, even longer, the man thought as he continued down the path.

Along the way the path became extremely narrow and barely recognizable so he had to stop and fetch the knife from his bag and chop his way through. At one point he was sure the trail had ended and was about to turn back, disappointed, when he noticed it had resumed a little way beyond. He cut his way across to it and continued on.

After a good thirty minutes, the man heard the gentle whishing sound of water and saw ahead of him a thin, steep creek which, he estimated, must help feed the main creek that runs along the mountain side. The path meandered towards the creek but, surprisingly, did not meet up with it as he had expected, choosing instead to climb further still into the forest, which was now so dense he began to reconsider.

Perhaps he should be heading back, he told himself, come another time with the boys in tow? But the adventurer in him begged him on and so he kept walking. He had heard the constant call of the Bird of Paradise as he walked, but it was a miracle he had not come across a deadly Papuan Black snake yet. He knew he had the rain to thank for that; they would be out a little later when the scrub dried out. He glanced at his watch. It was nearly noon and the forest was heating up. He would give the path ten more minutes and then turn back. For all he knew, it could lead right around the mountain to the grass airstrip behind it and he did not relish the thought of the long trek home.

Less than two minutes later he pushed aside some branches to find a rocky alcove come clearly into view. From where he stood he could make out the top of a cave but the base was blocked by a boulder and, thrilled at the discovery, he quickened his step. He had heard rumors of caves in the mountain but had never had the good fortune of finding one. Today's discovery was thrilling, exhilarating, and he edged his way closer, keeping one eye on the cave and the other on his trail.

That's when he saw the skulls.

There were thirty-two in all, perched upon the ledge like beacons on a hill. They were off-white and cracked, many with their teeth still firmly in place, and all facing what must have once been a spectacular view. The forest, while thick and indomitable, showed slight glimpses of the airstrip and the ocean beyond. Many years earlier these skulls would have been looking out at paradise.

The man dared not touch them. He counted them and surveyed them from every angle awestruck by the sight. *How long had they been here? Were they local skulls? Missionaries perhaps?* He had heard tales of the island's past, of headhunting and such, but never took much of it to heart. Perhaps he should have?

Slowly a small chill began working its way down his spine. How had these skulls managed to stay so perfectly aligned, so free of foliage and dust? He looked around then, frantically, searching for human traces. It was clear, now, that these skulls, while decades old perhaps, had not been neglected. Someone had been caring for them, and had done so recently.

He studied the cave floor. It had been swept clean and a pile of fallen teeth and bone fragments had been placed neatly to one side. Whoever knew about this cave was taking good care to keep it in order and, he thought a little angrily, a secret.

He had to find out more.

Then a wide smile filled his face. Hettie! It was obviously the local witch doctor. This kind of place was right up Hettie's alley, tending to the ghosts of the long dead. Why hadn't he thought of that?

But I wish she had shown me, he thought. *I wish she had trusted me enough.*

He stayed there for several minutes, taking in its magnificence and then, feeling a little intrusive, grabbed his backpack to begin winding his way down the hillside, toward the old pathway.

That's when a set of bright plume feathers caught his eye. They had been wedged under a rock to the side of the cave and he wondered how a bird could possibly have managed that. He reached for the feathers and noticed that they belonged to the Raggiana and there were, in fact, three sets, all neatly entwined with fishing wire.

Anger prickled back down his spine. *What was going on?*

Hettie would know better than to hunt the Bird of Paradise. It would bring her bad luck. He looked around more closely and then, through the foliage, spotted something bright red. He reached for it. A cap with the word Pepsi on it.

What the hell was going on?

The feathers, the cap, the bush clearings and small fires all suggested that someone had been up here recently, and probably hunting the birds. They were likely doing it late at night or early in the morning, when they thought the coast was clear. He knew then what he had to do.

That evening Jamie lied to Genevive for the first time in his life. He had some work to do with Toia, he told her, not wanting to worry her, not now, not with young Villy's flu and doctors so far away. And he wondered again, as he

233

strapped on his backpack and snuck his way up the mountainside, if he had done the wrong thing, dragging his young bride so far away from home.

"It's just until we get our own money put away," he had told her over dinner, no longer heir to his father's great fortune and feeling liberated because of it. "We'll be fine, Gene, everything will be okay."

And for the first time since they'd arrived in Papua New Guinea, he really felt she believed him. That she was beginning to warm to the place at last. She had smiled at him, her usual frown nowhere to be found.

The moon was clear and bright that night but little use under the thick, forest canopy and he was grateful for his torch as he slipped and slid his way through, determination and anger fuelling him on. The rushing of the creek served as his guide and eventually he spotted the rocky alcove and the hidden cave came into view. He waited behind some bushes, listening for life. Reassured, he stepped out into the clearing and looked around for the best place to hide.

To the side of the cave, a smaller outlet offered some seclusion. He could sit in there until someone came by. He checked his watch. It was almost 9:00 p.m. He could be in for a long wait.

Jamie removed his backpack and checked the contents. His water bottle was full and he had pinched some fruit from the back garden, just in case. There were spare batteries, too, and a bottle of RID and, right at the bottom, his wife's journal. It must have been left there from their trip to Samarai.

He massaged the insect repellent into every part of his exposed skin, across his face and neck, his ankles and hands, then slowly peeled a banana and waited.

Just after 4:00 a.m., Jamison awoke with a start. It took him some minutes to get his head in order. His back was aching from the rocky wall against which he had dozed and two banana peels lay beside him. He reached for his watch but an odd sound froze him mid-movement. Men's voices, low. Some laughter, too. A familiar laugh that stabbed at his heart.

He waited a few minutes, not daring to move, and listened to the sounds of men making a fire. Eventually curiosity got the better of him. He shuffled to the edge of the alcove, trying to peer around the side. He needed to confirm what he already knew to be true.

Sharpening a long, wooden spear around a smoky fire, Francis sat, legs crossed, brow furrowed. Beside him, another black man, unfamiliar to Jamison, was cradling an axe. And standing over them both, peering up at the trees, was a rough-looking American called Texas. He was Dick O'Brien's right-hand man.

"Not long now," Texas told the men. "We just need two more today. No fuckin' around, this time, you got it? Riley's waiting for our signal so let's not keep him, okay!"

They both just shrugged and didn't look his way.

Jamison felt sick to the stomach. He had seen enough. More, in fact, than he had wanted to see. He could expect it of Dick O'Brien, perhaps even Riley, but Francis was his trusted employee, his friend.

His head was spinning, his temper rising, but he kept it together as best he could, waiting for their next move. About twenty minutes later, the sun showed its first signs of light and Jamie heard the fire being kicked out, followed by footsteps leading away from the clearing and up into the dense forest.

He peered around the alcove. It was empty. All that remained were the gleaming white skulls looking out at the hidden view. He grabbed his backpack and slipped out, edging his way along the cave wall and then back down the muddy path towards the creek and away.

The rainforest tangled towards him as he ran, and he grabbed at branches, vines, anything, to stop from slipping on the slimy undergrowth. The skulls were at least a kilometer behind him now but every hair on his body stood to attention reminding him of what he'd seen and imploring him to keep on.

And so he ran, stumbling, sweating, screaming wildly within.

Perhaps that's why he never heard the axe swoosh towards his neck and rip his head off with one clean swipe.

PART 8

KUNOO POINT REVISITED— FALLING IN

Vilia stopped to catch her breath and to wait for Boroko to continue clearing the scrub ahead. In her hand she clutched the old bit of rag that bore the map she once mocked. They were closely following the path to Kunoo Point—the original, steeper path on the other side of the island, near the air strip.

She could hear the whooshing of a creek nearby now, and the kwa-kwa sound of the island's treasured birds. She felt, then, that she could have melted into the greenery, never to be seen again. It was fluorescent, vibrant, alive. And the air was cool with the stale smell of rotting undergrowth mulching over time to feed the rainforest above.

At first, Boroko had hesitated when she asked him to take her there.

"I know there's a path on that side," she said the morning after her return from Samarai. "And I believe it leads to the skull cave. I need to see that cave."

He had stared into her eyes for some time, giving nothing away.

Eventually he said, "I no go for many years. Not since I was *liklik*. Little boy."

"Do you think you can still find it?"

He thought about this and then nodded warily. "Papa bilong mi say no one must go there. *Sanguma*. Sorcerer put evil spell on cave."

239

"Do you mean Hettie?"

It took him a few moments but eventually he nodded again.

"Yes, Hettie. Witch doctor."

"And who told your dad about the evil spell? Francis?"

Boroko looked surprised and then nodded slowly, yes. She shook her head angrily. Of course Francis didn't want them near the skull caves or the original Kunoo Point path. It had nothing to do with lazy tourists or evil spirits, at least not of the supernatural kind. He was just keeping the evidence hidden away. He had insisted on searching around that area the day after her father disappeared, and was probably the one who switched the maps and changed the route to the lookout so his evil deeds would never be uncovered.

Too bad, she thought, staring hard at Boroko.

"I need to go there," she told him. "And I'll find my own way if you don't help me. It's very important. To me. To my dad."

Boroko paused and then he simply walked away. Vilia sighed heavily, could feel the tears welling up in her eyes, but then she saw him return, a gleaming machete in hand.

"Okay," he said, "it is time."

This trek, she realized, was not unlike the newer path to Kunoo Point, one she did just a week ago, and indeed, it was all part of the same mountain range. They were simply clawing their way up the other side, the side that was deliberately forgotten.

Today, however, everything was clearer. All around her she saw a myriad of shapes and colors, textures and tones that she had not noticed before. There were tiny yellow mushrooms sprouting out of rotting tree trunks and fluorescent gray-green vines that looked like faux plastic plants, the sort you see in tacky shopping malls, perfectly winding their way up brown and red speckled rainforest trees. But it was the trees themselves that really took her breath away. Where once she just saw a mass of green, today she saw layers of contrast. There were skinny trees with knobbly knees that were covered in boil-like bumps. And flaky, orange trees, wrapped in vines that reached so high you could barely see their heads. And everywhere, ferns that spread out for meters or that rested like a wild mop of hair atop the tallest, lankiest of limbs.

This trek was tougher than the last, though, and not only because it was so badly overgrown. It was much steeper and certainly less tourist-friendly. No wonder Francis had no trouble convincing everyone to change the route.

At one stage they were climbing almost vertically straight up, scratching at trees for support and meeting elaborate spiderwebs and stinging mosquitoes in their path. But none of it dampened her spirits. She thought of the tribesmen, centuries ago, carrying their dead to their final resting place, and it spurred her on, giving her the courage she needed to keep breathing, keep climbing, keep slowly making her way.

And she recalled three conversations from the night before, not long after she had jumped off the boat from Samarai. Liam's voice had been surprised at first, a little aloof, perhaps, and then slowly softening, warming, happy to hear from her at last. He marveled at the story of Tubu.

"I'm glad you went back," he said down a scratchy line from New York, "it must've taken a lot of courage, but it was the right thing to do."

And her eyes filled with tears because she knew he'd understand. He was one person who always expected more of Vilia than she ever expected of herself.

She thought of Alex, too, a dear friend but one who had never quite expected enough. He had been her crutch over the years, the one who would tell her she was okay just as she was, she didn't need to change. But Vilia knew now how insidious that had been. She couldn't keep living like that, laying blame. She needed to do as Liam had urged her to do. She needed to stand up for herself and then, more incredibly, to let herself fall again. Because through the falling, she realized, you learn that you can survive.

And so she had rung Alex, revealed what she had learned and told him good-bye. She wasn't cutting him off so much as keeping him in his place.

And then, finally, she had poured Jonah and herself a gin and tonic and they had sat out on the veranda watching the sparkling horizon and marveling at the dancing fish and the busy fireflies.

"I won't be selling, at least not for a long while," she told him and he, too, didn't seem surprised.

"Thought you'd fall in love with the place. Ya mum was right all along. It's a bugger that way."

"Yeah, old Gena was right about a lot."

"What ya gonna do now? Hang around for a bit?"

"Unfortunately, I can't. I have some stuff to clear up in Cairns and New York first, but I'll be back, sooner than you know it." Then she smiled. "Unlike my mum, I don't intend to stay away."

He laughed. "Good, I reckon a certain neighbor'll be happy to see you back."

She blushed. He was right, Kyle O'Brien had already said as much. They'd had a surprisingly easy dinner the night he'd dropped her off and she could feel a connection with him that she'd never felt with anyone else. Not even Liam.

They were comfortable together, despite being relative strangers, and had talked for hours about their childhoods while sitting out on the veranda watching the sea. He'd opened up about the hardship of being an O'Brien around these parts and she'd asked him why he hadn't fled.

"Why should I?" he'd replied. "It's their bullshit, not mine. Besides, I love this country. Don't know where else I'd go. This is my home."

Then he'd turned to her with his cerulean blue eyes and said, "You can't escape your past, Vilia, might as well embrace it."

She'd nodded her head. He was right.

Kyle O'Brien was like a kindred spirit and she knew, now, that they would be connected for life.

"Just one thing," Vilia said, to Jonah, shaking herself out of her reverie. "Eventually, when you've retired, I'm giving Tubu to the villagers. They might not be the original landowners, but it's more their place than mine."

And Jonah had smiled widely at this.

"You know what Tubu means, don't you?"

"No," she said, wondering why she hadn't thought to ask.

"It's a local word. It means *to grow*, and I reckon you've done just that."

Then he raised his glass and toasted her to the darkening sky.

Vilia took a generous swig of her water bottle, preparing herself for this final leg of her long, tumultuous journey. They had trekked for what seemed like hours, her nerves growing with every step, but now they were just meters from the cave and she could already see the gleaming skulls, lined up along the rocky ledge, scores of eye sockets looking out at the lush greenery. Above them, moss and ferns hung down like an unruly fringe, and deep inside the craggy walls looked almost like papier mache.

Waves of emotion buckled Vilia about the knees, and she grabbed on to a tree and tried hard to blink back the tears that were threatening to burst forth.

Boroko, too, was teary-eyed and had stopped and turned his face away.

They both knew this was now her journey, it was time for her to lead the way, and so she shook herself out and gently brushed past him, to walk the final leg alone. She trod carefully towards the cave, to confront the faces of a past many thought—hoped—was long erased.

There was an eerie beauty to the skulls. She felt hushed and placated but strangely unafraid, and she placed her backpack to one side and turned to take a closer look. The heads, she noticed, were covered, stubble-like, in a thin layer of green mold. They were all missing their lower jaws and so appeared to be munching on the rock face below, some boasting as many as five teeth still clinging to their bony upper gums like dried kernels of corn. Hornet nests now occupied the empty nostrils and eyes, and some had strange bumps and cracks across them, from past tribal wars, perhaps?

Yet these skulls still seemed at war, she thought, jawbones crashing into eye sockets where they had fallen into each other over time. She reached for her torch and jumped at the sound of crushing bone beneath her shoes. She stepped back, retrieved a sliver of jaw, and propped it back in its place.

On the furthest side of the ledge, she spotted a solitary skull sitting slightly to one side and she flashed the light upon it. Then stepped back again with a start.

Part of Vilia wanted to run then, back down the slope and away. She wondered if not knowing was preferable to this pain. But images of her mother staring hopelessly out to sea were all she needed to spur her on, towards that lonely, fleshless face.

Vilia breathed the cool air long and hard and then lowered herself down to take a closer look. She surveyed the jaw structure, the eye sockets, the teeth, some still stuck to the jawbone, one crowned in gold. It didn't take an anthropologist to know that this one didn't belong. And you didn't have to be a detective to work out who it was.

This skull had been watched over, cared for, ritualized. Around it a collection of dusty, cobwebbed shells were scattered in an imperfect circle, and to one side several small, faded plastic bags had been placed. The brand was barely legible now but she could just make out the words *Chocolate Crackers*. She softly laughed at this and then sat down.

"Hi, Dad," she said to the lone skull, and "Thanks, Hettie," and "It's okay now, Mum," before dropping her head into her hands and sobbing at last.

Vilia stayed like this for almost an hour and Boroko stood quietly, patiently, waiting on the side, and when at last she was ready to leave, she wiped her eyes, scooped up the torch and flashed it around the cave one last time.

And that's when she spotted it.

Propped under a rock behind his skull, almost hidden and covered in decades of dust, was a small, leather-bound journal. She gasped, hesitated, and then, placing the torch to one side, still shining in the cave, she gently picked the book up, holding it in both hands as though it might break.

Suddenly, quite unexpectedly, her torch snapped off. Vilia swung around with a start and then looked back at Boroko whose eyes were now wide, the color almost drained from his face.

She placed the book down, picked up the torch and gave it a good shake. The batteries, she recalled, were fresh. She reached for replacement batteries, popped them in and switched the torch back on. But it didn't work, would never work again as it turns out. So she took the old journal and moved back out of the shadows of the cave, to a stream of sunlight that was filtering through the foliage.

The book was small, bound in leather and bore the hand written words *Genevive Lea*.

Vilia choked back a sob. She had no idea her mother had ever kept a journal, wondered why she had stopped, but she recalled now how Gena had nurtured the habit in her. She had forgotten that.

How many other things, she wondered, had her childhood anger helped erase from her mind?

She pried open the front cover, flipped gently to the first page and began to read, tears streaming down her face as she realized that her mother had been as lonely and lost in this wilderness as she had. She skimmed the pages, flipped towards the end, noticing as she went how the mood was lightening, how her mother was inevitably falling in love with Tubu. Just as she had.

She turned, at last, to the final entry.

May 5. A trip to Samarai.

Gena had been happy, delighted, upbeat. Vilia didn't recognize that voice, a voice she would never use again. Underneath it, she noticed a few simple words had been added in a different scrawl: *My darling Genevive. We will be alright.*

A final sense of hope before fate slashed it all away.

That afternoon as Vilia wandered along the beachfront, she came across a giant, gramophone-shaped Nautilus with reddish brown stripes across a smooth, pearly shell. And she placed it to her ear, as her mother had done, and laughed aloud with joy because now she could hear it.

"HuuuhhhhhHhhhuuuuhhhhHuuuhhhh."

The shell was still singing in unison with the tides. It had crashed onto shore, its voyage now complete, but it would forever breathe in tune to the ocean of its birth. She listened for some time before placing the shell aside and slipping off her clothes. Then she waded, naked, into the water's depths and fell back into its folds letting the liquid roll her about like a giant waterbed.

And as she lay there squinting up at the sun, she thought again of the Asaro Mudmen, falling into the muddy river and coating themselves in the earth's wet skin before returning to the place of their downfall.

They did not just scare away their conquerors. They were victorious in their defeat.

~~~~~~~~

CPSIA information can be obtained
at www.ICGtesting.com
Printed in the USA
LVHW110121230720
661323LV00002B/257

9 780987 187246